W9-AFZ-966

Secrets of a Victorian Household

One family. Four unexpected romances!

The Fairclough Foundation, situated in the backstreets of Westminster in London, has become a vital safe haven for women down on their luck. At the helm is resilient widow Lilian Fairclough. But now Lilian and her two daughters, Millie and Lottie, find themselves in trouble, having not heard from Millie's twin brother, Silas, for over six months...

With their dwindling funds threatening the foundation, the urgency to find out where exactly Silas is is greater than ever. And as they fight to save their livelihood, each family member is about to uncover scandalous, dangerous secrets...and find unexpected romance along the way!

Discover more in

Miss Lottie's Christmas Protector
by Sophia James
November 2019

Miss Amelia's Mistletoe Marquess
by Jenni Fletcher
December 2019

Mr. Fairclough's Inherited Bride
by Georgie Lee
January 2020

Lilian and the Irresistible Duke
by Virginia Heath
February 2020

Author Note

I've really enjoyed collaborating on this Victorian series with my fellow authors Sophia James, Georgie Lee and Virginia Heath, all of whom have inspired and supported me. It's not easy juggling characters and plots, especially across continents and in different time zones, but I've fallen in love with the whole Fairclough family and I can't wait to read their stories!

JENNI
FLETCHER

—

*Miss Amelia's
Mistletoe Marquess*

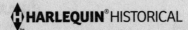
HARLEQUIN HISTORICAL

If you purchased this book without a cover you should be aware that this book is stolen property. It was reported as "unsold and destroyed" to the publisher, and neither the author nor the publisher has received any payment for this "stripped book."

Special thanks and acknowledgment are given to Jenni Fletcher for her contribution to the Secrets of a Victorian Household series.

ISBN-13: 978-1-335-63552-5

Miss Amelia's Mistletoe Marquess

Recycling programs for this product may not exist in your area.

Copyright © 2019 by Harlequin Books S.A.

All rights reserved. Except for use in any review, the reproduction or utilization of this work in whole or in part in any form by any electronic, mechanical or other means, now known or hereafter invented, including xerography, photocopying and recording, or in any information storage or retrieval system, is forbidden without the written permission of the publisher, Harlequin Enterprises Limited, 22 Adelaide St. West, 40th Floor, Toronto, Ontario M5H 4E3, Canada.

This is a work of fiction. Names, characters, places and incidents are either the product of the author's imagination or are used fictitiously, and any resemblance to actual persons, living or dead, business establishments, events or locales is entirely coincidental.

This edition published by arrangement with Harlequin Books S.A.

For questions and comments about the quality of this book, please contact us at CustomerService@Harlequin.com.

® and TM are trademarks of Harlequin Enterprises Limited or its corporate affiliates. Trademarks indicated with ® are registered in the United States Patent and Trademark Office, the Canadian Intellectual Property Office and in other countries.

Printed in U.S.A.

www.Harlequin.com

Jenni Fletcher was born in the north of Scotland and now lives in Yorkshire with her husband and two children. She wanted to be a writer as a child but became distracted by reading instead, finally getting past her first paragraph thirty years later. She's had more jobs than she can remember but has finally found one she loves. She can be contacted on Twitter, @jenniauthor, or via her Facebook author page.

Also by Jenni Fletcher

Harlequin Historical

Married to Her Enemy
Besieged and Betrothed
The Warrior's Bride Prize
Reclaimed by Her Rebel Knight

Secrets of a Victorian Household

Miss Amelia's Mistletoe Marquess

Whitby Weddings

The Convenient Felstone Marriage
Captain Amberton's Inherited Bride
The Viscount's Veiled Lady

Visit the Author Profile page
at Harlequin.com.

To Andy, my best chum.

Also, thanks and love to my other partners in fictional crime, Therese, Rachael and Jeev.

Chapter One

December 1842

Forty-five minutes!

Millie Fairclough stared at the enamelled bronze carriage clock above the fireplace in astonishment. She would never have imagined such a feat of verbosity were possible, but apparently it was. Lady Fentree and her five middle-aged companions really *had* been talking about bonnets for forty-five minutes. Not to mention fifteen before that on hemlines and almost a full hour on sleeves!

'Personally…' Lady Fentree intoned with the air of a woman about to make some momentous pronouncement '…I favour a wide peak. Poke bonnets are far too restrictive. I tried on one of Vanessa's the other day and I could barely turn my head!'

'Oh, I agree completely.' The woman on Millie's left nodded her head so vigorously that her lace cap flopped forward over one eye. 'But you know young girls like to follow the latest fashions and your Vanessa would look charming in anything.'

'True…' Lady Fentree smiled complacently '…and I suppose we were the same once. Only one learns to appreciate practicality over appearance at *our* age.'

Millie looked down at her hands as half-a-dozen ladies laughed, somewhat surprised and faintly chagrined to be included in the latter category. She could only presume that their hostess had forgotten she was there, given that she hadn't uttered more than a few murmurs of agreement for the past hour and a half.

It wasn't that she *didn't* like bonnets, or hemlines or sleeves for that matter. On the contrary, she had a keen and, she was afraid, somewhat sinful interest in fashion. It was her guilty pleasure. She couldn't afford to buy new clothes very often, no more than a pair of new gloves or a few ribbons anyway, but she could still look at and appreciate the sartorial choices of others.

Truth be told, she knew a quite shameful amount about bonnets. Straw bonnets, cottage bonnets, spoon bonnets, drawn bonnets… She had an opinion on each and every one of them—maybe not forty-five minutes' worth—but still, more than she cared to admit. There were certainly things she *might* have contributed to the conversation, but the whole subject seemed far too shallow compared to her everyday life at the Fairclough Foundation, the institute for down-on-their-luck women her parents had founded more than twenty years before. Now, no matter how hard she tried to relax and enjoy the evening party, she found herself unable to indulge in a little light-hearted discussion. She was a serious person with a serious reputation to uphold and serious matters to consider. Whatever would people say if they discovered that the dutiful, virtuous and, above all, self-sacrificing Miss Amelia Fairclough had opinions on bonnets?

Not that there was anything inherently sinful about the subject, she reminded herself. After all, people needed clothes even if they didn't necessarily need fashion. That was the reason she gave sewing lessons at the Foundation, as well as weekly tutorials in embroidery and crochet. It was thanks to those very skills that she'd managed to transform her best dress, now in its seventh year of service, into something vaguely fashionable for this evening's outing. It had taken all of her ingenuity, but she'd finally succeeded in reducing the gigot sleeves into short puffed ones, even fringing the cuffs with a layer of white lace and adding a matching trim to the hem. It wasn't perfect. The bodice was too high and the overall shape nowhere near full enough, but she'd thought it had looked reasonably presentable.

Less than a minute inside Lady Fentree's imposing Georgian mansion had been sufficient to destroy that illusion. All of the other young ladies were dressed in the very height of fashion, in off-the-shoulder silk gowns with bell-shaped skirts and low, pointed waists, as if they'd come to the party straight from their modistes. As a casual observer Millie thought she might have enjoyed the spectacle, but to be seated amid so much splendour made her feel like a gaudy weed in a flowerbed full of lilies. It was hard not to feel a little bit jealous, especially when the new vogue for pastel shades was far better suited to her pale skin and auburn hair than the recent craze for bright colours. Even harder not to feel self-conscious when everything about her, from the sensible, unadorned bun at the nape of her neck to the practical ankle boots poking out from beneath her skirts made her feel hopelessly dowdy.

'What do *you* think of Pamela hats, Miss Fairclough?' Lady Fentree's voice penetrated her thoughts suddenly.

'Me?' Millie flushed, embarrassed to have been caught with her attention wandering. 'Oh, I like them very much, especially the ones with wide ribbons.'

'Indeed. They're so flattering, especially when one wears the back of one's hair in ringlets. It stops them getting flattened.'

'Yes, I suppose it does, although I'm afraid I've never worn ringlets.'

'*Never?*' Lady Fentree sounded genuinely shocked. 'Well, how extraordinary.'

'Is it?' Millie looked around the group in dismay, wishing she'd kept her mouth shut, after all. Judging by the looks being exchanged, everyone else thought it extraordinary, too. As if she'd needed another way to prove how drab and boring she was!

Which was nothing but foolishness and vain self-regard on her part, she chided herself, sitting back in her chair as the conversation moved on without her. There was no cause to feel jealous of the other young women either. Clothes were simply the external trappings of a person and not a reflection of the soul beneath. Self-sacrifice and duty were the things that really mattered in life and she for one could survive perfectly well without new gowns or elaborate hairstyles. It was only being in society that made her feel this way and she'd be back out of it soon enough, as soon as she and her mother returned to the Foundation, where *nobody* had forty-five minutes to waste in idle chatter about bonnets.

For once, however, the idea of noble self-sacrifice failed to provide its usual consolation. Looking around a room filled with smiling, chattering faces, she still couldn't help but feel just a little bit…well, boring. *Was* she boring? She didn't want to be, but compared to everyone else, her impulsive younger sister Lottie especially, she couldn't help but suspect that she was. Lottie wasn't there, of course, having stayed behind in London with a cold while she and their mother came to spend Christmas in the country, but Millie still knew what she'd say. She'd tell her to stop behaving like an old maid and just enjoy herself for once. That was the whole point of this holiday, after all, even if Millie suspected their mother had ulterior motives.

They were staying at the house of her father's cousin, Lady Alexandra Malverly, the only member of his family who hadn't disowned him after his marriage to her bluestocking mother, Lilian. Despite rigid opposition, the two women had become close friends and remained so even after his premature death from typhoid ten years before. Since then, Alexandra had issued regular invitations for them to visit, but her mother had generally refused, being unable to make reciprocal offers herself. This year, however, she'd said yes, claiming that she needed a change of scene and a rest. Given how worried they were about Millie's twin brother, Silas, that was hardly surprising, but it was still out of character enough for Millie to wonder if there was something else behind it.

'I really think you *ought* to try ringlets, Miss Fairclough.' Lady Fentree's fan tapped her knee, startling her anew. 'A little more width at the sides would make your face look rounder. Yes, indeed, you *must* try ringlets and with a Pamela bonnet, too. I shall advise your mother to purchase one.'

'Oh, no.' Millie lifted a hand in protest. The last thing her mother could afford was a new bonnet for her. 'I'm perfectly happy as I am. There's really no need to trouble yourself.'

'It's no trouble…'

'But I'd *prefer* it if you didn't.'

'Well, I'm sure I was only trying to help!' Lady Fentree tossed her head and gave a loud, affronted sniff. 'In any case, it seems that your mother is otherwise occupied.'

Millie followed the direction of her gaze across the drawing room to where her mother was deep in conversation with a strikingly handsome, dark-haired gentleman. Now that she thought of it, she'd been talking to him the last time she'd looked *and* the time before that. Which was…surprising. Even more so the fact that her mother was actually laughing, something she rarely did at the Foundation. Or at all any more. In fact, in the decade since her mother had been widowed, Millie didn't think she'd ever seen her talk to any man, family members excluded, with anything other than polite interest.

'She does look rather engrossed.' The woman on her left tittered. 'I'm sure bonnets can wait.'

'My mother has far more important matters to concern herself with than bonnets.' Millie stiffened defensively.

'Oh, yes, Lady Malverly told me all about your *Foundation*.' Lady Fentree looked pointedly around at her companions and gave an exaggerated shudder. 'Mrs Fairclough and her husband set up an institute for women of *questionable* virtue a number of years ago. I understand that Miss Fairclough here assists in its running.'

'I do, but it's for women *in need*,' Millie corrected her, 'virtuous or otherwise. In particular, it's for women with nowhere else to go. Our Foundation provides them with a place to stay and helps them get back on their feet.'

'Very laudable, but I don't think I'd like my Vanessa to involve herself in such matters. A young lady ought not to know too much about *that* side of life.'

'No, far better to learn about bonnets,' Millie heard herself snap, 'but I've been raised to believe that we can't just ignore things—or people—that we might prefer not to notice. We have a duty to help others.'

'But surely we can do both?' Her cousin Alexandra appeared at her side suddenly, wearing a placatory smile. 'Personally I've never understood why we can't help those less fortunate than ourselves *and* wear the latest fashions.'

'Quite!' Lady Fentree's voice had the force of a small cannon. 'Although I might suggest that this Foundation teach a few lessons in manners as well!'

'What a splendid idea.' Alexandra placed a restraining hand on Millie's shoulder. 'I'll suggest it to Lilian later, but now I'm sorry to say we must leave you. It seems the weather is conspiring against us.'

'Why, whatever do you mean?'

'It's snowing. Quite heavily, too. If we don't leave now, then I'm afraid we might become stranded and

I wouldn't want to trespass on your hospitality overnight.'

'No indeed.' Lady Fentree narrowed her eyes at Millie. 'I prefer not to share my roof with revolutionaries.'

'But we've had a perfectly lovely evening, haven't we, Millie?' Alexandra's grip on her shoulder tightened.

'Yes…thank you.' Millie rose to her feet and bobbed a dutiful curtsy. 'Please forgive my bluntness, Lady Fentree. I meant no offence.'

'Mmm.' The look on the other woman's face was anything but forgiving. 'In that case, I hope you enjoy the rest of your stay in the country, Miss Fairclough, though I very much doubt that our paths will cross again.'

Millie gritted her teeth as she followed Alexandra and a few other guests from the village out into the hall. They'd all travelled together to save the need for individual carriages, but now the thought of sitting in a constricted space and reviewing the evening's entertainment made her want to scream.

'Millie dear…' Alexandra's voice was gently chiding.

'I know. I was unforgivably rude.'

'Not without provocation. It might do Lady Fentree good to be reminded that there are other people in the world, but perhaps it was a little tactless to do it under her roof.'

'I'm sorry, Cousin.'

'Never mind.' Alexandra patted her arm sympathetically. 'It'll be forgotten soon enough, but it's not like you to be so sensitive. Are you feeling all right?'

'Yes… *No.*' Millie looked down at the floor in consternation. 'Not really. I thought Mama might have told you I received an offer of marriage last week.'

'She *did* mention it, yes…' Alexandra paused tactfully. 'From the local Curate—although I understand it's not a love match.'

'No. It's not romantic for either of us. Gilbert's a good man and he says he wants a wife who can work alongside him, but we're not in love.'

'But you're thinking of accepting him?'

'I suppose so…yes.'

Millie drew on her gloves with a sigh. Yes, she *was* considering it, although considering was as far as she'd got. Practically speaking, it was an advantageous offer. Gilbert was good and intelligent and serious. A little too serious perhaps, pedantic even, and a little overzealous on occasion, but still…*good* and surely that was the quality she ought to want most in a husband? Only she couldn't help but worry that two serious people together might become a little *too* serious. Which would make her even more boring…

'I believe your mother is afraid you might accept him simply to alleviate her current financial difficulties.' Alexandra's gaze was a little too focused.

'*Our* financial difficulties. Her problems are mine, too.'

'Ye—es, but the last thing she wants is for you to sacrifice yourself to a loveless marriage just for her sake. Or the Foundation's, for that matter.'

'I know.' Millie glanced back towards the drawing room. 'I think she hoped I might meet someone else, but it seems unlikely. All the men here tonight could talk about were the newest inventions and how much money they might make from them.'

'You didn't give them much of a chance, dear.'

'No, but why would they look at me anyway?' She bit the inside of her cheek at the words. She hadn't meant them to sound quite so self-pitying.

'I can think of a lot of reasons, but I think what you need more than anything else at this moment is a rest. You look exhausted.'

'Do I? I don't feel tired. I usually do much more in a day.'

'I didn't say tired, I said exhausted. There's a difference and you, my dear, are the latter. You work far too hard at the Foundation.'

'I don't mind. It's too much for Mother to manage on her own.'

'Perhaps, but she wants you to be happy more than she wants your help.' Alexandra touched her chin gently. 'Self-sacrifice is all very well, but not if it causes you to make foolish decisions.'

'I'm not...'

'In any case,' Alexandra spoke over her, 'you're staying with me for a fortnight. There'll be plenty of time to think about the future and make a decision after Christmas. In the meantime, I want you to rest.'

'Yes, Cousin.'

Millie smiled half-heartedly as they put on their bonnets and capes and went out on to the front steps of the mansion into a world transformed. The moon was full and high, making the sky shimmer with snowflakes that danced and spun like falling stars all around them. It was hardly like night-time at all, Millie thought, catching her breath in wonderment. It was beautiful, as if a white cloak had been draped over the landscape. Even the air tasted different. Crisp and clean, utterly unlike that of London.

'Here we are.' Alexandra put an arm around her shoulders as three carriages rolled alongside the front steps. 'You go ahead with the others. I'll wait for your mother.'

'No, you go.' Millie looked at her pleadingly. 'If you don't mind, I don't think I can bear any more conversation tonight. I'll wait for Mama.'

'Are you certain?'

'Yes…' she smiled ruefully '…and I promise to go straight to bed when I get back.'

'All right. If that's what you want, then I'll see you in the morning. Goodnight, dear.'

Millie waved goodbye, waiting until the first two carriages had rattled away before turning back into the house. Her mother had made it as far as the hallway, though she seemed in no hurry to leave, *still* engrossed in conversation with the handsome gentleman. Something about the way they were standing made her avert her face again quickly, too, struck with the distinct impression that she was interrupting something private.

She looked up at the falling snow again, wondering what to do next. She *could* climb into the last carriage, she supposed, but she didn't want to shut herself up inside just yet, not when the world looked so breathtaking. And surely a quick stroll through the gardens wouldn't hurt?

She threw a swift glance over her shoulder and then hurried down the mansion steps, over the gravel drive and across the lawn. It was positively luminescent, she thought delightedly, the snow beneath her feet making soft crumpling sounds as she wandered into a small grove where a line of willow trees obscured any view of the house. It was like a fairy-tale grotto, secret and silent and peaceful, the trees all bedecked with sparkling crystalline pendants. A memory popped into her mind, of throwing snowballs in the park with Silas and Lottie as children. They'd charged around like hoydens while their parents had watched arm in arm from the path. It was a happy memory, but bittersweet, too. She'd been so much more carefree and adventurous back then, always running about and getting into scrapes. What had happened to her? As a woman, she obviously couldn't expect the same freedom allowed to her brother, but Lottie still managed to be fun. Why—*when?*—had she become so dull?

She didn't have time to think of an answer, whirling around at the muffled sound of wheels and hooves coming from the direction of the driveway. Catching up her skirts, she ran back out of the grotto just in time to see the last of the carriages roll away from the house.

'Wait!'

She started to run and then stopped. Even without the snow slowing her down she doubted she'd be able to catch it. Obviously her mother had thought that she'd left with the others and taken the carriage by herself. Which was a reasonable assumption, given the weather and the fact that, foolishly, she hadn't told anyone except Alexandra that she was waiting behind. It was her own fault for straying so far from the house, but surely once her mother got back to the village and discovered her mistake, she'd send the carriage back? *Unless* her mother assumed that she'd gone straight to bed…and if Alexandra assumed the same thing…and she'd told the maid not to wait up for her… Well, then there was a very real chance that no one would realise she was missing until morning.

Millie closed her eyes in mortification, weighing up the choices before her. The thought of throwing herself on the mercy of Lady Fentree and begging a room for the night made her shudder, as did that of admitting her mistake and asking for another carriage. No, *those* alternatives didn't bear thinking about, which meant the only other thing she *could* do was walk. Which, since she was wearing practical boots, didn't seem like too much of a hardship. It was only a couple of miles to the village, after all—three at most—and the snow wasn't *so* heavy, nothing to worry about anyway.

She turned her feet in the direction of the gate and started purposely towards it. The more she thought about it, the more appealing the idea of a walk became. It wasn't what sensible and boring Miss Amelia Fairclough would do, but it was right up the alley of her previous incarnation, Millie Fairclough, intrepid twin and plucky explorer.

She loosened the strings of her bonnet and tugged at the pins of her bun underneath, letting the auburn tresses unravel about her shoulders. *There*, she didn't have to be so strait-laced all of the time. Alexandra was right, there was no need for her to think about the future just yet. Tonight, she wouldn't think about the future at all. Tonight she would forget the rest of the world even existed, stick her tongue out at the Fentree mansion and be Millie again.

And a moonlit walk in the snow sounded like a perfectly wonderful idea.

Chapter Two

Cassius Whitlock, the thirteenth Marquess of Falconmore, stretched his legs out in front of the fire and refused to open his eyes. It was the only way to pretend that the knocking he could hear on his front door was a figment of his imagination and not what—or more precisely *who*—he suspected it was.

The blasted woman had followed him.

After half a minute or so the knocking stopped and he slid deeper into the comfort of his armchair, breathing a sigh of relief and ruthlessly suppressing any feeling of guilt. There was no need to feel guilty, after all. The chances of Sylvia walking any distance on foot were about equal to those of her flying. She could simply take the carriage she'd doubtless commandeered back to the hall. And who was to say that he *hadn't* dreamed the knocking sound anyway? He'd been dozing beforehand so perhaps it really *had* been a figment of his imagination, although what that implied about his current mental state he didn't want to consider, not tonight anyway. He'd already drunk far too much port to come up with anything coherent, let alone helpful.

No, overall it was far better to leave thinking until tomorrow and then find another reason not to.

Delaying, deferring, dragging his heels—those were the things he'd become good at over the past year. Avoiding subjects he didn't want to think about had become his speciality. Why else would he be hiding away like some frightened schoolboy in an empty property on the edge of his estate rather than confronting his problems face to face?

At least the gatehouse was warm and dry, two of the most important considerations on a foul night like this one. The temperature seemed to have dropped several degrees just in the half-hour it had taken him to walk up the drive. Now that he was firmly ensconced in his armchair with the aforementioned bottle of port, however, he felt quite cosy. Frankly it was worth the effort just for the peace and privacy, both of which qualities were becoming signally elusive at Falconmore Hall. Given a choice, he might actually have opted to live here instead, but then he hadn't been given a choice. Not about any of it.

He scowled as the knocking started again, even louder and more insistently than before. This time he *definitely* wasn't imagining things and he could hardly pretend not to hear it either. A herd of cattle outside his front door would have made less commotion.

He surged to his feet, muttering a stream of the most obscene words he could think of. What in blazes was wrong with the woman? Didn't she have *any* pride? It was bad enough hounding him out of his own house, but to pursue him here in his refuge was too much! This time she'd gone too far. This time he'd tell her exactly what he thought of her and her all-too-obvious intentions. Maybe he'd tell her what his cousin would have thought of her behaviour, too. *That* ought to be enough to send her and her daughters running away from Falconmore Hall once and for all. To the other end of England preferably!

He grabbed a candle, took one last fortifying swig of port and then strode out into the hallway, an inadvertent glimpse of his reflection in the hall mirror revealing a wild visage and untidy apparel. Which was hardly surprising really. He'd changed into some old clothes in order to clean out and rebuild the fireplace and hadn't bothered to change back, even after he'd smeared coal across the front of his shirt. All the better, he thought sardonically, running a hand through the dust and then deliberately ruffling his hair to coat the thick, blond strands in black. He was through with behaving like a gentleman. Since Sylvia failed to appreciate subtlety, maybe she'd understand rugged and dishevelled instead!

'What?'

He flung open the front door, bellowing the word before his port-addled senses had a chance to take in the woman before him. It was...*not* Sylvia, though as to who else it was... He blinked a few times, searching his memory and failing to find any answer... No, he had no idea who she was. Only she looked somewhat like a snowman. A pretty, red-cheeked and slightly desperate-looking snowman.

'I apologise for d-disturbing y-you.' Her teeth chattered as she spoke. 'But I'm l-lost.'

He looked past her into the night, too surprised to answer. There was no horse, no trap, nobody else in sight, only a raging blizzard and what appeared to be a foot of snow. When had *that* happened? It had been cold earlier, but he hadn't noticed any flakes, at least not before he'd drawn the curtains…

'Would you m-mind letting me inside for a f-few minutes? Just to warm up? P-please?'

'Yes… Of course.' He remembered his manners at last, stepping aside to let her into the hallway.

'Oh, dear.' A flurry of snow fell from her skirts as she passed him. 'I should have shaken myself off outside.' She looked down at the rapidly swelling puddle in dismay. 'If you have a mop, I'll clean it up for you.'

'There's no need.' He closed the front door against the freezing air. 'I'll deal with it later.'

'Thank you. I'm s-sorry to barge in on you like th-this. I was on my way to the village, but I must have taken a wrong turn somewhere.'

'You mean Rayleigh?'

'Yes.' She rubbed her hands vigorously over her arms as if she were attempting to restore circulation. 'Is it f-far?'

'About a mile down the road. You turn left out of the gate.'

'Oh.' A look of chagrin crossed her face. 'Well, at least I was going in the right direction. Only I didn't think it was so far and the snow was lovely at first, but then it got so heavy I couldn't see the carriage tracks any more.'

'I see.' He looked her up and down incredulously. 'Do you mean to say that you were out walking in the dark on your own?'

'Yes. Not intentionally, but there was a misunderstanding with the carriages and…well…' she scrunched up her pink-tipped nose and lifted her shoulders, send-

ing a fresh flurry of snow tumbling to the floor '...here
I am.'

'Indeed. Here you are.'

He set down his candle on the hall table, mentally
reviewing the amount of port he'd consumed over the
course of the evening. Surely not enough to make him
hallucinate, although the whole situation seemed unlikely. Incredible. Downright unbelievable, in fact, but
here she was, his very own damsel in distress, standing
shivering in his hallway, asking for help. Which, as a
gentleman, he ought to give her. Only, as a gentleman
he really ought to have a chaperon, too.

'Perhaps I might speak to your wife?' The thought
seemed to occur to her at the same moment. 'So that I
can explain to her?'

'Unfortunately not.' He folded his arms behind his
back. 'I don't have a wife, or a maid for that matter.
You find me all alone here.'

'Completely alone?' Her eyes flickered back to the
door, though her expression was conflicted. 'Then perhaps I should...'

'Perhaps you should, but considering the weather it
might be somewhat foolhardy.'

He tapped his foot on the tiled floor, considering
what to do next. However extraordinary the situation,
it was hard to be irritated with someone who looked
quite so thoroughly bedraggled and he could hardly
send her back out into the night. On the other hand,
letting her stay didn't seem like a particularly judicious
idea either. She was a young and presumably unmarried lady, though he couldn't see her ring finger, and he
was a bachelor, and they were alone together in a house
that contained a bed, at night. Not that society gener-

ally required the presence of an actual bed to think the worst, but still the situation could hardly have looked any more compromising. A suspicious man might have thought her arrival some kind of scheme to entrap him, but the way that she'd been shaking definitely hadn't been play-acting and surely no one, not even Sylvia, would have put themselves into such a perilous situation deliberately. Besides, whoever she was, she had an honest as well as a pretty face and he had enough on his conscience without adding anything else, especially another dead body. Which meant that he had no choice but to let her stay.

Damn it. No choice. *Again.* The realisation made his voice gruffer than he'd intended.

'You'd better give me your wet things and come into the parlour.'

'Thank you.' She looked somewhat taken aback by his tone, pulling off her gloves and cape to reveal a conspicuous absence of wedding band and a lithe, willowy figure dressed, somewhat incongruously, in an evening gown. Both of which details paled into insignificance as she removed her bonnet to reveal a cascade of long, lustrous and, more surprisingly, loose hair.

'Oh, dear.' She put one hand to her head self-consciously and then started to rifle in her reticule. 'I must have dropped my pins somewhere.'

'Under the circumstances, I believe unbound hair may be the least of our worries.' He cleared his throat and then gestured for her to precede him into the parlour, trying not to stare at the way the auburn tresses seemed to shimmer in the candlelight. She looked as if she'd just stepped out of a painting by Titian. 'Take the armchair.'

'Oh, no, that's yours.' She sank down on to her haunches in front of the fire and held her hands out to warm them instead. 'This is wonderful.'

'I can't just allow you to sit on the floor, Miss…?'

'Millie. *Just* Millie and I'm more than happy here, honestly. I feel as if my insides have been frozen, Mr…?'

'Whitlock.' He paused in the act of draping her damp cloak across a straight-backed wooden chair in the corner, taken aback by the question. No one had asked who he was since he'd come back to England. Young ladies especially seemed to know his identity without introduction. It made a refreshing change to meet one who did not. Liberating even, as if her words had just freed him from the constraints of the past year. It made him feel oddly grateful.

'*Cassius* Whitlock at your service, although I'm afraid I ought to apologise for my reception. It's not much of an excuse, but I thought you were someone else.'

'I guessed.' She peered up at him through her lashes, her gaze faintly ironic. 'You looked quite ferocious.'

'It was ill mannered of me.'

'Perhaps, but it would be churlish of me *not* to forgive the man who just saved my life.'

'I merely opened a door.'

'Which probably saved my life. Please accept my gratitude. It was silly of me to even think of walking back to the village in this weather. You've no idea how relieved I was to see the smoke from your chimney. I don't think I could have managed another step.'

He harrumphed and sat down on the edge of his armchair. 'You're not from this area, I take it?'

'No, I live in London. My mother and I are staying here for Christmas with a relative.'

'Won't they be worried about you?'

'Ye—es.' Her expression turned anxious. 'If they've realised I'm gone, that is. Only there's a good chance they won't notice until morning.'

'Really?'

'Not that I make a custom of wandering around in the dark on my own, but…it's complicated.'

'I see.' He looked from her to the fireplace and back again. 'Can I fetch you anything? Some soup, perhaps?'

'Thank you, but I've already inconvenienced you enough.' She pressed her lips together for a moment. 'Are you a gamekeeper?'

'I'm sorry?'

'A gamekeeper?' She pointed towards the painting of a stag above the fireplace. 'Or a gardener, perhaps? Only I notice you like pastoral scenes.'

'Ah…yes.'

He threw a swift glance around the room. In all honesty, he hadn't paid a great deal of attention to the decor before. The fact that the house was habitable had been enough for him, but on closer inspection he noticed a veritable profusion of stags and pheasants, somewhat at variance with the spartan furnishings. It was no wonder she assumed he was a gamekeeper, especially considering the somewhat weathered state of his attire. He certainly didn't look much like a marquess.

'Estate manager.' He decided to stretch the truth rather than lie directly. After all, he *was* an estate manager of sorts, even if he employed someone else with the same title.

'How fascinating.' She looked duly impressed. 'Is the estate very large?'

'About fifteen hundred acres. Falconmore Hall is at the other end of this drive.'

'Really?' She sat up hopefully. 'Then perhaps I ought to seek shelter there?'

'I'm afraid it would be quicker to walk back to the village.'

'Oh, dear.' She sighed and sat back again. 'Well, perhaps it's for the best. I think I'd like to avoid halls for a while. I offended the hostess at the one we visited this evening.'

'Indeed? Who was that?'

She glanced sideways, as if she were questioning the wisdom of telling him. 'Lady Fentree.'

'Fentree?' He gave a bark of laughter. 'It doesn't take much to upset that old battle-axe, believe me. She was probably just annoyed at you for overshadowing the Honourable Miss Vanessa.'

'*Me?*' His companion looked genuinely shocked. 'I don't think I overshadowed anyone.'

'Then you don't give yourself enough credit, *Just Millie.*'

He surprised himself with the comment, aware of an unfamiliar tingling sensation in his chest as their eyes met and held. Hers were a bright summer-grass green, he noticed, uncommonly clear and direct with pale lashes that made a striking contrast with her hair. The more he looked, the more he thought that she overshadowed almost every other young lady he'd ever met, or could think of for that matter. Even when she'd looked like a snowman there had been something appealing about her. Something intriguing… Unless it was just the port making him think so. Or the fact that she didn't know who he was. Or that any woman was preferable to Sylvia. Whatever the reason, he was finding it difficult to look away.

Fortunately, she did it instead, her cheeks reddening slightly as her gaze drifted towards the bottle on the table beside him. 'My father used to say port was the best way to warm up on a cold night.'

'I'm inclined to agree. Certainly better than soup. Would you care for a glass?'

'Me?' She looked even more startled, her mouth forming an O shape as if she were about to refuse, then changed her mind. 'Maybe just a small one…if you're sure that's all right?'

'I wouldn't have offered if it wasn't.'

He poured a small measure into a tumbler and handed it to her, refraining from taking a glass for himself. Given how much he'd already drunk, the effects of which he hoped weren't *too* obvious, it was probably wise to abstain. He was having trouble believing the evidence of his own senses as it was.

'Well, then, *Just Millie…*' he watched, the tingling sensation in his chest intensifying, as she lifted the glass to her lips '…after you've finished that I suggest you get a good night's sleep. Given the depth of the snow, I'd say we're stranded here until morning.'

'I suppose so…' She sounded anxious. 'But what if my mother sends out a search party? I'd hate for people to be out in the dark searching for me.'

'How long were you out walking?'

'An hour, perhaps.'

'Then I'd venture to suggest that if your relatives

were going to come looking, they would have done so by now.'

'Yes.' Her brow creased. 'You're probably right.'

'Of course we *could* fashion some kind of sign, hanging your bonnet from the gatepost, for example, but it might be prudent for us to be a little more discreet.'

She drew her knees up to her chest and took another mouthful of port. 'I suppose if anyone knew I was here it *would* look a little compromising.'

'More than a little.' He shifted in his seat, distracted by the way she ran her tongue over her bottom lip, soaking up the last of the liquid. 'Fortunately, it's nothing that can't be fixed with a little harmless deception.'

'What do you mean?'

'There's a disused cottage in one of the fields between here and the village. If, theoretically speaking, you were to have taken shelter inside it, it would be entirely plausible if I, again theoretically speaking, were to find you there in the morning. Then I could take you back to the village without anyone being any the wiser.'

'I see.' She nodded slowly. 'That *does* sound like a good idea, but there's no need for you to escort me anywhere. I'm sure I can find the way on my own.'

'More than likely, but I can hardly just wave you goodbye and hope for the best. You've already admitted you were lost this evening.'

'Only because it was dark.'

'None the less, I'll escort you. My conscience won't be easy otherwise. In the meantime, you can sleep in my bed.'

'Then where will you sleep?' She shook her head adamantly. 'No, I couldn't possibly do that.'

'But I'm afraid this time I have to insist, especially since you've already refused my armchair. Which is surprisingly comfortable, I might add. I won't suffer at all.'

She looked hesitant for a moment and then gave an appreciative smile. 'That's very kind of you and I confess I *am* tired. I never realised that walking in the snow was so exhausting.'

'Yes,' he murmured in agreement, only half-aware of what he was saying as the warm sensation in his chest seemed to escalate by a few degrees and then spread outwards through his body. As smiles went it was extraordinary, lighting up every part of her face and making her look quite exceptionally pretty. Captivating, in fact. In all his thirty-two years, he could honestly say that he'd never seen another smile like it. Not once. Not ever. Not even in his dreams. Back when his dreams had been pleasant ones, that was.

'Then I hope you sleep well, *Just Millie*. I'm afraid that I don't have any women's clothing to lend you, but feel free to make use of whatever you can find.' He inclined his head and then coughed as his voice turned unexpectedly husky, stirred by the thought of her in one of his nightshirts.

'I'm sure I'll manage.' She swallowed the last of her port and stood up. 'Goodnight, Mr Whitlock. Thank you again for opening your door. I do believe that you've saved me from myself.'

Chapter Three

Millie jolted upright with a gasp, her heart hammering against her ribcage at the sound of a shout, followed by glass shattering downstairs. In another instant, she was out of bed and on to the landing, so disorientated that she was halfway down the stairs before she remembered that she was only wearing her shift and petticoat and her situation was shocking enough without her running around in her underwear. But she still had to hurry. If Mr Whitlock was in some kind of trouble, under attack by the sound of it, then she had to help him as he'd helped her!

Quickly, she returned to her room and fumbled around on the back of the bedroom door for the dressing gown she'd noticed there earlier and then ran down the stairs as fast as the moonlight streaming in through a pane of glass above the front door would safely allow. The parlour door was closed, but there were still noises coming from within. Not shouts any more, but angry, expletive-laden grunts and muttering. She looked around for a weapon, her gaze settling on an umbrella in one corner.

It wasn't much, but it was better than nothing, enough to give someone a painful jab in the ribs if necessary.

She hoped it wouldn't have to be necessary.

Gritting her teeth, she steeled her nerve, put on what she hoped was a suitably frightening expression, grabbed the door handle and burst in.

'What the—?' Mr Whitlock spun around at once. He was crouching down by the fireplace, picking up pieces of glass as she lunged forward, brandishing the umbrella like a sword in front of her.

'Oh!' She looked around the room in surprise. Everything was just the same as it had been when she'd gone to bed. There were no signs of a struggle, no broken windows and, apparently, no one else there.

'Millie?' He stood up, his expression almost comically confused.

'I thought you were in trouble. There was a shout.'

'Ah.' He deposited several shards of glass into the coal scuttle and then brushed his hands together. 'I'm sorry for disturbing you. It appears I flung an arm out in my sleep and knocked the bottle over.'

'Oh.' She lowered her arm, belatedly realising that she was still brandishing the umbrella. Now she thought about it, there was a distinct aroma of plums and alcohol in the air. 'The port?'

'I'm afraid so.'

'Can I help?'

'It's not important. I'll deal with the rest in the morning.' He dropped down into his armchair and pressed a hand to his forehead. 'You can go back to bed.'

Millie stood where she was. In all honesty, she was feeling slightly ridiculous, but he seemed…different. When he'd first opened his front door he'd looked positively thunderous, his nostrils flaring so wildly that she'd almost turned on her heel and run away into the snow, but now he seemed to have gone to the other extreme. With the candles all extinguished the only light came from the fire, but his features looked unnaturally pale and drawn, as if all the energy had been drained out of him, too. No matter what the impropriety, her conscience wouldn't let her leave him like that.

'Are you feeling unwell?' She put the umbrella aside and advanced a few steps into the room.

'No.' He gave an indistinguishable sigh.

'Was it a nightmare?'

This time he moved his hand away from his face to look at her. 'I suppose so. Although that suggests something imagined, doesn't it? This was a memory.'

'You have bad memories?' She crouched down on her heels in the same spot she had earlier.

'One or two.' His lip curled, though there was no merriment behind it. 'But I won't disturb you again, I promise.'

'Because you don't intend going back to sleep?' She tipped her head to one side, seeing the answer in his eyes. They were a bright and piercing blue, the very first thing she'd noticed about him on the doorstep, but now they looked haunted. 'I doubt I'll be able to for a while either. It's hard to calm down after a shock, especially when you've been fighting imaginary assailants with umbrellas.'

He looked faintly amused, the barest hint of a smile softening the harsh lines of his face. 'I do appreciate your coming to rescue me. Nothing scares intruders away like an umbrella, I understand.'

'Ah, but I was simply creating a diversion. I intended

for you to do the rest. Unless you were indisposed, of course, in which case I would have hurled the umbrella at whoever it was and gone for the poker instead. I had it all planned out.'

'Evidently.' He actually chuckled.

'Would you like to talk about it?'

'About what?' A shutter seemed to slam down over his eyes, turning the blue into shards of silver, as wintery cold as the snow outside.

'Whatever it is you were dreaming about. My younger sister used to have nightmares after our father died. We shared a bed so I always knew, but talking about it soothed her.'

'What happened to your father?' The shutters lifted slightly, though he didn't answer her question.

'Typhoid. There was an epidemic in London ten years ago and he was one of the victims. Lottie was only twelve and it wasn't easy for her to witness.'

'Or for you, I should imagine. I doubt you were much older.'

'No. I was fifteen, but I had to be strong for her and my brother and mother.' She winced at the memory of that dark time. 'My parents were devoted to each other, you see. They ran a charitable institution, but after he died, my mother couldn't bear to face the world for a while. Someone had to be practical and keep things going.'

'I'm sorry.' His gaze seemed very intense all of a sudden. 'For all of you.'

'Thank you.'

She rocked back on her heels as they lapsed into a pensive silence, without so much as the crackle of a log in the fireplace to relieve the atmosphere of tension. Maybe she ought to go back to bed, after all, Millie thought. If he didn't want to talk, then she didn't want to push him, although for some reason she didn't want to leave so soon either. Despite the tension she felt strangely comfortable with him.

'What did you say to your sister after her nightmares?' he asked finally, his voice softer than before. 'How did you make her feel better?'

'I'd tell her that the pain would ease in time, that Father wouldn't have wanted us to be sad and that we had to take care of each other the way he would have wanted us to. But mostly I just let her talk.'

'And that helped?'

'It seemed to.'

He nodded and stared down at the floor as if he were considering something, his brows contracted into a straight, hard line. 'What do you know about the military campaign in Afghanistan?'

She blinked, taken aback by the change of subject. 'Only what I've read in the newspapers. It sounded awful.'

'It was.' He looked up again, the muscles in his jaw and neck clenched tight. 'I was sent there two years ago as a captain in the Army of the Indus, twenty-one thousand men sent to play "the Great Game", as Melbourne and the rest of our politicians called it. It wasn't a game for us. That was the real nightmare. Things happened that I wish I'd never seen, things done by both sides, but I was one of the lucky ones. I was sent back to India after a year. I wasn't in the Khyber Pass.'

'Oh.' She lifted a hand to her mouth, horrified by the mere mention of it. 'That was terrible. Just one survivor.'

'Out of thousands of soldiers.' He nodded grimly. 'Our generals were over-confident and didn't understand the terrain. They delayed the retreat for far too long, until winter. The whole campaign was a disaster. There were skirmishes on our march back to India, too. My unit was attacked several times.'

'Were you injured?' For some reason the thought made her breath catch.

'Not badly, but…almost.' A muscle in his jaw seemed to spasm. 'I had a friend who saved me from a knife in the stomach. Unfortunately it got him in the shoulder instead.'

'Did he recover?'

'We carried him back to India on a stretcher, hoping he'd somehow pull through, but…' He dropped his gaze to the floor again. 'I sat by his bedside for four days, telling him he'd been a damned fool to save me and doing whatever I could to repay the favour, but it wasn't enough. All I could do was watch him die.'

'I'm sorry.' She didn't know what else to say.

'So am I.'

'I'm sure he was glad to have a friend by his side.'

'I don't think he was aware of much by the end.' He ran a hand over his brow. 'He was thirty years old with a fiancée waiting at home and his whole life ahead of him. I was going to be the best man at his wedding. It was all such a waste.'

'Yes.' She couldn't argue with that. 'What was his name?'

'Towse, Captain Edward Towse.' He grimaced as he reached for the bottle of port that wasn't there. 'He was like a brother to me and I…'

'You blame yourself?' She finished as his voice broke.

'Yes.'

'It was his choice to save you.'

'But he shouldn't have taken the risk. I didn't ask him to.' The look in his eyes was stark. 'He gave up his life for mine. That's not an easy thing to live with.'

'No, I don't suppose it is.' She shook her head sympathetically. 'Is that what you dream about?'

He nodded. 'Not every night, but often. I watch the whole scene in my head, only slowed down. I see the glint of the blade heading towards me, I see my own sword come up and then I see Edward push me aside. Then I can't see anything because his back is in the way and then...then I see him fall. Over and over again, like I'm trapped in those few minutes. It's as though my mind thinks if I watch it enough times then I'll be able to change things somehow, to stop it all from happening, but I can't. Nothing ever changes. Not the result or the guilt. Some nights I'm afraid to go to sleep.' He gave a ragged laugh and shook his head. 'A grown man, afraid of his own dreams.'

'They're not dreams.' She repeated his earlier words. 'They're memories.'

'Ah.'

'Is that why you left the army?'

'Part of the reason, but I was needed back in England, too.' He shifted forward, bracing his arms over his knees. 'A few days after Edward's funeral, I got word that my cousin had taken a bad fall from his horse. By the time I returned to England, he was dead.'

'How dreadful. Were you very close?'

'Not so much in recent years, but as boys we were

inseparable. We grew up together, you see, but after university our lives went in different directions. Magnus married and had children and I joined the army. I wish I'd made more of an effort to stay close to him.' He stared down at the purple-stained hearth and made a face. 'Now you see why I drink. Guilt is a terrible thing, *Just Millie*, but you're quite right.'

'What do you mean?' She drew her brows together. 'I didn't say anything.'

'Ah, but you thought it and you're right. Edward sacrificed himself to save me and all I do to repay the favour is wallow in self-pity and alcohol. It's downright ungrateful.'

'I don't recall thinking any of that.' She stiffened, offended by the implication. 'Everyone grieves in their own way.'

'But I suspect that *you* wouldn't behave like this. I ought to be practical like you were, don't you think?'

'I still have emotions, Mr Whitlock. Just because I threw myself into work when my father died doesn't mean I didn't love or mourn him. A person can be practical and still *feel*.'

'Forgive me—' he reached forward suddenly and caught one of her hands '—I didn't mean to suggest otherwise. It takes strength and courage not to let your emotions get the better of you, to carry on with life even when you're in pain. Sometimes I'm afraid that I'll never be able to move past what happened, that I'll never find peace or joy again.' His gaze burned into hers. 'You have fortitude, *Just Millie*. I admire and envy you for that. On top of which, you're an excellent listener. Your sister is very lucky to have you.'

'Thank you.' She looked down at their joined hands.

Hers looked so small and weak inside his, yet he said he envied *her* strength. 'And things will get better for you, I'm sure of it. Even the memories will fade eventually. You'll find peace and joy again.'

'Will I? Why do I deserve those things when he's gone?'

'Because everyone deserves those things. And you will because wounds scar over.' She strove to sound reassuring. 'You were wounded that day you lost your friend, just like I was when I lost my father. They might not have been injuries anyone could see, but they were still real. Some wounds might be mortal, but the rest heal and scar over in time. You might not be the same person you were before, but you'll be able to move on some day.'

'Move on...' he repeated the words, his fingers tightening imperceptibly over hers. 'I'm almost afraid you're a part of some dream, too, *Just Millie*, only a good one this time. Are you sure you're real and not a figment of my imagination?'

'I think so.' She nodded, though she had to admit she was feeling somewhat light-headed. Probably because her pulse was accelerating to a positively alarming rate. She tried drawing in a breath to slow it down, but the room seemed unusually lacking in air. It made her feel as if she were panting instead.

Desperately, she shifted her gaze away from their hands and then instantly regretted it. His shoulders were broad and muscular and the neck of his shirt was open, revealing the strong column of his throat as well as the top of his chest and a dusting of pale golden hair beneath. Her gaze continued downwards, as if drawn of its own volition, certainly against her own better judgement. He must have woken up in a sweat because his shirt was stuck to his skin in places, making the stomach muscles beneath as visible as if he were naked.

She ran her tongue nervously over lips that felt bone dry all of a sudden. Their close proximity was utterly inappropriate, even more so than her being there was already, but his hand was still holding hers, his fingers warm and strong, and she felt an almost irresistible impulse to stroke the inside of his palm with her thumb.

'I'm very real—' she cleared her throat instead '—but I don't deserve your admiration. Sometimes I feel trapped, too, not in the past, but in the present. I don't compare my situation to yours, of course, but there are days when I want to scream at the very top of my lungs. If I hadn't found your house this evening, I might actually have done it, just to see how it feels.'

'Go ahead.'

She looked up in alarm. 'I'm not going to scream, Mr Whitlock.'

'Why not? It's the perfect opportunity. There aren't any other houses within hearing distance, just a lot of trees. You might frighten a few badgers and squirrels, but we can live with that.'

'I still can't scream.'

'Why not?'

'Because I don't do things like that. It's not who I am. Once maybe, but not any more.'

'Then who are you, *Just Millie*?'

'Who am I?' The very question made her feel reckless. 'I'm Miss Amelia Fairclough, teacher of sewing and housekeeping at the Fairclough Foundation. I'm practical, virtuous and self-sacrificing.' She drew her fingers away from his to tick the qualities off one by one. 'Which I know because everyone tells me so.'

His lips twitched as he lifted an eyebrow quizzically. 'Aren't they supposed to be positive qualities?'

'They are, but put all together like that they just sound so utterly boring.'

'Surely people don't tell you *that*?'

'Not to my face, but it's implied. *Self*-sacrificing, as if I don't have a *self*!' She dug her nails into her palms in frustration. 'It's not that I'm unhappy, at least not exactly. My work is very rewarding and it pleases me to know that I'm doing something useful and helping others, but I want to be *more* than just practical and virtuous! I *used* to be, only those things have become habits and now everyone expects them of me. I feel so...'

'Trapped?'

'Exactly! And boring. I feel as if I've become someone I didn't want to be, someone I'm not even sure that *I* like. My sister and brother are both far more interesting than I am.'

'Are you the eldest?'

'Only by half an hour. Silas is my twin.' She drew in a deep breath and then sighed it out again. 'It sounds ridiculous, but I was trying to be different and rebellious tonight and look what happened! I got lost in a snowstorm and ruined your evening.'

'You haven't ruined anything. I'm glad to have met you, *Just Millie*.'

'You are?'

'Extremely.' He sounded surprisingly genuine. 'You've made me feel better.'

'I'm glad.' She peered up at him. 'Although in that

case I probably shouldn't tell you the most boring thing of all.'

'But now I'm curious.' There was a hint of a smile in his voice. 'Tell me.'

'All right…' She sighed again. 'It's that at this precise moment, what I'd like more than anything else in the world is a cup of tea.' She screwed her mouth up apologetically. 'That's not something an exciting woman would say, is it?'

'I don't know. It sounds like a quite genius idea to me.' He pushed himself out of his chair, started towards the door and then stopped, turning around to bob down beside her. 'For what it's worth I don't think you're boring at all. In fact, I think you might be the most intriguing woman I've ever met.' His gaze dropped. 'And my dressing gown suits you, by the way.'

'Oh!' She pressed a hand to the throat of the peacock-green-and-blue garment self-consciously. It swamped her slender shoulders and trailed several inches along the floor, looking more like a ceremonial robe than a housecoat, but it was soft and surprisingly comfortable, so much so that she'd forgotten she was wearing it. She even liked its musky smell. 'I was rushing to get downstairs, but I didn't want to do it in my unmentionables and this was the first thing that came to hand.'

'Well, that's certainly a relief. We wouldn't want any unmentionables on display.' His gaze drifted to her mouth and then back to her eyes, his own glowing with some indefinable emotion. Only it brought the word *smouldering* to mind. 'Now wait here and I'll see what I can find in the kitchen.'

Millie waited until the parlour door had closed before swallowing hard. His face had been so close to hers that for the space of a few unsteady heartbeats she'd thought that he was going to embrace her. To kiss her. The idea ought to have been shocking, but it wasn't. On the contrary, it had been quite decidedly tempting.

She pressed her hands to her furiously blushing cheeks, feeling as if his gaze itself had scorched her. Ironically after her evening's adventure in the snow, now the whole room felt too hot. She stood up and moved away from the fire, trying to distract herself from the fact that she'd just poured her heart and soul out to a man she'd only just met. It was outrageous! Though on the other hand, it had felt good to talk to someone about her feelings for once, and it wasn't as if she'd done anything very wrong. She'd only told the truth and it was an unusual night, after all, a break from her real life of virtue and self-sacrifice, a snow-covered secret that no one else ever needed to know about.

And he'd called her intriguing. *That* was the best secret of all.

Chapter Four

'Tea is served,' Cassius announced, lifting the pot and pouring out two cups of steaming amber liquid.

'Thank you.' Miss Amelia Fairclough, as she was apparently called, clasped her hands around the rim with a pleased-sounding sigh.

'Sugar?'

'Two lumps, please.'

'Two lumps.' He dropped them into her cup and stirred. 'I'm rather good at playing mistress of the house, don't you think?'

'Very proficient.' Her lips—perfect, bow-shaped, rosy-red lips—spread into a smile. 'All you need now is an apron.'

He chuckled and sat down on the hearth rug beside her, leaning against the armchair for comfort. It was strange how relaxed he felt in her company now. Positively serene, in fact. Since returning to England, he'd barely spoken about his time in Afghanistan and India to anyone, no more than was necessary anyway. He preferred that nobody knew how much the experience had affected him. Part of the reason he chose to sleep in the gatehouse was so that his staff, never mind Sylvia and her daughters, wouldn't overhear his nightmares. He didn't want anyone else to know that he had them at all, only Miss Fairclough had somehow guessed the truth. As to why he'd chosen to tell her the details, he had no idea. It wasn't simply because she'd been there in a moment of weakness. It was *her*. She'd made him *want* to talk, to be listened to as well by someone who'd seemed like she might understand. She'd truly made him feel better. So much so that he wanted to help her, too.

'Now I have a question for you, *Just Millie*, if you'll permit me?'

'I will.' She lifted her cup and blew across the surface of the tea to cool it. 'But I've told you my full name. You're permitted to use it.'

'But I prefer *Just Millie*. It suits you and Miss Amelia sounds far too formal. In my mind you'll always be *Just Millie*, umbrellaed avenger!'

'Now you're being ridiculous.' She laughed. It sounded soft and soothing, like water trickling over stones in a brook. 'Very well, then, what's your question?'

'What do you want?'

She gave him a baffled look. 'Pardon?'

'You said that you've become someone you didn't want to be so...' he opened his hands, palms upwards '...what do you want? If you could do anything with your life, what would it be?'

'Anything at all?'

'Anything. Be Queen of England if you want.'

'I believe the position is taken, but if I could do anything...' She tapped her chin thoughtfully. 'I'd like to be decadent, just for one day. I'd lie on a *chaise longue*, eat macaroons, read novels and have a cat.'

'A cat?' He lifted an eyebrow. 'Did I mention that you could do *anything*?'

'Yes, but I don't have any regal ambitions and I've always wanted a pet cat. My brother sneezes around them so it was never possible growing up.'

'So you're saying that you want a cat more than you want to be Queen?'

She nodded her head firmly. 'I'd call it Electra or Orestes, depending on whether it was male or female.'

'I see you've put a lot of thought into this.'

'I have.' She leaned forward conspiratorially. 'I tried keeping a stray once. She was mewling so pitifully at the back door so I made her a little bed in the coal shed, but I must have carried her hair inside on my clothes. Silas still sneezed.' She sighed plaintively. 'Fortunately, I found her a home with an old lady on our street. They were both very happy.'

'And why the Greek names?'

'Oh, I've always liked Greek mythology. When I was little I had a book filled with stories and legends. I read it so much that eventually the cover fell off.'

'You don't think that Electra and Orestes have somewhat bloodthirsty connotations?'

'They're still nice names.'

'I suppose so.' His lips twitched in bemusement. The conversation was so odd he half-wondered if he was dreaming again. 'Well then, can't you have a cat now? Or does your brother still live at home?'

'No.' Her expression turned anxious. 'He went to America to seek his fortune just over a year ago. He sent several letters at first, but now we haven't had any word in seven months. We're all worried.'

'Naturally.'

'I'm sure there are all kinds of good reasons why we haven't received any letters, but if I were to get a cat, it would be like admitting he wasn't coming back at all.'

'I see.'

'But maybe I'll get one if—' She stopped mid-sentence, her cheeks flushing a pretty pink colour.

'*If...?*'

'If I marry.' She lifted her teacup and held it at chin level. 'A friend of the family, our local Curate, asked me to marry him last week.'

'Indeed?' He felt a jolt in his chest, a reflexive stab of something like disappointment. 'You don't sound very enthusiastic.'

'Because he's a friend. I know we could get along perfectly well together. He's a good man and I respect him, but I don't know if I could ever care for him in the right way. As a husband, I mean.'

'Have you told him that?'

'Oh, yes, and he said he's had similar thoughts about me as a wife, but overall he considers friendship more important than love.' She took a sip of tea and then looked up abruptly. 'Isn't that odd? If you were married, wouldn't you want your partner to be more than just a friend?'

Yes. Unquestionably. Undoubtedly. Unequivocally.

The words were on the tip of his tongue, but he swallowed them with a mouthful of too-hot tea. 'I suppose so. *Some* people might even say it was integral.'

'He's never even tried to kiss me.' She murmured

the words as if to herself and then blushed violently again. 'Forgive me, I shouldn't have said that.'

'Why not? Kissing is another important aspect of marriage.'

'Oh, dear.' Her eyelashes fluttered. 'That's what I was afraid of. Only he doesn't seem to want to and every time I even *try* to imagine kissing him, my mind just shies away from the idea. Last week I polished all the brass in the house just to avoid thinking about it! I know I oughtn't to say it, especially to another man, but it just doesn't feel right.'

'Then I believe you might have your answer to his proposal.'

'It's not as simple as that!' She sounded indignant. 'I wish it were.'

'But surely if you don't feel the right way…?'

'How I feel has nothing to do with it. My mother and sister and I are almost down to the last of our savings. Without my brother's money coming from America, we can't afford our rent, let alone food, at least not without taking money from the Foundation and Mother would hate to do that. If I don't marry, then we could be destitute.'

'You can't marry just for a place to live.'

'Says the man who's allowed to make his own living.' She gave him a scornful look. 'Having a place to live is the reason why a lot of women marry. We have to be practical.'

'Can't you strive for happiness, too?'

'Keeping a roof over my family's heads *will* make me happy.'

'Even if it makes you want to go out into the woods and scream?'

She knitted her brows together, taking another sip of tea before answering. 'Even if it does that, yes.'

'What about love? Your suitor might not think it important, but what do you think?'

If he wasn't mistaken, her breath caught at the word *love*. 'That would be another sacrifice, but I believe marriages without love are quite common.'

'Pardon my saying so, but you sound very cynical about it.'

'I suppose I am. Only I've met all kinds of women at the Foundation and I've listened to their stories. I *know* the real world isn't romantic.'

'On the whole I'd agree with you, but you seem a little too young to give up.'

'I'm twenty-five.' Her eyes shot to his and then softened. 'Forgive me, you might be right. I know that true love exists because I saw it with my parents, but I can't let my mother and sister be thrown out of our home just because *I* want the same thing. It would be selfish of me. Besides, what if I never meet a man I can fall in love with?'

'What if you do?'

'And what if we all starve or freeze to death in the meantime?'

'I still say that marrying this suitor of yours is a sacrifice too far.' He felt suddenly determined to convince her. If she was so desperate for money, then he would be more than happy to help, though he could hardly make the offer at that moment without it sounding somewhat indecent. Perhaps what she needed was a different kind of convincing.

'All right, *Just Millie*, tell me this.' He leaned closer towards her. 'Do you think you could *ever* love this man?'

'As a friend or a brother, yes. As a wife, no.'

'Because you can't imagine kissing him?'

'In part.'

'Have you *ever* been kissed?'

'Mr Whitlock!' Her body jerked so abruptly that tea sloshed on to his dressing gown.

'Don't worry about that.' He reached for her cup, putting it aside as she started to wipe herself down. 'I shouldn't have put the question so bluntly, but have you considered that it might just be the thought of kissing itself that puts you off? If you've never tried it, perhaps you're simply nervous?'

'Perhaps.' She pulled her shoulders back stiffly and folded her hands in her lap, seeming to make a concerted effort to regain her composure, though her expression was still flustered. 'Yes, I suppose it *could* be that.'

'In which case, maybe I can help.'

Green eyes widened like saucers. 'What do you mean?'

'Just that if you'd *like* to try then I'd be more than happy to oblige.'

'You would be...' He hadn't thought that her eyes could get any bigger, but apparently he'd been wrong. Fortunately, the expression in them was more bewildered than offended. 'Are you offering to kiss me, Mr Whitlock?'

'Yes.'

'Why?'

'Because...' He started and then stopped, considering for a moment. In all honesty, he was somewhat surprised by the suggestion himself. He couldn't even blame it on the port since he'd sobered up a good hour ago. It wasn't a gentlemanly offer. On the contrary, it was downright *un*gentlemanly, only now that he'd made it, he found himself somewhat ardently hoping she'd say yes. 'Well, for a start, because you helped me earlier and now I'd like to help you. I admit that kissing isn't something I'd usually suggest to a young lady, but we might consider it as a practical experiment, a way to work out how you feel about the whole process.'

'I see.' She lifted her chin, looking down her nose at him. 'So kissing me would constitute your good deed for the day?'

'I wouldn't put it quite like that. I told you, I'm more than happy to do it.'

'How gallant of you to say so.'

'Forgive me—' he couldn't help but smile at her sarcasm '—I didn't mean to imply any selflessness on my part. I'm sure I would enjoy the experience, too. It would just be one kiss, one single, solitary, utterly harmless kiss.'

'Something tells me Gilbert wouldn't see it that way.'

'*Gilbert?* That's the name of your suitor?'

'Yes.' She blinked. 'What's wrong with Gilbert?'

'Nothing, only I'm *Mr* Whitlock.'

'Because we've only just met!'

'True, but since you're thinking about kissing me, you might at least call me Cassius.'

'I never said I was thinking about kissing you.'

'But you are?'

'No!' She shook her head so emphatically that auburn hair tumbled forward over her shoulders. 'I couldn't possibly.'

'Why not?' He let his eyes follow the lustrous waves

downwards. They reached to just below her breasts. If she were naked, the sight would be quite tantalising. His imagination was already running riot... 'I don't suppose you could shake your head again?'

She ignored his request. 'How could I marry Gilbert after kissing someone else?'

'You wouldn't have to tell him.'

'That would be even more wicked!'

'All right then, tell him the truth: that you needed to know what the experience was like.'

'Then he'll say that I should have asked him to kiss me.'

'Exactly!' Cassius grinned triumphantly. 'Only he shouldn't have *needed* to be asked. He should have done it already. That's as good a reason as any for *not* marrying him, in my opinion. The man's clearly insane.'

'Mr Whitlock...' she pursed her lips, looking and sounding like an archetypal schoolmistress '...either you're teasing me or you're a Lothario.'

'Millie...' he shifted closer, emulating her tone '...if I were a Lothario, then I wouldn't have *asked* if you wanted to be kissed, I would simply have done it. Then I would have found us another bottle of port and made some excuse to escort you upstairs. *You* were the one who came down, remember? And I believe you were also the one who first mentioned kissing?'

'Oh, yes...' her brow wrinkled '...so I did.'

'And, as for teasing, I assure you that my offer is entirely genuine.' His leg brushed inadvertently against hers, though since it was there he didn't bother to move it away. 'The truth is I'd rather *like* to kiss you. Your lips look quite extraordinarily kissable, especially now.'

'Why especially now?'

'Because you look so surprised.' He brought his face alongside hers, murmuring into her ear, 'Is it really so inconceivable that I might want to kiss you?'

'Honestly?' A small tremor seemed to run through her before she moved her head back to look him in the eyes again. 'Yes.'

'Why?'

'Nobody's ever wanted to before.'

'Only as far as you know.'

'Well, yes, but…' She drew her bottom lip into her mouth and sucked, unconsciously, he was certain, though the gesture struck him as intensely sensual. '*Just* one kiss?'

'Just one and we'll stop whenever you want. We don't even have to talk about it afterwards. We can talk about something else entirely. The East India Company in China, for example. Personally I consider their behaviour reprehensible, but Peel and his government seem deter—'

'Cassius?'

'Yes?'

'I think I'd prefer not to talk about the Prime Minister right now.'

'As you wish. I'm a Whig myself…'

'Cassius?'

'Yes?'

'You can kiss me. *Just* once…' her pupils seemed to swell as she spoke '…and *just* as an experiment.'

'With pleasure.'

He lifted a hand to her cheek and drew her face gently, but steadily, towards him. Her eyes opened wide for a split second and then closed as his lips touched against hers, though she didn't pull away as he'd half-expected she might. On the contrary, she swayed closer, actually increasing the pressure of the kiss as she let out a small, barely distinguishable sigh. The sound seemed to warm his insides, heating his blood and making his heart skip a beat and then start to pump at twice its usual speed. Her lips were just as kissable as they'd appeared, velvety smooth and tasting of hot, sweet tea. Perfectly delicious, in fact. He slid his tongue between them, stroking the inside of her mouth, *also delicious*, then brought his other hand up to slide through the soft red waves of her hair.

She reached for his shoulders and a bolt of desire, startling in its intensity, shot through him with the force of a bullet. Damn it. He let his hand fall from her hair. This was a mistake. So much for one *utterly harmless* kiss. With this woman, he had a feeling that one kiss would never be anywhere near enough. He wanted more, *much* more, several hours' worth of more, in fact. Which meant that he had to stop now before all the blood rushed to the lower half of his body and he lost the ability to make rational decisions.

He broke away, clearing his throat to disguise the ragged sound of his breathing.

'Well…' He picked up his cup and drained the contents in a few short gulps, doing his best to adopt a suitably detached expression. 'I think, as experiments go, that was quite satisfactory.'

'Ye—es.' Her own breath emerged in shallow gasps as she looked at him dazedly for a few moments and then seemed to come back to herself, wrenching her hands away from his shoulders. 'It was…illuminating.'

'Good.' Apparently his throat needed clearing a

second time. 'Then I hope it helps you come to a decision.'

'A decision?' She looked confused. 'Oh, you mean about Gilbert. Yes, perhaps I've misjudged him, after all.'

'What?'

'Well, as you say, the experiment was quite satisfactory. Perhaps kissing him won't be such a problem.'

'But that wasn't the point!'

'Yes, it was. We were trying to establish if I liked kissing in principle.'

Cassius rubbed a hand over his jaw, feeling unreasonably offended. *Had* they been trying to establish that? Now that he thought of it, he'd said something similar. Only he'd been so intent upon kissing her that perhaps he hadn't thought the idea through...

'Well, yes, I suppose. Or at least I was trying to prove that kissing can, *should,* be pleasurable, but kissing one person isn't the same as kissing another.'

'Why not?'

'Because everyone is different.'

'Then why didn't you tell me that before?' Her tone was accusing. 'You said that kissing you would help me to imagine kissing Gilbert!'

'Did I?'

'Yes!' She blinked. 'Didn't you?'

'I'm not entirely sure I remember.' He clamped his brows together. 'Perhaps you should try imagining it now?'

'I can't right now! It wouldn't be right.'

'No, perhaps not. Here.' He picked up her cup of tea and handed it to her. What was it his aunt had always said? Nothing like a cup of tea in a crisis. And if this wasn't a crisis he didn't know what was. 'Drink up before it gets cold.'

'Thank you.' She took a few sips, watching him warily out of the corner of her eye before putting the cup down again and standing up. 'I ought to get back to bed. It's very late.'

'Of course.' He stood up, too, making a small, awkward bow. 'I hope that you sleep well, Miss Fairclough. I apologise for the misunderstanding.'

'Not at all.' She seemed to have trouble meeting his gaze. 'It was my fault, too. Perhaps we should just forget it ever happened?'

'Consider it done.'

'Thank you.' She started towards the door and then stopped, half-twisting her face back towards him. 'When you say it would be different with Gilbert, how different exactly do you mean?'

'Well…' He felt an unmistakable pang of jealousy. 'I suppose that depends on how much you feel like polishing some brass right now.'

'Oh… I see. Well, goodnight then, Mr Whitlock. I hope that you don't have any more bad dreams.'

Cassius waited until the parlour door had closed shut behind her before dropping into his armchair. No matter how bad they'd been before, he had a feeling his dreams for the rest of the night were going to tell a whole different story.

Chapter Five

Millie crept through the hall on tiptoe, tensing as she lifted the latch of the front door and then lowered it with a soft click behind her. The sun was just coming up over the treetops and in the early hush of dawn even that tiny sound seemed too loud. Pulling her cloak tighter around her, she hurried through the gates that stood next to the house and out on to the road, relieved to be away from the scene of her disgrace. Thankfully the snow had stopped some time during the night and the village was only a mile down the road, or so Cassius had told her when she'd first appeared on his doorstep. Now she just had to hurry before he woke up and came after her.

Would he come after her? She glanced nervously back over her shoulder, a wave of heat washing through her body at the thought. He'd been fast asleep in his armchair when she'd crept into the parlour to retrieve her cloak, but she was afraid it was something he *might* do if he woke up and found her gone. He'd said that his conscience wouldn't be easy until he'd escorted her to her door, but the thought of seeing him again made her feel mortified. After the scandalous way she'd behaved, she doubted she'd be able to look him or any other man in the face ever again. She hadn't even dared look at *herself* in the bedroom mirror that morning.

She was a scarlet woman! Or if not completely scarlet, then definitely pink. Salmon-coloured maybe. She'd *kissed* a man, a man she'd only just met! A man with hypnotic blue eyes that had seemed to peer into her very soul and whose lips had unleashed a torrent of new and extraordinary responses in her body, each more shocking than the last. For a few wicked seconds she'd surrendered completely to a feeling of light-headed, breath-stealing, almost painfully intense pleasure. And why? Because for one brief moment curiosity had got the better of her. Because she'd liked him and the way he'd talked to her as if she really *were* intriguing. But mostly because she'd wanted to know how it would feel to be kissed.

Well, she'd certainly achieved that. She hadn't been able to get a wink of sleep afterwards, her whole body wide awake and tingling all over. Now the problem was going to be trying to forget it.

She shook her head, determinedly attempting to displace the memory. She wouldn't think of him or his lips or eyes, hypnotic or otherwise, ever again. She wouldn't think of *him* at all. She only hoped that he wasn't invited to any of the festive events her cousin had planned…

Her steps faltered at the sight of a young woman, bundled up in a woollen shawl, trudging towards her from the direction of the village.

'Good morning.' Millie nodded her head as she

passed, doing her best impression of a woman out for an entirely plausible jaunt in the snow.

'Morning, miss.' The woman's gaze darted quickly to her face and then away again.

Seized with an even greater sense of trepidation, Millie pulled her bonnet forward and increased her pace, making her way as quickly as her impractical evening gown would allow through the snowdrifts. Fortunately, she didn't meet anyone else before she reached her cousin's red-brick manor on the outskirts of the village.

'Millie!' Lilian Fairclough came flying out of the drawing room, flinging her arms around her the moment she entered the front door. 'What on earth happened? Where have you been? We've been so worried.'

'You have?' Millie looked at her mother in surprise. She'd taken the absence of search parties on her way as a good sign.

'Well…yes.' Her mother looked shame-faced. 'Or at least we have been since five minutes ago when I came down to breakfast and Alexandra asked me how you'd been on the journey home. I had no idea you'd stayed to wait for me.'

'It didn't occur to me to mention it last night.' Alexandra came to stand behind her mother. 'I just assumed that you'd gone straight to bed.'

'I thought that might happen…' Millie kissed her mother's cheek reassuringly '…but it's all right. I'm here now.'

'Did Lady Fentree send you home in her carriage?' Alexandra peered out of the window. 'Has it left again already?'

'No. I walked back.'

'She let you *walk*? In this weather?'

'Actually she doesn't know anything about it. I was out in the garden when I heard the last carriage leave and I thought it would be pleasant to make my own way home, although in retrospect I suppose that was somewhat foolish of me.'

'But surely you haven't been out in these temperatures all night?' Her mother looked horrified.

'No, I came to a house and the owner gave me shelter.' She made a show of removing her outer garments, horribly aware of her cheeks reddening. 'Is breakfast still out? I'm famished.'

'You can have all the bacon and eggs you want.' Alexandra took hold of one arm while her mother took hold of the other, leading her through to the dining room. 'We're just so relieved that you're all right.'

'Ah, there she is!' George Malverly waved a fork from one end of an oval-shaped mahogany table. 'Didn't I tell you she'd show up in her own good time? She's resourceful, this one.'

'I appreciate your confidence.' Millie took a seat beside him with a smile. Alexandra's husband was a good twenty years older than his wife, but their marriage had been, and remained, a love match. At seventy years old, his figure was becoming increasingly portly and his nose a somewhat startling shade of red, but the roguish glint in his eye never failed to make her laugh.

'Been out for a morning's perambulation, eh?' He nudged her arm across the corner of the table. 'Good for the complexion, I should imagine.'

'*Fresh air* is good for the complexion, George.' Alexandra sat down opposite. 'A snowstorm is dangerous.'

'What? Oh, yes, quite right, but she's here now and looking as fit as a fresh-faced fiddle. No damage done, I'd say.'

'Where was it you found shelter, dear?' Her mother sat down beside Alexandra.

'Just a house on the road. Could you pass me the toast, please?'

'Well, that certainly narrows it down.' Her mother exchanged a glance with her cousin. 'It's mostly woodland between here and the Fentrees, isn't it?'

'Nearly the whole way.'

'Where's the butter?'

'There's only one house I can think of and that's empty.'

'I think I'd like marmalade this morning…'

'Who was it that sheltered you, dear?'

'Oh, I meant jam. Strawberry preserve if you have any?'

'Millie?' Her mother lifted an eyebrow. 'Forgive me for saying so, but you're being rather evasive.'

'Am I?' She smeared butter on to a piece of toast and then put the knife down, acutely aware of two pairs of eyes watching her like constables across the table. 'Oh, very well. It was a gatehouse. There was a drive leading somewhere, but I couldn't see any other buildings close by.'

'It must have been the one belonging to Falconmore Hall.' Alexandra looked surprised. 'The drive's a good two miles long, but I didn't think anyone lived in the gatehouse any more.'

'They don't.' George speared his fork into a piece of kipper. 'Not for the past two years.'

'Well, there was someone there last night.'

'Yes, but who?'

'Who?' Millie took a deep breath, scooped up some strawberry jam and dolloped it on to her bread. 'I believe he said he was the estate manager.'

'A *man*?' Alexandra pressed a hand to her mouth with a look of horror.

'An estate manager?' George looked thoughtful. 'Falconmore must have hired somebody new. Seems odd when Linton's been doing the job perfectly well for fifteen years, but there you go. New man, new ideas, I suppose.'

'What do you mean?' Millie paused with the toast halfway to her lips.

'Oh, the former Marquess died just about a year ago. Tried jumping a fence he shouldn't have, poor fellow. I suppose the new Lord Falconmore thinks it's time for some changes.'

'George!' Alexandra interrupted her husband sternly. 'Falconmore's staffing situation is irrelevant. Millie spent the night alone in a house with a man!'

'Did she, by Jove?'

'Yes…' Millie swallowed a mouthful of toast '…but under the circumstances, I was very grateful to see him. I don't know what I would have done if he hadn't let me stay.'

'Well, yes…' Alexandra leaned forward over the table '…but *a man*? Wasn't there anyone else in the house?'

'I'm afraid not.' She straightened her shoulders defensively. 'I know it looks bad, but I couldn't have walked another step and there was a blizzard. I almost collapsed on his doorstep as it was. The situation was regrettable, but unavoidable. Fortunately, only he and

I and now the three of you know. Surely that's safe enough?'

'Do you think you can trust his discretion?'

'Yes.' For some reason, it hadn't occurred to her to doubt it.

'And nobody saw you leave?'

'No, and I saw only one other person this morning, a maid on the road, but I was halfway back to the village by then.'

'Yes, but the snow stopped during the night.'

'What difference does that make?'

'Your footprints.' Her mother looked anxious. 'They'll lead straight back to the gatehouse.'

'Oh…dear.' She stared at her toast for a few seconds and then put it down, losing her appetite suddenly. *Oh, double dear…*

'Well, that doesn't mean the maid will have noticed—' George's tone was reassuring '—and even if she did, how would she know who Millie is?'

'That's true.' She grasped at the idea eagerly. 'Thank you, George.'

'Always glad to be of service.'

'Mmm.' Alexandra sounded doubtful. 'We *were* going to call on a few acquaintances this morning, but under the circumstances it might be best for you to stay here, just in case you were recognised. Your hair colour is quite distinctive, after all. We'd better give it a couple of days to make sure.'

'In that case, we'll have coffee and biscuits in the library.' George winked at her. 'How do you fancy a few games of backgammon?'

'That sounds lovely.' Millie smiled, trying to quell a nagging sense of disquiet. 'Just lovely.'

* * *

Cassius knocked twice on the bedroom door with his knuckles and then twisted the handle. The cup of tea he'd left outside earlier was untouched despite his having knocked then, too, and he couldn't wait any longer. He'd given it a full hour, but without any sound from upstairs, not so much as the faintest creak of a floorboard, he was becoming somewhat anxious.

'Miss Fairclough?'

He nudged the door open slowly, though even a brief glance showed that the room was completely empty, albeit tidier than it had been before. The furniture had all been straightened, the bed completely made up and his dressing gown folded neatly across it. He walked in and picked it up, lifting the velvet collar to his face with a curious sense of loss. It smelt like her, of soap and some other floral perfume, like bergamot and orange blossoms. She was gone, though as to when and why she'd left without as much as a goodbye... He grimaced. The answers to both of those questions were obvious. *When* had been after he'd finally drifted into a deep and surprisingly restful slumber and *why* was in all likelihood due to his ungentlemanly behaviour. She'd probably been afraid he might pounce on her again.

He hung the dressing gown where it belonged on the back of the door and then crouched down, spotting something shiny on the rug beside the bed, a garnet-and-emerald-studded gold brooch shaped like a butterfly. He held it in his palm, studying it for a few seconds, then tucked it inside his jacket pocket and made his way determinedly down the stairs, stopping only to pull on his greatcoat, boots and top hat at the door. There was nothing else for it. Even if she'd run away in the early hours, then the least he could do was make sure she'd made it back to the village safely.

Fortunately for him, her footprints were still perfectly clear in the snow, leading him all the way back to Rayleigh and her front door. Which answered the question of who her relative was. George, Viscount Malverly, and his wife, Alexandra, were passing acquaintances. If he knocked now, then he could be certain that they'd receive him, at least. The question, however, was not *would*, but *should*, he, whether it wouldn't simply be better for him to turn around and go. Miss Fairclough's early departure made it abundantly clear that she didn't want to see him again and, much as he ought to apologise, respecting her wishes was more important.

He turned on his heel, marching back the way that he'd come. And that, he supposed, was that. Footprints in the snow would be the last he would see of her. Which was probably for the best, all things considered. Any attraction he'd felt, that she'd seemed to feel, too, for that matter, had likely just been the result of the tense situation in which they'd found themselves.

Besides, no matter how beguiling or intriguing he found her, he had enough on his hands dealing with Sylvia. He certainly didn't need another woman in his life, especially one who knew all about his past, not to mention his nightmares. And it wasn't as if his finer emotions were involved. His heart was a battered and broken organ, incapable of feeling anything positive to any great degree, love especially. Love, in his experience, led to loss and pain. He'd lost too many people he cared about and seen too many terrible things for it to recover again, even for someone as intriguing as *Just Millie*. He didn't regret what had happened between them. His time with her had been enjoyable—he might even say special—but it was over and done with. She would remain a bittersweet memory in his consciousness, but that was all. Which was clearly the way she wanted it, too. Under the circumstances, running away had probably been the wisest course of action.

Now that he had his thoughts in order, he felt an unaccustomed spring in his step that morning. Who would have imagined that talking could have such a calming, therapeutic effect? Well, talking and one deeply arousing kiss. The whole experience had been strangely invigorating, leaving him ready to face the world anew. He even felt ready to face Sylvia, which wasn't something he'd *ever* thought before.

It was forty bracing minutes before he finally reached the steps of Falconmore Hall and strode up to the front door where his perpetually stony-faced butler stood ready to greet him.

'Breakfast has been kept out in the dining room, sir,' Kendrew intoned solemnly. 'Lady Falconmore's orders.'

'Thank you, and Lady Falconmore is…?'

'Already in the drawing room, sir.'

'Excellent.' Cassius shrugged out of his greatcoat and rubbed his hands together, heading straight for the dining-room sideboard and loading a plate high with eggs, bacon and sausages. Even his appetite felt better this morning, though doubtless that was just due to the morning's exercise. Now if he could just eat in peace for once…

'Cassius!' The shrill tones of his cousin's widow rendered that hope impossible, making him flinch and almost drop his plate in surprise. 'You're back! Finally! How could you put me through such a night?'

'Good morning, Sylvia.' He inclined his head in greeting before seating himself at the head of the table. 'What exactly have I put you through now?'

'Worry, of course. It started to snow so soon after you left yesterday evening. I was afraid you might have been trapped in a snowdrift. I barely slept a wink all night.'

'How unfortunate, although I must say you look very well for it. Nobody would imagine you had lost any sleep at all.'

'I have bags under my eyes, I'm certain.' Perfectly coiffed blonde ringlets bounced indignantly. 'I do wish you wouldn't take such risks. Magnus was always behaving recklessly and look what happened to him.'

'I'm perfectly aware of what happened to my cousin, thank you.' Cassius gave her a hard look. 'There's no need to remind me.'

'I just couldn't bear to lose you, too.' She flounced into the chair beside him and clasped her hands together piteously. 'Even a chill can become serious.'

'I believe the camp surgeon mentioned that once or twice in the army.'

'Hermione and Isolde have been quite distraught, too. You know they think of you as a second father.'

'That would explain their rushing to greet me, I suppose?'

'They're at their piano practice now, but they'll be vastly relieved to know that you're back.'

'Glad to hear it.'

'You know…' A small foot coiled its way around his ankle. 'I don't know why you insist on taking such long walks and sleeping who knows where. There are plenty of ways we could amuse each other without leaving the house. I never lock my bedroom door.'

'But I do.' He shifted his legs to one side. 'As I believe we've already discussed. Twice.'

'If it's because of Magnus, then you needn't be so squeamish. *I'm* his widow and if *I* don't mind, then I really don't see why—'

'Enough!' Cassius laid both his hands down flat on the table. 'It's about time we discussed your living arrangements. It's been more than a year since the funeral. Maybe it's time for you and your daughters to…'

'You wouldn't be so cruel!' Sylvia practically leapt out of her chair. 'This is our home. Surely you wouldn't throw us out on to the street?'

'The Dower House is hardly the street. It's perfectly comfortable and—'

'Stop it!' She put her hands over her ears. 'I can't listen. I won't listen!'

'Oh, for pity's sake, we can't go on like this.'

'No!' She uttered one last piercing wail and then ran headlong from the room.

Cassius tossed his napkin aside with a sigh of disgust. Why was it, he wondered, that every conversation with the woman had to end in either a seduction attempt or hysterics or both? She hadn't been so bad for the first six months of his living there, but ever since he'd suggested a move to the Dower House she'd seemed positively determined to flirt with him instead. If he wasn't mistaken, she actually wanted to marry him! He supposed he ought to be flattered, but the

thought of marrying, let alone bedding, his cousin's
widow was abhorrent. This was at least the dozenth
time he'd broached the subject of her moving out, but
she doggedly refused to listen. It was a wonder to him
how Magnus had ever put up with her, but then his
cousin had never been able to resist a pretty face.

An image of Miss Fairclough's notably *un*dramatic
face floated into his mind. It wasn't as pretty as Sylvia's, somewhat on the long side, in fact, but just the
memory served to make him feel calmer again. She,
he was quite sure, never threw tantrums. It was hard to
imagine her being dramatic at all. Strangely enough, he
actually *missed* her. After only a few hours he wanted
to see her again, to hear her voice, too. Now that the
chance had passed he wished he'd told her about his
predicament with Sylvia. Something told him that *Just
Millie* would know exactly what he should do.

He reached into his jacket pocket and felt for the
butterfly brooch. He'd forgotten about it in front of
the Malverly house earlier, but it needed returning at
some point. He could send a footman, he supposed.
That would probably be the discreet thing to do. Or
he could take it himself, but what would Miss Fairclough think of that? He had no idea what she'd told
her family about him…and hadn't he already decided
that seeing her again was a bad idea? After one night,
she already knew more about him than he felt comfortable with. Except for the one significant fact of
his real identity, of course, and if he met her again in
more formal surroundings then he'd have to explain
who he really was…

He sighed and tucked the jewellery away again. No,
sending someone else was a much better idea. It would

probably be best for both of them if he avoided the village for the foreseeable future. He'd send a footman this afternoon, or tomorrow maybe, certainly at some point. For the time being, however, and just for a while, he wanted to keep the brooch in his pocket next to his shrivelled heart.

He had no idea what to think about that.

Chapter Six

Millie walked out of Rayleigh's Norman-built church arm in arm with her mother, smiling brightly while Alexandra and George exchanged greetings with the Vicar. She was already feeling ten times better than when she'd first arrived in the country. Alexandra had been right, she'd needed a holiday and some rest. The evening after her adventure in the snow she'd gone to bed straight after dinner and slept through until noon the next day, something she'd never done in her whole life.

The rest of that day she'd occupied herself with reading, eating and playing backgammon with George. In between time she'd done her best *not* to think about the night she'd spent in the gatehouse. She certainly hadn't let herself think about the kiss she'd shared with Cassius, though during the night her mind had seemed determined to relive the moment over and over again. She had a sneaking suspicion that that was part of the reason she'd slept so late yesterday morning, although she refused to think about why that might be. Maybe one day she might let herself think about it, when the memory wasn't quite so stirring, but for now she needed to concentrate on the future. She still hadn't come to any decision about that, but she was in a better frame of mind at the *prospect* of making it, which was a start.

'Dearest?' Her mother tugged gently on her elbow, drawing her closer as they walked along the path to the gate. 'Have you noticed anything unusual this morning?'

'Unusual?' She drew her brows together. 'No, although I have to say I found the Vicar's choice of sermon rather curious for this time of year. I expected something festive rather than a stricture on the perils of sin, but I thought maybe you'd called on him to discuss the Foundation.'

'No, I haven't spoken to him at all, although he was glancing in our direction rather often, don't you think?'

'I suppose so and, come to think of it, we got some rather strange looks when we arrived, too. Maybe it's because we're guests here?'

'Maybe.' Her mother sounded doubtful. 'Or perhaps your adventure the other night didn't go unnoticed, after all.'

'But surely you don't think…?' Millie looked over her shoulder just in time to see a dozen heads turn quickly in the other direction. 'Oh!' A wave of mortification swept over her. 'You mean you think the Vicar was directing those words at me?'

'I'm afraid he might have been, dearest, yes.'

'Lilian!' Alexandra caught up with them, her manner brisk. 'Have you noticed it, too? I think that perhaps you ought to take Millie home. George and I will stay and find out what's being said.'

'Eh?' Her husband looked startled. 'What do you mean? What's going on?'

'Correction.' Alexandra rolled her eyes. '*I* will find out what's going on and my husband will escort me. I'll do my best to fix it, too.'

'Thank you, Cousin.' Her mother nodded in agreement. 'I think that would be best.'

'But he was talking about *fornication*!' Millie looked between them, appalled.

'Quite.' Alexandra thrust her shoulders back like an Amazon preparing for battle. 'Only try not to worry just yet. You go on home and we'll see you there for luncheon. *I* shall see to this.'

'The time has come to worry!' Alexandra announced, throwing her bonnet aside and wrenching at the leather ends of her gloves. 'We have a rather substantial problem.'

'You mean everyone *knows*?' Millie stopped pacing in the centre of the drawing room, grabbing the back of her mother's chair for support as the abrupt halt made her dizzy.

'I'm afraid so. It turns out the girl who saw you works as a laundry maid at Falconmore Hall. She followed your footprints to the gatehouse and found out who else was staying there. Then when she got back to the village that night she told her sister who recognised you from the description.'

'Oh, no.'

'Oh, yes. If you'd only had blonde or brown hair we might have got away with it.' Alexandra finally succeeded in removing her gloves and clasped one of her hands instead. 'The only question, Millie dear, is why you didn't tell us the whole truth?'

'What do you mean?' She felt every muscle in her body tense at once. The *whole* truth wasn't something she'd intended to tell anyone ever, but how could the maid have found out about the kiss?

'You told us the man you stayed with was an estate manager.' Alexandra's tone was mildly admonishing.

'He was.'

Alexandra glanced towards her mother and back again. 'Is that what he told you?'

'Yes. He said his name was Cassius Whitlock.'

'Alexandra?' Her mother clasped her other hand supportively. 'Are you saying that Millie was misled?'

'I say.' George followed his wife into the room, wearing a baffled expression. 'This is a curious turn of events. Calls for sherry, I'd say.'

'I think it might require something stronger.' Alexandra looked somewhat perplexed herself. 'At least he gave you the right name, although as to why he'd tell you he was an estate man—'

'Cousin!' Her mother interrupted. 'What are you saying?'

'I'm saying that the man in the gatehouse that night *was* Cassius Whitlock, only he isn't an estate manager. He's the Marquess of Falconmore.'

'What?' Millie dropped down on to the sofa, wondering if she were the butt of some practical joke. 'The *Marquess*?'

'Yes.'

'Of *Falconmore*?'

'Yes.'

'But that's ridiculous! Why would a marquess be

sleeping in his gatehouse? There must be some mistake. He said he'd been a soldier.'

'He was, only he came back from India a year ago. As for the rest, I admit it does seem rather eccentric, but perhaps he *is* eccentric. He grew up at the hall, but I can't say I've spoken to him more than a couple of times.'

'I have.' George paused in the act of pouring brandy from a decanter. 'Decent fellow. A bit melancholy these days, though I can't say I blame him under the circumstances.'

'If he were decent, then he would have escorted Millie home the other morning and explained himself!'

'He couldn't.' She winced, aware of how incriminating the words sounded. 'I crept out of the house while he was still asleep.'

'You crept?' Alexandra's eyebrows almost disappeared into her hairline.

'I thought I'd inconvenienced him enough during the night.'

'Was he at church this morning?' her mother asked Alexandra.

'No, although his cousin's widow and their daughters were both there in the family pew. Her aunt, a Mrs Moore, I believe, was there, too. She moved in when Lord Falconmore returned from abroad for propriety's sake.'

'Oh, yes, the old lady sitting with the very pretty blonde lady and the two sweet-looking girls? Yes, I saw them, but they didn't give us any strange looks, I think.'

'Perhaps they didn't know anything about it at that point, although they certainly will by now. I'm afraid to say it was the talk of the churchyard.'

'Maybe I ought to go and call on Falconmore, eh?' George handed his wife a tumbler. 'Ask him what he intends to do about the situation?'

'No!' Millie sprang back to her feet. 'There's no situation and definitely no need to *talk* to anyone. All Mr Whi—*Lord Falconmore*, that is, did was offer me shelter in a blizzard. We didn't do anything wrong.'

'Of course not.' Her mother's expression was sympathetic. 'In that case, that's what we'll say and what we'll keep saying until we're blue in the face, if necessary. People just like to gossip.'

'Thank you, Mama.' Millie subsided back on to the sofa gratefully. It was all too, *too* awful. Worse than that, it was all her fault! If only she hadn't decided to be impulsive and walk home in the snow that night. If only she hadn't tried to be someone she wasn't any more. Now she'd brought disgrace on herself and her whole family. 'I'm sorry for involving you.' She looked up at her cousin apologetically.

'Oh, never mind that.' Alexandra tossed back the contents of her tumbler in one gulp. 'The day I stand by and let people criticise my family is the day I sprout wool from my ears. Now, let's put the subject behind us for a while and have some luncheon. Judging by the smell, it's roast beef. And don't say you're not hungry! If we're going to defeat the gossips, then we'll need *all* of our strength, believe me.'

Cassius glanced at the library door. As far as he could tell, Sylvia and her aunt and daughters had arrived home almost a quarter of an hour ago and so far none of them had come to disturb him. Which was definite progress, he thought optimistically, even despite the high-pitched, keening wail that seemed to be emanating from the direction of the hallway.

He turned his attention back to the ledger book spread out on the desk in front of him. His *real* estate manager, Linton, had provided him with all of the accounts for the past ten years and he was working his way through them methodically. Not that he didn't trust the man, but since the estate was now effectively his job, he wanted to do it properly and he couldn't do that without understanding how things worked. It was actually quite fascinating, or it would have been if the wailing wasn't distracting so much of his attention. It seemed to be getting louder.

'I've brought your coffee, my lord.'

He jerked his head up in surprise as his butler laid a small tray on the edge of the desk. The man's preternatural ability to pass through closed doors without making a sound never failed to amaze him.

'Thank you, Kendrew.' He gestured in the direction of the hallway. 'I might regret asking this, but would I be right in assuming that charming noise is somehow related to Lady Falconmore?'

'Indeed so, sir. I believe that she's been in some distress since returning from church.'

'Do we know what the matter is?'

'I couldn't say for certain, sir, but if you'll permit me I might hazard a guess.'

'And what would that be?'

'I believe she might have become aware of certain, ah, rumours.' Kendrew's usual impassive features looked somewhat pained. 'On a not-unrelated note, I feel it my duty to inform you about some rather salacious gossip below stairs.'

'*Salacious?*'

'I'm afraid so, sir. Naturally Mrs Turner and I have made it clear that such talk won't be tolerated, but I fear the damage may have already been done.'

'I see.' Cassius put down his dip pen and pinched the bridge of his nose with his fingers, aware of a tangible sinking feeling. 'I hope this is strong coffee, Kendrew.'

'Indeed so, sir. I made sure of it myself.'

'Good.' He took a deep breath, bracing himself for the worst. 'All right, then, out with it. What are these rumours?'

Kendrew's gaze settled on the bookcase behind him. 'I'm sorry to say that they concern yourself, sir. More specifically, your stay in the gatehouse two nights ago.'

'I see. Not that it particularly matters, but might I enquire as to how these rumours began?'

'One of the laundry maids who lives in the village passed the, ahem, *lady* in question on the road. She noticed that her footprints led away from the gatehouse and apparently felt compelled to share that information with others.' Kendrew sniffed disapprovingly. 'Mrs Turner and I are of the opinion that she ought to be dismissed.'

'On what grounds?'

The butler stiffened as if the answer ought to be obvious. 'Betraying the secrets of the household, sir.'

'That does sound serious.' Despite the circumstances, Cassius felt a strong temptation to laugh. 'On the other hand, she was only reporting the truth. Those footprints *did* lead away from the gatehouse.'

'None the less, the family honour is at stake, sir.'

'Family honour be hanged. Give the girl a repri-mand, but that's an end to it. I don't want anyone dis-missed, especially this close to Christmas.'

'As you wish, sir.'

'And for the record, Kendrew, the lady in question *is* a lady. You might mention that fact below stairs.'

'I'll make a point of it, sir.'

'Good.' Cassius drained his coffee and then pushed his chair back, tugging at the edges of his waistcoat as he stood up. 'Well, I suppose there's only one thing to do now.'

'That wouldn't be for me to say, sir.' Kendrew's ex-pression was impassive again. 'Shall I ask the stables to prepare a horse?'

'I think you'd better. I probably ought to get changed, too.'

'Forgive my contradicting you, sir, but it might be wise not to tarry within the house. And if I might be so bold as to suggest a departure via the orangery? Only Lady Falconmore is in the drawing room and the front windows are somewhat large. If she sees you prepar-ing to depart and guesses the reason, I fear she might do something…dramatic.'

'Good point.' Cassius threw his butler a grateful look. 'Remind me to increase your wages, won't you, Kendrew?'

'I wouldn't dream of it, sir, only if you'll forgive my presumption in mentioning it, the former Marquess always used to throw a party for the staff at this time of year.'

'Ah. Yes, remiss of me not to think of it. By all means, have a party. Do whatever you like. I'll pay for everything.'

'Very good, sir. Mrs Turner will be most gratified to hear it.' Kendrew held out a top hat that seemed to have materialised out of thin air. 'Best of luck with the young lady, my lord.'

Chapter Seven

'Falconmore!' George Malverly came striding across the hallway to greet him. 'How d'you do? In good health and all that?'

'Excellent health, thank you, sir.' Cassius shook the older man's hand. 'I trust I find you the same?'

'Eh? Oh, tolerable, I suppose. Better than I deserve, no doubt, but you're not here to discuss rheumatism with me. You're here about the rumours, I presume?'

'Indeed. I've only just learned of them or I would have been here sooner.'

'It's a bad business.' Malverly shook his head sympathetically. 'Damned unfortunate for both of you.'

'Naturally I've come to make amends.'

'Well, of course you have! Never doubted that for a second, although what's this about you being an estate manager, eh? Well, never mind. She's in the library.' Malverly stepped closer and lowered his voice confidentially. 'The other ladies are in the drawing room, but I'd keep out of their way if I were you. We've just finished luncheon and they're on the warpath, proverbially speaking.'

'I appreciate the warning, sir.'

'Jolly good, carry on then. The library's that way. We were just about to play a game of backgammon, but I suppose this is more important.'

Cassius bowed and then strode purposefully towards the door indicated. There was no point in dallying, after all, since walking slowly would only delay the inevitable. Just as there was no point in acknowledging his own reluctance to be there, let alone to ask the question he was about to ask. If a proposal *had* to be made, and there was no doubt in his mind about that, then it was better to do the honourable thing at once and consider his own feelings later. In all honesty, he didn't *dare* think about those just yet. All he knew was that he had to do the decent thing and after his behaviour the other night perhaps it was only what he deserved. Still, it struck him as vaguely ironic that after all his efforts to avoid being trapped by Sylvia he'd walked headlong into a different trap. Not a deliberate one, he was certain, but still a trap none the less. For richer or poorer, in sickness and in health, for as long as they both should live…

He repositioned his cravat, adjusted his expression to that of a suitor rather than a man walking towards impending doom and lifted a hand to the library door. It was slightly ajar, allowing him a glimpse of Miss Fairclough curled up in a plump, button-backed armchair by the fireplace. Her face was averted and yet for a moment the scene looked so strikingly familiar that he felt a nostalgic tug in his chest as if, despite their situation, he was actually glad to see her again.

He pushed the door open with one hand and propped

his shoulder against the frame. 'You didn't say good-bye, Miss Fairclough.'

If he'd launched a firework into the room he didn't think she could have sprung out of her chair any faster or looked any more horrified to see him. He had the impression that if he hadn't been blocking the door she would have made a run for it.

'Mr Whitlock! I mean… Lord Falconmore?'

'One and the same.' He pushed himself upright again and made a formal bow. She looked markedly different from the way she had the other evening, dressed in a high-collared, dove-grey morning gown with her auburn hair tucked away neatly into a bun. *Too* neatly, in his opinion, without so much as a strand out of place. Not so much Titian as…well…tame. She looked exactly the way she'd described herself as, a prim, proper and somewhat dull model of respectability. He missed bedraggled. 'I see that my secret's out. I thought it might be.' He forced a smile. 'Forgive my simply walking in. I didn't mean to startle you.'

'How did you find me?' She didn't bother with pleasantries, her green eyes widening with a look of definite panic.

'It wasn't too hard. Even if I hadn't followed you back here the other morning, there aren't many young ladies from London staying in the village.'

'You *followed* me?'

'I wanted to make sure you'd got back safely, especially with it being so early.' He advanced a few steps into the room. 'I hope you at least waited until it was light before you left.'

'It was just after dawn.' She looked faintly sheepish. 'I wanted to leave a note, but I couldn't find any paper.'

'Ah. Was I such an ogre that you were afraid to say goodbye face to face?'

'Of course not. I just didn't want to disturb you.' She folded her hands neatly over each other. 'I'm sorry if I caused you alarm.'

'Apology accepted.' He paused meaningfully. 'Although I believe you know I have a different reason for calling.'

'No.' This time the flash of panic was unmistakable. 'I don't, but if it's about the rumours then you're being ridiculous.'

'Ridiculous?'

He lifted an eyebrow in surprise. After the way Sylvia had pursued him, he'd expected that any offer of marriage he might make would be snapped up in a heartbeat. *Some* maidenly modesty he might have anticipated, but he certainly hadn't expected to be called ridiculous. He wasn't sure whether to be offended or impressed, but he wasn't prepared to be dismissed quite so easily. Oddly enough, her refusal made him *want* to convince her.

'You don't think we ought to discuss the situation?'

'There's absolutely no need.' She shook her head and reached for a small bell on the table. 'Now I believe that hospitality demands I offer you some tea. Would you care for a cup?'

'Is that wise?' He felt a sudden urge to provoke her. 'After what happened the last time?'

'Cassius!' Her eyes flew to the door. 'We agreed to forget about that.'

'So we did.' He shrugged, gratified to see her prim-and-proper demeanour lapse for a moment. 'Only for some reason I don't seem able to. I've tried and tried to no avail. I never realised my memory was so intractable.'

'Try harder!'

'Pity. I thought perhaps you might still remember it, too. I even thought it might have been the real reason you left so precipitously. You were afraid that you might be tempted to throw yourself at me.'

'Throw myself?'

'It seemed a logical explanation,' he teased, pleased with the distinctly *improper* flash of her eyes. 'It was a *very* satisfactory kiss, after all. We both agreed.'

'I don't recall saying any such thing.'

'No. *Illuminating* was your word, I believe.'

'Illuminating isn't the same as satisfactory.'

'It still sounds positive.'

'Not necessarily. It could simply mean educational, no satisfaction implied.'

'Ah.' He put a hand over his heart. 'Then I'm duly chastened.'

'Lord Falconmore…'

'Cassius.'

'*Lord Falconmore*, as we discussed the other night, I don't make a habit of kissing men I've only just met. Or men at all, for that matter!'

'I never doubted it for a second.'

'Furthermore, I'm sure that any gossip about us will blow over in time. As for our…indiscretion, nobody else knows about that and I'd prefer for it to stay that way. I implore you not to say anything else on the subject.'

'As you wish,' he agreed with faux solemnity. 'In that case, I promise not to kiss you again. Today, that is, and not on the lips. I will, however, give you this.'

He reached into his jacket pocket and pulled out her brooch. 'Yours, I believe?'

'My butterfly!' She gasped and rushed forward, indignation evaporating as she broke into a smile. It was the same wide smile he remembered from the gatehouse and just as stunning as it had been the first time. 'You found it!'

'On the rug next to the bed. I presume it fell from the table.'

'Thank you.' The tips of her fingers brushed against his palm as she took it, their warmth searing into his skin and making it tingle unexpectedly. 'I thought I'd picked it up, but I was in such a hurry. Then I was afraid I'd dropped it in the snow.'

'Is it valuable?' He found himself swaying slightly towards her. Standing this close, he could smell orange blossom again. It made him want to stand closer still. Right up against her, in fact.

'I doubt it.' Her eyes looked suspiciously bright, a hint of moisture swirling in the green depths as she ran a finger over the jewelled surface. 'But it's priceless to me.'

'Indeed?'

She nodded, though her expression was bittersweet. 'It was a present from my father on our last Christmas together. He gave one to me and one to Lottie. *Schmetterling* was his pet name for us, you see. He spent time in Germany when he was a young man and he liked the language. It means butterfly. Whenever he tucked us into bed at night he would say that the blankets were our cocoon and that we had to sleep so that our wings would grow. Then he'd blow out the candle and say that we'd fly away some day, but not yet, not until we were ready.'

'That's a charming story.' Cassius held out a handkerchief, wanting to comfort her somehow. 'I suspected you had hidden depths the first time we met, but now I'm even more impressed. Are there purple wings beneath that gown?'

'Naturally...' she dabbed quickly at her eyes and then peeked at him '...and antennae trapped beneath this bun. Don't all ladies have them?'

'I must have been spending time with the wrong ladies.'

She gave a small laugh. 'Thank you for returning it. I'm very grateful.'

'You're welcome.'

'Even so, I don't think we ought to see each other again. My being seen leaving your house was regrettable, but I have a perfectly good explanation and I'm only here for Christmas. I'm sure any rumours will fade away once I go back to London.'

'I'm afraid that may be overly optimistic. Rumours have a way of following people.'

'Then I shall ignore them.'

'What about your Gilbert? What will he think?'

Her facial muscles all seemed to freeze. 'I'll tell him the truth. The *whole* truth.'

'Very laudable. Only I would have thought that a curate's wife might need to be above reproach?'

'Perhaps, but if he's the man I believe he is then he'll understand and forgive me.'

'He sounds quite the paragon.' Cassius felt a flicker of irritation. 'Did you try imagining it, by the way?'

Her eyes shot to his and then quickly away again. 'I've no idea what you mean.'

'I think you do. Did you imagine kissing him?'

'That question is impertinent.'

'Extremely, but you still haven't answered. Did you imagine kissing him?'

'No, as it happens.'

'Is that so?' He felt smugly pleased by the answer. 'And why not?'

'Because I haven't got around to it yet.'

'You've had time.'

'I've been busy.'

'Or perhaps you're *still* putting it off?'

'Perhaps it's none of your business!'

'Millie.' He stretched an arm out, blocking the way as she made to move past him. 'Forgive me, I didn't come here to tease you. I came to ask you to marry me.'

'I know…' her eyelashes fluttered closed '…but I'm afraid I have to decline.'

'On what grounds?' He lowered his arm again. 'The other night you said that you needed to be practical to avoid being destitute. I would have thought that marrying a marquess was nothing if not practical.'

'It would be extremely practical. Indeed, it's a very good offer and I'm grateful to you for making it, but I still have to say no. Practicality needs to work both ways and what could I possibly bring to a marriage with you? I may be poor, but I still have my pride.' She opened her eyes again. They looked very clear and bright, like unblemished emeralds. 'Most of all, however, I don't want to trap you. *I* was the one who made the foolish decision to walk home on my own in the snow and *I* was the one who turned up on your doorstep. That means *I* am the one who ought to face the consequences.' She tilted her chin upwards. 'All of this was my doing and I refuse to let you pay the price!'

'Pay the price?' He lifted an eyebrow suspiciously. 'Are you being self-sacrificing again?'

'If one of us needs to make a sacrifice, then it *should* be me.'

'So you'll marry your Gilbert instead?'

'If he'll still take me then, yes.' She sounded exasperated, as if her reasoning ought to be obvious. 'Gilbert asked me to marry him of his own free will. You're only here because your honour compels you to be. I appreciate that fact, truly, but I refuse to force any man into marriage. I'd rather that my reputation *was* ruined!'

'But I wouldn't.' He folded his arms, surprised by his own persistence. Given that she'd just offered him an escape route—she'd even agreed to marry another man!—he ought to be halfway back to Falconmore Hall and basking in a sense of relief by now. Only for some reason he was still there and determined not to let her marry someone else either. 'You forget that both our reputations are at stake, Miss Fairclough. Yours might not mean a great deal to you, but mine does to me. I consider *that* a rather important consideration, too.'

'Yes, but...'

'And what if your Gilbert *doesn't* want to marry you, are you really prepared to be a social pariah for the rest of your life? Because that's what you'll be. All because of one small indiscretion. Personally I don't believe that to be fair.'

'Well, no...'

'Then are those your only objections, that you believe you've trapped me into marriage and that you think you can't offer me anything in return?'

'I…' She looked taken aback for a few seconds and then put her hands on her hips. 'No! You lied to me!'

'Did I?' He frowned. 'Ah, about being an estate manager. I like to think it was more of an exaggeration.'

'I believe that's what a lawyer might call a technicality.'

'You might be right, but I *do* manage my estate in a way and I've found that most people, young ladies especially, tend to speak somewhat differently to a marquess.'

'*I* wouldn't have.'

'I believe you. That's a big part of the reason I'm still here. I believe they call it integrity. Which is something you *can* bring to our marriage, incidentally.'

'But you're a marquess and I don't think you quite understand who *I* am. My father was cast out of his family for marrying beneath him. My mother's father was an inventor, respectable but somewhat eccentric. Then my parents set up a charitable institution for women in need. That means *all* kinds of women, Mr Whitlock, from all kinds of backgrounds. Do you really wish to be associated with such a place?'

'I believe the more pertinent question is whether you believe me to be a heartless monster?' He felt irritation give way to anger.

'I didn't mean to imply…'

'None the less, you just did. If you believe that maintaining a veneer of aristocratic dignity means more to me than philanthropy, then I believe that's *exactly* what you just implied.'

'You're right.' Her brows puckered. 'I shouldn't have

judged you, but you still ought to know the truth. The rest of your family might not approve of me.'

'The rest of my family consists of one maternal great-aunt and some distant cousins in Devon. I've met the aunt once and the cousins not at all. Their opinion is perfectly irrelevant to me.'

'What about your cousin's widow? Doesn't she live with you?'

'She and her daughters, yes, but they'll accept it.'

'Really?'

'Yes.' His lips curved with a flash of sardonic humour. 'In fact, Sylvia's constantly suggesting I ought to get married. At least this ought to silence her on the subject.'

'But Lord Falconmore—*Cassius*—do you *want* to marry me?'

He drew in a breath and then let it go again. 'No. To be perfectly honest with you, Miss Fairclough, no, I do not.'

'There you go, then.'

'However, it *is* my duty to marry some day, or so I've been told anyway. This may be sooner than I would have liked, but I'm sure I'll get used to the idea.'

'But you could marry someone more suitable. Someone more suited to you, too. We barely know each other. For all we know we might be completely incompatible.'

'Not completely, I think.' He reached for her hands though they appeared to be curled into tight balls. 'As for finding someone more suitable, I'm afraid that doesn't sound like something I'd enjoy at all. Dinner parties and trips to the theatre and all that.' He started to unfurl her fingers one by one. 'Besides, I don't see why I should go out looking for a prospective bride when I have a perfectly good candidate standing right in front of me.'

He held on to her gaze, somewhat taken aback to realise the words he was saying were true. 'I admit that our situation isn't ideal. Neither of us intended for this to happen, but it has and now all we can do is make the best of it. I can't offer you my heart. In all honesty, I don't believe I have one to give. I'm not capable of love any longer, but if you agree to marry me then I promise to respect and honour and be faithful to you for the rest of our lives.' He gave an ironical smile. 'You said yourself that plenty of marriages succeed without love. I enjoyed your company the other evening and I believe that you enjoyed mine. Given time, I think we might get along very well together.'

'Yes.' She sounded surprised by her own admission. 'I think we might, too.'

'Good.' He shrugged his shoulders. 'The blunt truth is that I intend to make a sizeable donation to your Foundation whether or not you intend to marry me.'

'You don't have t—'

'But I *will*, enough that you don't have to marry anyone if you don't want to, but gossip won't just go away.' He squeezed her hands. 'What do you say then, *Just Millie*? Will you do me the honour of becoming my wife?'

She was so still that for an alarming moment it looked as if she'd stopped breathing. And for some reason, he was holding his breath, too…

'Yes,' she answered at last, though her lips barely moved. 'Yes, I will.'

Chapter Eight

It was funny, Millie thought, the difference a name could make. If Cassius had called her Amelia, then she would have continued to refuse his proposal. She would have thanked him again, but said that she couldn't in all conscience accept it, especially since he'd just freely admitted that he didn't want a wife. Miss Amelia Fairclough's future was in London. That was where she belonged and where she would dutifully remain, no matter what the damage to her reputation. And if Gilbert didn't want to marry a ruined woman, then she would remain a spinster and rebuild her reputation day by day through a life of good work and virtue. But Cassius *hadn't* called her Amelia. He'd called her Millie. And Millie Fairclough was prone to following her instincts and inclinations no matter what her prim-and-proper alter ego might tell her to do. Only *she* would have the nerve to say yes.

So she'd said yes. Which had brought her here to the Malverlys' drawing room, standing stock-still in front of her family while Cassius formally announced the news of their engagement. What had she done?

She was aware of a disorientated feeling as if the two sides of herself were fighting for dominance inside her own head. Cassius was holding her arm as if to steady her, which was fortunate since she was feeling very unsteady indeed. Internally, she was a quivering mass of unsteadiness, as if her insides—her very *self*—was rearranging itself. There had been so many reasons to say no to his proposal, but the longer he'd talked, the more persuasive his arguments had become until finally the way he'd held her hand, squeezing her fingers softly between his, had caused the last of her resistance to crumble. Shameful as it was to admit it, the pressure of his touch on her skin had caused such a spine-tingling physical effect that she might have agreed to almost anything, but added to that he'd called her Millie, appealing to the selfish side of her that had suddenly wanted, very much, to say yes.

Not that she'd allowed feeling to overcome reason completely, she assured herself. Given the circumstances, marrying him *was* the sensible thing to do and it was still a sacrifice of sorts since she was going to have to leave her home and family and move to the country. Even if it didn't seem like very much of a sacrifice since she *did* like him, she *could* imagine kissing him and she was going to be a marchioness, for pity's sake! He was the one sacrificing his freedom, not to mention the chance of making an advantageous match with somebody of his own class. No matter which way she looked at it, she was being selfish, but he was right, she hadn't intended to trap him and she didn't want to be a social pariah for the rest of her life. Perhaps all they *could* do was make the best of it.

'Congratulations to you both!' George was the first

to stand up and offer his hand. 'Is it too early for champagne, do you think?'

'By several hours, dear, yes.' Alexandra's tone was less effusive, though she still managed to produce a smile. Unlike her mother, Millie noticed.

'I still appreciate the sentiment, sir.' Cassius took the proffered hand with what appeared to be genuine good humour. Standing at her side he looked almost too good to be true, the perfect model of a fiancé. Tall, slender and almost ridiculously handsome, with arguably the finest bone structure she'd ever seen and one errant lock of gold hair that persisted in curling forward over his forehead, he looked more like a character from some romantic novel than a real man of flesh and blood. Not to mention muscle, judging by the form-fitting cut of his suit. There was only one thing spoiling the picture. One sentence in fact. *I'm not capable of love any longer...* What kind of romantic hero would say that?

'You're a lucky fellow, Falconmore, that's all I have to say.' George pumped his hand a few times. 'Between you and me, this one's always been my favourite. One of the best backgammon players I've ever met, too. Beats me nine times out of ten.'

'Indeed?' Cassius's gaze darted towards her, flickering with interest and amusement. 'Then I look forward to playing with you, Millie.'

'I...' her tongue felt oddly frozen, as if there were a block of ice sitting on top of it '...yes.'

'But now I'm afraid I must leave you to make the arrangements.' He finally succeeded in retrieving his hand from George. 'I'll need to ride to London to procure a special licence.'

'A special licence?' her mother and cousin exclaimed at the same moment though he appeared nonplussed.

'Yes. We've decided to marry as soon as possible, before the end of the week hopefully. I trust that should put an end to all the gossip. With your permission of course, Mrs Fairclough?'

'Of course, if Millie's agreed…?' Her mother's enquiring expression suggested that she was waiting for her daughter to contradict the statement. 'Well then, I've no reason to object. I trust my daughter's judgement.'

'In that case, I'll leave at once, but perhaps you'd care to join me and my cousin-in-law for tea at Falconmore Hall the day after tomorrow?'

'We'd be delighted.' There was a brief but definite pause before Alexandra answered for all of them.

'Excellent. Then I can show you around your new home, Millie.' He let go of her arm and took hold of her hands again, smiling into her eyes. 'You can tell me if it passes muster.'

'Yes.' It was all she could manage to say.

What on earth was the matter with her tongue?

'Until Tuesday then.' He lifted one hand to his mouth, though this time his lips only skimmed the surface. 'I'll look forward to it.'

Millie waited until he'd left the room, then until the front door had closed, then until the sound of his horse's hooves had finally faded before putting her hands to her face and peeping out through her fingers.

'I don't know!'

Her mother and cousin rushed forward at once.

'What don't you know, dearest?' Her mother was at her side first.

'How it happened!'

'Never mind how.' George sounded as jovial as ever. 'It's all worked out rather well, I'd say.'

'Honestly, darling.' Alexandra gave him a pointed look. 'If you can't say anything helpful, then perhaps you ought to go for a walk.'

'Eh? What did I say?'

'Millie's trapped in an engagement with a man she's only just met!'

'A marquess.'

'Yes, well, it could have been worse, but no one wants to be trapped into marriage.'

Millie groaned aloud.

'Are you sure about this, dear?' Her mother's tone was sympathetic. 'You can still change your mind if you're not certain.'

'I don't know what I am. I *told* him all the reasons why it's a bad idea. I even told him that I'd prefer to marry Gilbert, but he said it was a matter of honour. Now I don't know if it's the right thing to do or not.'

'Of course it's the ri—'

'*George!*' Alexandra seized hold of her husband's arm and bundled him towards the door. 'That's quite enough. You *and* I shall take a walk.'

Despite herself, Millie managed a faint laugh as they departed. 'What do *you* think, Mama?'

'I can't deny it's a shock, but it says something for his character that he came, I suppose. Do you like him?'

'Yes, insofar as I know him.'

'Would you really prefer to marry Gilbert?'

'No, and I don't suppose that Gilbert will want to marry me once he finds out how I've behaved.'

'You don't have to marry either of them.'

'It'll reflect badly on the Foundation if I don't.'

'Forget the Foundation for a moment. Your happiness is far more important and it's better to be poor and happy than rich and miserable. Your father always said that and he knew it better than anyone.'

'I know, but he also said that a promise oughtn't to be given lightly.' She pulled her hands away from her face finally. 'No, I've given my answer and I must stick to it.'

Her mother smiled. 'You always were strong-willed. Millie dearest, whatever shall I do without you?'

'Oh, please don't.' She threw her arms around her mother's shoulders and clung there. 'Or I'll start to cry. I'll miss you so much, Mama.'

'And I you…' her mother's voice sounded suspiciously tremulous '…but at least you'll be living close to Alexandra.'

'Lady Fentree, too,' Millie sobbed.

'Oh, dear, yes.'

'She said that she doubted our paths would cross again.'

'I think she might change her mind once you're a marchioness.'

'That's the most ludicrous thing about all of this!' She laid her head against her mother's shoulder. 'Can you imagine *me* as a marchioness?'

'Yes, actually.'

'You can?' She lifted her head again in surprise.

'Yes. It's always been my opinion that good breeding has nothing to do with birth or titles. It's inside us, in the way we behave.'

'But it's *my* behaviour that's caused such a mess. All of this has happened because I wanted to take a walk in the snow!'

'Hardly the worst motive in the world, dear.'

'No.' She sighed. 'Isn't it ironic that if I'd frozen to death in the snow everyone would have lauded my virtue, but because I took shelter with a man, my reputation is ruined?'

'Those of us who love you are very pleased you *did* take shelter. And nobody who truly knows you will think badly of you.'

'Thank you, Mama.' She smiled gratefully. 'Maybe I ought to follow the Queen's example and wear white for the wedding. It would be rather fitting in this weather, don't you think?'

'I suppose it would. We'll go to the village store to-morrow for fabric.'

'Oh, no.' She shook her head quickly. 'You mustn't spend money on me.'

'But I *want* to and for once you're going to let me buy you a present.'

'All right then, and I admit I *would* like to wear white. That way if I change my mind and make a run for it, at least I'll be camouflaged.'

'Millie...'

'I know.' She lifted her fingers to touch her butter-fly brooch. It was pinned back where it belonged, just below her throat. 'Father always said that I would fly away some day, but I don't think he meant like this. It wasn't meant to be like this at all.'

Chapter Nine

'I refuse to meet her!' Sylvia stood in the middle of the hallway, five feet of blonde ringlets and heaving bosom, a handkerchief pressed to her eyes. 'I can't bear the thought of it!'

'If that's what you want.'

Cassius passed his travelling cloak to a footman with an exasperated sigh. He'd only just arrived back from London, had been inside Falconmore Hall for less than thirty seconds, in fact, and already he was sick of his cousin-in-law's histrionics. If he'd been having second thoughts about his engagement, this spectacle alone would have silenced them. He tapped his breast pocket, reassuring himself that the special licence was tucked safely inside.

'You mean you don't care if I *don't* meet her?' The handkerchief fell from Sylvia's grasp and floated to the floor.

'Not particularly. Hide in your room, if you wish. Of course, she'll be living here in a matter of days so it might make the domestic arrangements somewhat difficult, but you're perfectly at liberty to move out.

As I've mentioned, the Dower House is entirely at your disposal. Then you'd never have to meet her at all.'

'Move out?' Sylvia's blue eyes narrowed to slits. 'Is that what *she* thinks I should do?'

'*Miss Fairclough* has said nothing of the sort, but it's certainly something to think about.'

'She trapped you!'

'No…' Cassius handed his hat and gloves to another footman and started towards the library. 'The maid who spread rumours about her staying in the gatehouse trapped us.'

'Which one of them was it? Whoever it was, I'll wring her neck.'

'You'll do nothing of the sort.' He stopped mid-step. 'I believe you can leave reprimanding the servants to me. As for Miss Fairclough, she had no intention of trapping anyone.'

'If you believe that…'

'I do, implicitly, and I won't hear a word to the contrary. Not from anyone.'

'But isn't there *anything* I can do to change your mind?'

'No. I'm engaged, Sylvia. In a few days there'll be a new mistress of Falconmore and this…' he waved a hand between them '…needs to stop. *Now.* Sooner if possible.'

'I don't know what you mean.'

'You know perfectly well what I mean.'

'Don't you find me attractive?' Her wailing tone turned wheedling. 'Because if you'd only tell me what it is that you want then I could—'

'I *want* the woman I've asked to marry me!' He spun around with his hand on the library door handle. 'Now

I have a duty to take care of you and your daughters, but in return I expect you to let me live my own life. You can meet Miss Fairclough or not as you choose, but if you *do* meet then I expect you to treat her with the courtesy and respect she deserves. Is that understood?'

Sylvia pouted. 'Yes.'

'Good. Now if you'll excuse me, I have some important matters to attend to before our guests arrive.'

He pushed open the library door and closed it firmly and with one last scowl behind him. He was aware of one of his black moods descending, though as usual there was nothing he could do to stop it. At least *that* conversation with Sylvia was over with. It had actually gone better than he'd expected. Definitely better than Sunday when the news of his engagement had resulted in screaming loud enough to bring half-a-dozen maids running from downstairs. He'd paid a quick visit to the nursery to assure the girls their mother was all right, given a quick nod to Mrs Moore, and then made his escape to London as swiftly as his valet's packing and his horse's hooves would allow, Sylvia's howls still ringing in his ears.

It had been a long ride there and back, but the snow had mostly melted and the fresh air had been bracing, a welcome respite from the worries that had nagged at him ever since he'd proposed to Millie. At the time, he'd been reasonably content with the outcome, admittedly not overjoyed and yet calm about the decision. After all, he liked her, he certainly found her attractive and he felt a grudging respect for the way she'd tried to refuse him.

Now, however, he was feeling somewhat unsettled. He didn't regret it exactly, but he was having…concerns. That was probably the best word. Not about the bride herself, but about what she knew about him, about what she'd witnessed in the gatehouse on the night they'd met and what he, foolishly, had told her.

He walked around his desk and collapsed into his chair. He might as well have written her out a list of his fears and weaknesses, but it was too late to retract any of it now. She already knew the worst, which meant that all he could do was try to re-establish some kind of distance between them. The marriage could still go ahead. He just needed to set out some boundaries, which meant being polite and courteous, but making it clear that certain subjects, mainly those involving his feelings, weren't up for discussion.

He rested his arms on the leather desk-top and sank his head down. *Too much.* She knew too much, saw too much, too, with those clear green eyes that made him feel as if she could see into the deepest hiding places of his soul. And in a few short days he was going to marry her and bring her back here to spend the rest of their lives together. Then at some point in the future he'd bed her and hopefully beget an heir… He glanced at the grandfather clock in the corner. In a couple more hours he'd be seeing her again. Until then it was undoubtedly best to put his worries, not to mention the thought of bedding her, out of his mind.

The latter task proved a great deal harder than he'd expected.

'Oh, no!' Millie drew her head back in through the carriage window.

'What is it, dear?' Her mother leaned forward, craning her neck to peer outside. 'Ah.'

'What's the matter?' George, sitting opposite, looked perplexed.

'I believe they're somewhat surprised by the size of the house.' Alexandra patted his knee.

'Somewhat?' Millie was aware of her voice rising several octaves. 'It's the same size as our street!'

'Yes, it's certainly impressive.' Alexandra nodded tranquilly. 'I remember it being built fifty years ago. Of course I was only a child, but I've always thought it rather elegant. All those Doric columns and Palladian windows.'

'But look at the size!' Millie peered out of the window again, hoping the fresh air would do something to lower both her voice and her galloping heartbeat. Cassius hadn't exaggerated the length of the drive either. It seemed endless, meandering through rolling, oak-filled parkland before descending into a shallow valley where a perfectly symmetrical, neo-classical style house stood a hundred yards back from a lake.

'You'll adapt, dear.' Her mother seemed to have recovered her equilibrium. 'You've always been able to rise to a challenge.'

Millie glanced down at her outmoded plum-coloured muslin gown and closed her eyes in dismay. A challenge was one thing, but this was a bigger change than she could ever have imagined, for her *and* her whole way of life! Once she married Cassius, this would be her home. She'd be the Marchioness of Falconmore, a lady of rank and property, a member of the peerage, for goodness sake. She'd have responsibilities and duties, not just to society, but to all the people who lived on the estate. More than that, she'd be expected to manage this house and all of its staff. It wasn't simply a challenge. It was terrifying.

But she'd given her promise and it was too late to change her mind…wasn't it?

'Here we are, dear.' Her mother's elbow nudged her subtly in the ribs as they rolled to a halt.

With a start Millie opened her eyes, just in time to see Cassius's blue ones appear at the window. They were really quite startlingly blue, she thought breathlessly, the brightest cobalt shade she'd ever seen. They seemed to have the power to make her heart jump, too. She'd almost forgotten how very handsome he was.

'Lord and Lady Malverly, Mrs Fairclough, Miss Fairclough, I'm delighted you all could make it.' He inclined his head politely, letting the steps down himself before holding a hand out towards her.

She took it, her stomach swooping and then twisting nervously as his fingers closed around hers. They felt warm even through her glove, sending ripples of heat through her whole body, though the tightness of his grip felt incongruent somehow. His touch had always been gentle before, whereas now…now he seemed different. Sterner and harder, more serious, too, if the frown lines between his brows were any indication, as if he wasn't as pleased to see them as his words suggested. As if *he* might be having second thoughts, too.

Suddenly the challenge before her seemed even more terrifying.

Now that she was out of the carriage, moreover, he appeared to have nothing further to say to her, waiting until the rest of her family had climbed out before gesturing towards the house. She swallowed, trying to ignore the fact that his fingers were still wrapped around hers, then gave a start of surprise as she turned and saw the lady standing at the top of the front steps. It wasn't just that she hadn't noticed her before. It was that she was, without doubt, the most beautiful woman Millie had ever laid eyes on, with platinum-gold ringlets framing both sides of a heart-shaped face that was as perfectly symmetrical as the building behind her. To heighten the effect, she was flanked by two little girls, both of whom appeared to be miniature versions of herself. *This*, Millie realised with a sinking feeling, had to be the former Marquess's widow, her predecessor. As if the house on its own hadn't been intimidating enough!

'This is Lady Falconmore.' The lines between Cassius's brows deepened even further as he introduced them. 'Sylvia, you already know the Malverlys. This is Mrs Fairclough and my fiancée, Miss Amelia Fairclough.'

'Miss Fairclough.' If she wasn't mistaken, the woman's pupils actually contracted.

'Lady Falconmore.' Briefly, Millie thought about offering a hand and then gave a small curtsy instead. 'I'm delighted to meet you. And these must be your daughters. It's a pleasure to meet you both, too.' She smiled down at the two girls, though they only stared impassively back.

'Their names are Isolde and Hermione.' Sylvia's expression didn't alter. 'Now shall we go inside? It's cold.'

Millie glanced nervously at Cassius, wondering if she'd said or done something wrong, but his face was set like stone, giving nothing away. Was he upset with her? That didn't seem fair, although if he were having second thoughts then perhaps he wasn't feeling particularly fair. She felt as if her stomach were actually tying itself in knots, dread turning to dismay. She hadn't expected the situation to be easy, but this forbidding man was nothing *at all* like the one she'd met in the gatehouse or the one who'd proposed two days ago either. He was as cold and reserved as a stranger, no doubt thinking that she didn't belong in a place like this, or next to a woman like that either.

The front door opened as if by magic, letting them into a vast, marble-floored hallway. The walls were divided into panels, pale blue paint interspersed with white plasterwork displaying elegant motifs of birds and dolphins, though what the two were doing together was, in Millie's opinion, somewhat baffling. There was a large, curved staircase to one side and, as she tilted her head back to look up, a domed skylight above, bathing them in sunshine. It was all perfectly beautiful and perfectly overwhelming. How could she ever live in a place like this? She felt like an impostor just visiting.

'Girls, you may go to the nursery.' Sylvia waved a hand dismissively, sweeping on through an archway to the left without so much as a glance back over her shoulder. 'Tea will be served in the drawing room.'

From within there came the sound of a bell ringing so violently that the rest of them barely had time to remove their outer garments before two maids arrived carrying trays laden with cups, cakes and a silver tea urn.

Millie faltered on the threshold of what appeared to be the drawing room, yet in contrast to the stark elegance of the hall there was almost *too* much here for the eye to take in, not just in terms of furnishings, but in the range of colours, too. Assorted porcelain vases arranged on small gilded tables were set off by turquoise walls, a red-and-gold patterned carpet, crimson-velvet curtains and an almost painfully bright display of citron-yellow furniture, every piece of which appeared to be fringed with tassels. Even the ceiling was painted, divided into red-and-yellow triangles that reminded her of a circus she'd once visited with Silas.

'Will you take a seat, Miss Fairclough?' Cassius led her across to the least gaudy-looking sofa, bowing courteously though he didn't join her, waiting until everyone else was settled before taking up a sentinel position beside the fireplace.

'Thank you.' She threw a surreptitious glance towards her mother and Alexandra. Judging by their somewhat strained expressions, she wasn't the only one taken aback by the decor.

'Do you mind if I pour, Miss Fairclough?' Sylvia reached for the tea urn before she'd finished asking the question. 'Since this will probably be my last opportunity as mistress of Falconmore Hall.'

'Sylvia.' Cassius's voice was barely a murmur though the note of warning was obvious.

'But it's only the truth! I *am* being replaced, aren't I?' Sylvia sighed dramatically and then peered up through her lashes at the only other man in the room. 'Can you imagine it, Lord Malverly? I'll be the *Dowager* Marchioness from now on. Do I look like a dowager to you?'

'Eh? What? No, not a bit of it.'

'How sweet of you to say so.' She passed him a teacup with a smile. 'It's just so hard to accept that one's life is over at five and twenty.'

'This is *such* a charming house, Lord Falconmore,' Alexandra interceded tactfully. 'We've had the pleasure of attending several balls here over the years.'

'While my poor Magnus was alive, you mean?' Sylvia's head spun towards her.

'Ye—es. I'm so sorry for your loss. It was such a terrible tragedy.'

'It was, but he was always reckless. I told him not to jump that fence any number of times, but he wouldn't listen. He always laughed and told me not to worry as if it were all a big joke.' A look of anger flitted across Sylvia's face. 'That's a painting of him above the fireplace, Miss Fairclough. Wasn't he handsome?'

'Very.' Millie looked up at the portrait in surprise. There had been so much to look at when they'd first come in that she hadn't noticed it before, but if she had, she would have assumed it to be one of Cassius. The resemblance between the two cousins was remarkable.

'I know what you're thinking.' Sylvia sounded smug. 'They could have been twins, couldn't they? You know, sometimes I look at Cassius and I almost forget...' She put a hand to her lips. 'But perhaps I shouldn't say so.'

'No, you shouldn't.' This time Cassius's voice was significantly more than a murmur, succeeded by an awkward silence that seemed to fill the whole room.

Millie looked between the pair with an even greater sense of misgiving. There was something decidedly possessive about the other woman's behaviour, almost as if she were jealous. Her own mind baulked at the idea, but it made sense in a way. Sylvia and Cassius had been living together under the same roof for a year, after all, and no doubt he'd comforted her after his cousin's death. It would only be natural if Sylvia had started to think of him as her friend and protector, her next husband even. That would explain the air of palpable tension between them, not to mention Sylvia's obvious hostility towards her… In which case, perhaps it explained Cassius's cold demeanour towards her, too? She pressed a hand to her stomach as it plummeted abruptly. What if there had been something more than friendship between them already, some kind of understanding even, before she'd turned up on his doorstep in the snow and ruined everything? What if he was in love with Sylvia yet honour-bound to *her*? What if they both resented her for trapping him?

A loud snore finally broke the silence. Millie glanced towards it, belatedly noticing an old lady dozing in an armchair.

'My aunt, Mrs Moore,' Sylvia explained with a pout. 'But don't worry. Nothing wakes her when she's napping.'

'What a very colourful room this is.' Millie's mother spoke up this time. 'Did you decorate it yourself, Lady Falconmore?'

'Oh, yes, I decorated several rooms when I first came here after my marriage. It was quite exhausting, but then I expected to be here for a long time, the rest of my life probably. I certainly never imagined being usurped and banished to the Dower House after just seven years.'

'Miss Fairclough.' Cassius put his teacup down with a clatter on the mantelpiece. 'Perhaps you'll permit me to show you the rest of the house?'

'That would be lovely, thank you.' Millie sprang to her feet, deciding on the lesser of two evils as she made her way quickly past Sylvia, not even waiting for her mother's permission before rushing out into the hallway.

Chapter Ten

'I apologise.' Cassius's eyes were like shards of ice as they stood facing each other in the hallway. 'That wasn't the welcome I'd hoped for.'

'No.' Millie looked away quickly. 'I think that Lady Falconmore isn't so pleased by the news of our engagement, after all.'

'She'll get used to the idea.'

'Are you sure? She seems to think—'

'Sylvia can think what she likes,' he interrupted her firmly, gesturing towards another door opposite. 'Now for that tour.'

Millie opened her mouth to say something else and then thought better of it, walking ahead of him into yet another drawing room. It was just as big as the other, but substantially less cluttered and painted in calmer tones of cream and pale yellow. It felt positively tranquil by comparison.

'*Much* better.' She sighed with relief.

'You mean you don't admire my cousin-in-law's taste in decorating?' Cassius lifted an eyebrow.

'Oh.' She bit her lip guiltily. 'I didn't mean…'

'Because if that were the case then I would agree with you. Wholeheartedly. That room makes my head ache.'

'It was certainly colourful.' She gave him a sidelong glance. He still looked stern, but he seemed slightly— *very* slightly—less tense now that they were out of company. 'But it's a beautiful house.'

He inclined his head, accepting the compliment before leading her on through four more reception rooms, an almost preposterously large dining room, a smaller but still slightly preposterous breakfast room, a music room and even an orangery. There was no need to ask which of the rooms Sylvia had decorated, though thankfully nowhere else was quite as vibrant as the first.

Millie fixed a smile on her face, trying to convey some sense of pleasure in their surroundings, though it was difficult to concentrate when she felt so horribly self-conscious and out of place. The more she saw of the house, the more miserable she became. The presence of her fiancé was no great comfort either. Cassius treated her with polite, but distant formality. He didn't offer his hand or his arm again, but she was painfully aware of his every movement. Each time he came within an arm's length of her, she felt as if all her nerve endings were standing on edge. It didn't help that he looked quite so handsome, in a fashionable grey suit and pale-blue waistcoat that only emphasised the vivid shade of his eyes and made her feel even more dowdy by comparison. Frankly it was downright unfair how attractive he looked—he *and* Sylvia—how much he seemed to belong there, too, whereas she...

Well, there was no point in denying the obvious.

She didn't belong there. Which was probably a good thing because nor did she *want* a fiancé who behaved so coldly towards her. No matter what she'd promised, if this was what marriage to him would be like then she didn't want anything to do with it. At that precise moment, she wanted nothing more than to go back to London and never see either this house or its master again!

At last they stopped in a long, wood-panelled corridor that appeared to be some kind of portrait gallery.

'Is that your mother?' Millie pointed towards a round painting of a woman with chestnut hair and kind-looking brown eyes. The woman was smiling, but there was a familiar pensive quality to her face, too.

'Yes.' He looked surprised. 'How did you know? Everyone says I take after my father's side of the family.'

'You do, only her expression reminds me of you. And she has a matching dimple in her left cheek. It's small, but it's definitely there.'

'Really?' He looked at the portrait as if he were seeing it anew. 'No one's ever told me that before.'

'Sometimes it takes someone new to notice such things.' She moved on a few steps to another, bigger painting of the same chestnut-haired woman, only this time she was seated next to a man in a soldier's uniform. 'Is that your father?'

'Yes.'

'He was in the army, too?'

'He was a colonel. Of course the army was fighting Napoleon in those days.'

'Did your mother follow the drum?'

He nodded. 'She was the daughter of a brigadier so she understood what a military life entailed. I was born in an army camp in Spain. Ten miles from Cadiz.'

'So you're Spanish?' She smiled and then drew her brows together. 'But I thought you said you grew up with your cousin? Did they send you back here to be educated?'

'Not by choice.' He cleared his throat, though his gaze never left the painting. 'Unfortunately conditions in camp weren't always sanitary. My mother died of blood poisoning when I was four.'

'I'm sorry.'

'Afterwards my father decided it would be safer for me to be raised here in his brother's household. He was probably right, but I cried for days after he left me behind. I was afraid that I'd never see him again.' His voice sounded distant. 'As it happens, I was almost right. I only saw him once more when he came home on leave.'

'What happened to him?'

'A bayonet wound, so my uncle told me. It's a strange memory. He'd always been such a stern and remote figure, but when he summoned me to his library that day there were tears in his eyes. He told me all about a battle at Waterloo and how proud I ought to be of my father.'

'I'm sorry.' She reached a hand out, but he jerked away, hunching his shoulders as if they were stiff.

'I had this idea that if I'd been there I would have saved him. Absurd, of course.'

'Is that why you joined the army? To follow in his footsteps?'

'That and because it's what second sons do. The first inherits the title and fortune and the second gets a commission in the army. I was raised like a second son so it seemed fitting.'

'And then you lost your cousin, too... I'm so sorry.'

'Miss Fairclough.' Cassius twisted sharply, turning his back on the painting. 'Contrary to our conversation in the gatehouse the other evening, it is *not* my usual custom to discuss my feelings. I have absolutely no intention of doing so again.'

'I'm sorry, I didn't mean to upset you.' She almost took a step backwards at the forbidding note in his voice. It sounded even more glacial than before. 'Of course, if that's what you want.'

'Good. Then we understand one another.' He strode on down the corridor, pausing with his hand on yet another door handle. 'What do you think of Falconmore Hall then, Miss Fairclough? Do you approve?'

Millie stopped mid-step, stiffening indignantly. The question seemed to imply that she *ought* to approve, as if she were there to carry out some kind of inspection. As if she ought to be revelling in her good fortune! As if she weren't thoroughly miserable with him and his house!

'*Should* I approve?' She glared at the back of his head. 'I'm afraid that I don't have much experience of *halls* and I've only seen Buckingham Palace from the outside. You'll have to tell me how it compares.'

He let go of the door handle again, turning around with both eyebrows raised. 'Sarcasm, Miss Fairclough?'

'And that's another thing!' She burst out angrily. 'I *thought* I was Millie!'

'You are.'

'Then stop calling me Miss Fairclough! If you do it one more time, then I promise I'll walk out of that *obscenely* large front door and go back to the Foundation where I belong!'

'Indeed?' His voice sounded infuriatingly calm. 'Is that what you want?'

'I don't know!' She folded her arms. 'Maybe. It depends.'

'On?' He folded his arms, too.

'On whether I'm Millie or *Miss Fairclough*, for a start.'

'I've just agreed that you're Millie.'

'All right then.' She gave a curt nod. 'Now I think we need to talk, especially if you're having second thoughts…'

'About?'

'What do you think, what about?' She stared at him incredulously. 'About our engagement!'

'I'm not.' His tone suggested the very idea was ridiculous.

'Then why are you being so…*different*?'

'I'm afraid you'll need to be more specific. As far as I can tell I'm simply being myself.'

She sucked in a breath, trying to control her temper, but his behaviour was maddening, as if he thought *she* was the one behaving differently! There was a door further down the corridor that led outside and she stormed towards it, wrenching at the handle and slamming it open.

'Millie?' She heard him call after her as she strode out on to a terrace. 'Come back inside. You'll catch a cold.'

'I might catch one in your company!' She hurled the words back over her shoulder, bracing her hands against a low wall where some residual snow was still gathered.

'We haven't finished our tour yet.'

'Yes, we have!' She spun around to find him standing in the doorway, frowning. 'I've seen everything I need to see and we are definitely finished! Now I'd like to leave.'

'All I asked was whether you approved of the house.'

'And all I've done is answer! But in case I haven't made myself clear, no, I do *not* approve of the house and I've no desire for this engagement to continue a moment longer.'

'Whatever the matter is, we should discuss it inside.'

'No!' She could feel her anger spiralling. It was so unlike her—Amelia, anyway—that she didn't know how to control it. The words seemed to be coming all by themselves. 'The matter is *you* and we'll discuss it now! You're behaving like…' she looked around as if she might pluck a word from the air '…like you're made of ice! No, I take it back, ice would show more emotion!'

'Is this because I said I don't want to talk about my feelings?'

'It's because of everything! You're not the man I agreed to marry. I don't know who you are now, but I've changed my mind.'

His glacial expression seemed to waver. 'Whoever I am doesn't change our situation. This marriage is a matter of honour and I told you I have enough on my conscience already. I *will not* add you!'

'You *will not*?' She clenched her fists at his imperative tone. 'It's my choice whether or not to marry you!'

'You're being childish! Come inside and—'

He didn't get any further as she bent down, scooped up a handful of snow and threw it as hard as she could towards his head. It missed, erupting on to his shoulder instead and scattering white flakes all over his suit, but the look of shock on his face was almost comical.

'*That's* childish!' She put her hands on her hips. 'And now I've given you a reason *not* to marry me. Consider your conscience appeased.'

'Do you think it's that easy?' He lifted a hand and brushed the snow from his arm, his eyes flashing now, too, though oddly enough not with anger. She didn't know what the emotion in them was, only for some reason it made her pulse quicken.

'Yes, I do think it's that easy.' She tried to ignore the feeling, stomping back towards him, irritated that he *still* managed to look handsome when her own nose and cheeks were doubtless in the process of turning a luminous shade of pink. 'I should never have agreed in the first place. I belong in London at the Foundation, not in a place like this, and I *can't* be a marchioness either. It's hopeless and we shouldn't marry just because—'

This time he was the one to interrupt, his mouth fastening on hers with a speed that took her completely by surprise. If it hadn't been for the hands that wrapped simultaneously around her head and waist she thought her knees might actually have buckled beneath her, but they held her upright, strong fingers caressing her neck and the small of her back as his lips moved fiercely over hers.

She opened her mouth to gasp and then gasped again as his tongue slid inside, startling her even more. She was vaguely aware that she was angry, in the midst of some kind of protest, too, but it was difficult to remember what about. Her mind seemed to be spinning, making it almost impossible to remember anything at all. Anything, that was, except the warm pressure of his lips against hers and the unusual but distinctly exciting sensation of his tongue as it stroked against hers. Not to mention the pressure of his arm as it coiled around her waist, drawing her close enough that she could feel the muscular contours of his chest through his shirt and against her breasts. She wasn't sure that she *wanted* to remember what she'd been protesting about anyway. All she wanted at that moment was to keep on being kissed, to kiss him back, too, to press against him and move her lips in a matching rhythm as her hands found their way around his shoulders and…

'There.' He pulled his lips away suddenly though his face remained close to hers, close enough that she could still feel and hear the quickened pace of his breathing. 'I believe *that* makes me honour-bound again.'

'Not necessarily.' She sank down off her tiptoes and pulled her hands away from his shoulders, willing her mind to clear, her memory to come back and her heart-beat to stabilise again. 'Nobody else saw.'

For the first time that day he actually smiled. 'If there's one thing we're not short of at Falconmore Hall, it's windows. Believe me, Millie, *somebody* saw. Now shall we continue? There's one last room I want you to see.'

'It's stunning!' Millie's jaw dropped the moment he opened the door. 'I've never seen anywhere like it!'

Cassius followed her appreciative gaze around the ballroom. There were floor-length windows on three of its sides and the walls between were covered in mirrors, making the space appear even bigger and brighter, especially with the last of the day's sunshine streaming in from the west. Three crystal chandeliers sparkled overhead and the floor was polished to within an inch, possibly a finger's breadth, of its life. He had to admit, as rooms went, stunning was probably the right word. Although he'd been feeling somewhat stunned *before* he'd entered.

So much for putting some distance between them! He wasn't entirely sure why he'd kissed her, except that the urge to do so had been gradually building, becoming more and more overpowering the longer she'd argued. She'd been positively bristling with anger, apparently unaware of the temperature outside, too, and there had been only one way he could think of to warm her up. No one had challenged him so bluntly since he'd inherited his title, let alone thrown snowballs at him. Then when she'd threatened to leave he'd felt a moment of panic. Strange as it sounded, every time she tried to get out of their engagement he found himself wanting to marry her more. Simply *wanting* her more. And this time, it had had nothing to do with honour or conscience.

Still, his own behaviour had surprised him. He'd convinced himself that his ardent response to their first kiss had simply been due to the tense situation in which they'd found themselves in the gatehouse. He certainly hadn't expected to feel the same way again, but if anything, his reaction this time had been even stronger, so much so that he was extremely tempted to do it again. Given that he had no idea what she was thinking, however, that probably wasn't a good idea. She'd seemed to enjoy their embrace and her anger had certainly diminished, but perhaps he'd simply taken her by surprise. Now she seemed to be avoiding his eyes.

'Have you danced here often?' She half-turned her head towards him, her side profile revealing still-flushed cheeks and kiss-swollen lips.

'A few times, although I'm afraid I'm an adequate partner at best. I never paid much attention to our dancing instructor.'

'You had an instructor?'

'For a while. Magnus and I were both educated at home so I was trained in everything he was.'

She darted a quick look over her shoulder, seeming on the verge of saying something before thinking better of it.

'What is it?' He moved a step closer. Now that he'd failed so spectacularly at re-establishing distance between them he seemed incapable of remaining more than an arm's length away.

'Nothing.'

'It's not nothing. I can practically hear you thinking.'

She shook her head. 'You said that you didn't want to talk about your past and I've no wish to be accused of prying.' She paused briefly. 'Again.'

'You won't be. I promise.'

'All right. I was just thinking that it can't have been easy to return here after what happened to your cousin. You must miss him.'

'I do.' He cleared his throat as a lump started to swell there. 'The day I set foot back in this house was one of the worst of my life. Hard though it is for some people to believe, I never coveted any of this. Not the house, the title or fortune. I could have made my own way in life.'

'I'm not *some people*.' She was looking straight at him now, her expression sympathetic. 'And I believe you would have.'

'I never wanted to disinherit his daughters either. This should be their home, not mine, but the property was entailed. There was nothing I could do about it except let them stay, but it's still hard not to feel guilty. Unfortunately I had no choice in the matter.'

'So you had no choice but to come back, no choice but to be a marquess and no choice but to propose to me. On top of everything else, no wonder you feel so trapped.'

He frowned, though he didn't deny it. 'Our engagement wasn't your fault. It was the weather that threw us together.'

'I'm still sorry if I've made things worse for you.'

'You haven't. As for the rest...' he swallowed '...I've told you more than I've told anyone, but it's not easy to talk about.'

'No.' She sounded thoughtful. 'Do you remember what I told you about my sister and how she would tell me about her nightmares after our father died?'

'Yes.' He lowered his brows. 'You said it helped her, but that doesn't mean...'

'Well, that wasn't the whole truth. That is, it *did* help her, but it only made things worse for me. We had so many visitors after the funeral. So many people who wanted to talk about what had happened and what he'd meant to them. They meant well, but it wasn't always helpful. Sometimes their attempts at consolation made me feel hollow inside. Here.' She laid a hand over her heart. 'Only my mother understood. She never made me talk about how I felt. It's part of the reason why she's so beloved in the Foundation. She can always tell who needs to talk and who needs silence. She taught me that everyone should be allowed to heal in their own way. I would never ask you to speak about anything you didn't wish to.' Her gaze fixed on his. 'But at the same time, *if* we marry, I'd be there if you needed to talk.'

'Thank you.' He felt a warm feeling in his chest, like gratitude and something more tender. 'And about what you said earlier, about my being cold... I apologise. The best way I can think to describe it is low spirits. I'm afraid there are times when all I want is to be left alone. I can be solitary and taciturn, often for days.' He grimaced. It was a strange way of wooing, telling her that he preferred isolation, but now that he'd started he felt he owed her the whole truth. 'If I've had second thoughts, that's the reason. You should know that I may not be the easiest man to live with.'

'I see.' She nodded slowly. 'Then do you wish to be left alone now?'

'I did.' He gave a guilty laugh. 'But at this precise moment? No. I just want to explain, to warn you, I suppose, but you should know that my moods have nothing to do with you, truly. If *you're* having second thoughts about our marriage, however, then I understand. I'd ask you to reconsider, but I would never force you into anything you didn't want. I can appreciate your reservations about taking all of this on, too. The estate is a lot of responsibility.'

'I don't mind responsibility, but, Cassius, you were raised in this house and this world, *I* wasn't. Ladies are taught almost from birth to manage households like this. I wouldn't have the faintest idea where to begin.'

'But you'd learn and you'd have plenty of help.' He clasped his hands behind his back, resisting the urge to reach for her again. 'Of course I won't deny it would be a lot of work. Just fixing all of Sylvia's damage would take a few months at least.'

'Her decorating, you mean?' Millie's lips quirked. 'I think you might be overestimating my abilities.'

'You could hardly make it any worse.' He started to smile and then frowned again. 'Only if you do choose to marry me there's one more thing I ought to warn you about. A favour to ask, really.'

'What kind of favour?' She sounded suspicious.

'I need to organise a ball.'

'A *ball*?' She looked as startled as if he'd just suggested something indecent. 'Here?'

'Yes. My butler asked if there could be a Christmas party for the staff and it occurred to me I ought to throw some kind of event for my tenants, too. The estate was in mourning for my cousin last year, but this time I thought I should throw a ball.'

'Well, that certainly sounds like a lovely idea…'

'Then you'll help me?'

'I would…' she clasped her hands together in front of her '…*if* I had any idea how to go about it, but I don't. I've never thrown a ball in my life.'

'No, you've only helped your mother run an entire institution.' He lifted an eyebrow ironically. 'I can see how that would be a lesser challenge.'

'That's different.'

'If it makes you feel any better, I've never thrown a ball either, but I believe they say there's a first time for everything.'

She twisted her face to one side and slanted a look

back towards him. 'Maybe you ought to ask Sylvia. She'd be much better at it.'

'But Sylvia won't be the Marchioness by the time of the ball—I hope.'

'You mean…?'

'I obtained the special licence in London. I was thinking of Friday?'

'For our…?' She seemed unable to finish the sentence, licking her lips instead.

'Wedding? Yes.'

'And the ball…?'

'Would be next week. Just before Christmas.'

'I see. So you want to hold a wedding and ball all within a matter of days?'

'Yes. I admit the timing is unfortunate, but my housekeeper, Mrs Turner, is very proficient. According to my butler, Kendrew, she's also bursting to meet you.'

'All right. I'll do my best.'

His heart gave a heavy, surely audible, thump. 'Does that mean what I think it means?'

'Yes. I gave you my promise. As long as there isn't any other *significant* reason why you can't marry me?' She let the question hang in the air for a moment. 'Very well, then. Friday it is.'

'Thank you. I'll do my best to make you happy, Millie.'

'I'll do my best for you, too.' Her eyes darted towards the door as if she were suddenly keen to escape. 'Before I forget, my cousin, Lady Malverly, suggested that you and Lady Falconmore and her aunt might wish to join us for dinner tomorrow evening. If that would be acceptable to you?'

'We'd be delighted.' He held out an arm. 'In that case perhaps we ought to return to the drawing room before all your relatives develop migraines?'

'Yes.' Her expression shifted to one of relief. 'I think that we'd better.'

Chapter Eleven

'Coffee, miss?'

'Thank you.' Millie took the proffered cup from a maid and stared into the inky-dark depths. The dinner party had been excruciating, but at least she could drink her coffee in peace. Or at least she hoped she could. It would be just her luck if Sylvia decided to come and sit next to her on the sofa and regale her with yet more stories about *dear* Cassius and how wonderful he'd been since returning from India.

The day itself had started out well. She'd woken up feeling almost optimistic about her impending marriage. Actually she'd woken up smiling thanks to a surprisingly lucid dream in which she'd relived both of their kisses in quite a shocking amount of detail. Naturally the smile had been superseded by a guilty, and yet somehow not quite sincere, frown, but she'd still felt better. Despite Cassius's initial coldness during her visit to Falconmore Hall, what he'd told her afterwards about his low spirits had pulled at her heartstrings and she'd seen enough damaged people at the Foundation to know the words had been sincere. She'd even convinced herself that she'd been mistaken about the nature of his relationship with Sylvia.

Unfortunately dinner had proven otherwise. Sylvia had talked endlessly about his finer qualities, how loving and considerate he was, not just to her, but to her daughters, even going so far as to lay a possessive hand on his arm several times. It was perfectly obvious that she was in love with him and he, no doubt, with her. That would also explain the way his expression had become steadily darker and sterner throughout the evening. He obviously felt divided, torn between doing the right thing by *her* while secretly yearning for the woman he already shared a roof with. Which meant that she was going to have to bring up the subject of second thoughts again!

She swallowed a mouthful of too-hot coffee and wished it were something stronger.

'You didn't seem to enjoy dinner.'

She gave a small jump at the sound of Cassius's voice. She hadn't noticed him approach, but he was already standing beside the sofa, dressed immaculately in a dark grey suit with his usual blue waistcoat and an elegantly knotted, pristine white cravat.

'It was perfectly…' She sought for an appropriate word and then gave up. 'Edible.'

'High praise indeed.' He gestured at the space beside her. 'May I sit?'

'If you wish. It's not my house.'

'True. In that case…' He sat down, one of his legs brushing lightly against hers. 'Is something the matter?'

'What makes you think that?' She shuffled pointedly to one side.

'Just your expression and body language and the fact that you barely spoke a word all throughout dinner.'

'Neither did you.'

'No, it can be hard to get a word in edgewise with my cousin-in-law.'

She glanced towards the table where Sylvia was holding court in a game of whist. In the glow of the candlelight, she looked so beautiful that Millie felt an unwonted pang of jealousy. No matter how indiscreet it sounded, she had to know the truth.

'Are you in love with her?'

'With *Sylvia*?' He sounded appalled by the very suggestion. 'She's my cousin's widow!'

'Yes, but the two of you were thrown together and… well, I wouldn't want to be the cause of a rift between you. If you had some kind of understanding before I came along, that is.' She lowered her voice as he stared blankly at her. 'Some kind of secret engagement, perhaps?'

'An engagement?' He looked thunderstruck. 'Why on earth would you think that? There could *never* be anything between us!'

'But she…and you…' She faltered, wondering if she'd misread the situation, after all. He looked as if he were telling the truth, as if she'd taken leave of her senses to even imagine such a thing, but it was hard to understand Sylvia's behaviour if there *hadn't* been some kind of understanding… 'Does *she* know that? Because she seems to think otherwise.'

She had the brief impression that he was about to say something dismissive, before his expression shifted and he ran a hand around the back of his neck. 'I've no idea what she thinks, but believe me, I am *not* in love with Sylvia. There's certainly been no suggestion of marriage, not on my side anyway.'

'But there has been on hers?' She heard the unspoken statement. 'Is that why she…*touches* you?'

He looked apologetic. 'Forgive me, I've tried talking to her about it, but she's surprisingly persistent. That would be the other reason I sleep in the gatehouse.'

She felt her mouth fall open in surprise. 'You mean you sleep there to avoid…*attentions*?'

'It's not very gallant of me to say so, I admit, but I promise you, there's never been and never will be anything between Sylvia and me.'

'I see.'

'Millie…' He cleared his throat. 'I only tell you this to reassure you. I hope that I can rely on your discretion.'

'Of course! I wouldn't dream of telling anyone. Only…' She drew her brows together.

'Only?'

'Well, it just doesn't make sense. Why would she be so persistent? She's so beautiful. Surely she could have her pick of men?'

'She's still in half-mourning.'

'That makes it even stranger! Unless she's lonely, I suppose, but still…' She spun towards him as a new thought occurred to her. 'Does she have an income of her own?'

He looked offended. 'I make certain she and her daughters don't want for anything.'

'Yes, but does she have the means to be independent herself?'

'Not that I know about. Unfortunately my cousin didn't leave a will.'

'Well then, *that* would explain it. She's probably

worried about her future, about where she'll live if you marry someone else.'

'*When* I marry someone else—*you*, in fact—and I've suggested she move to the Dower House, not debtors' prison. It's a perfectly fine house.'

'Where is it?'

'On the estate, about half a mile from the hall.'

'All on its own? Not even close to the village?'

'I suppose so. What's wrong with that?'

'*Cassius.*' She fought the urge to roll her eyes. 'Look at things from her perspective. She's already lost her husband and now I've come along to take her position in society and her home, too. Maybe she doesn't want to live in isolation in the country, especially if she's used to socialising.'

'Magnus did say she liked parties.'

'There you go, then. She's probably worried about being lonely.'

'She has her daughters.'

'Who are how old? Three and four?'

'Three and five.'

'Exactly. Lovely as they are, they aren't at an age to provide a great deal of mature conversation. It's no wonder your cousin-in-law is behaving so badly.'

'That still doesn't excuse it.'

'But maybe she's just trying to hold on to what she knows, the future she expected to have, too. Yesterday she said something about her life being over at twenty-five.'

'So what should I do?' He lifted a hand. 'Bearing in mind that she is *not* living with us.'

'No, that's probably not a good idea. Do you have any other properties?'

'A hunting lodge in Derbyshire and a house in London.'

'Then perhaps you should offer her one of those?'

'Perhaps I should.' He rubbed a hand over his chin. 'So if I'm following your argument correctly, you're suggesting that it was only a house and security she wanted, not me?'

'Probably.' Millie nodded emphatically and then froze, realising her mistake. 'Although I'm sure she liked you, too.'

'So you're *not* suggesting that she doesn't find me attractive?' He regarded her sternly for a few seconds before bursting into a laugh loud enough to draw the attention of everyone else in the room.

'Cassius!' She swatted his arm with her hand. 'I thought I'd offended you!'

'On the contrary, this might be the best news I've had all year.' He was still laughing. 'You have no idea how liberated I feel! All these months! But why on earth didn't she just tell me?'

'Maybe she didn't know how to.' Millie gave him a penetrating look. 'Maybe you're not easy to talk to.'

'Ah. You might have a point.' His expression sobered. 'In that case, I appreciate *your* telling me now. Hopefully it means I can do something about it.'

'Good. Only don't tell her what you were just laughing about and don't laugh again either. Be sensitive and remember what she's been through. You aren't the only one who's grieving for your cousin, remember, whether she shows it or not. She needs reassurance and she needs it *in writing*. She can't live the rest of her life entirely dependent on your good will.'

'Why do I feel like a chastened schoolboy?' Despite the words, his gaze warmed as he looked at her. 'I should have listened to you properly that first night. You told me then that a lot of women marry just to keep a roof over their heads.' He tipped his head towards her, so close that the warmth of his breath made her cheek tingle. 'From now on, I'll pay attention.'

'I know what you're going to say!'

'Do you?' Cassius propped his feet on the bench opposite as the carriage rolled away from the Malverlys.

'Yes and I'm not sorry.' Sylvia stared out of the window, her tone defiant.

'Really? Not even for the word *usurped*?'

'I don't recall using it.'

'Well, you did. Three times actually.'

'I'm upset.'

'So we all noticed. I'm not entirely sure why you chose to accompany me this evening instead of staying at home with your aunt, especially considering your earlier reluctance to meet my fiancée at all. However, it may have been a blessing in disguise.'

'What do you mean?'

'I believe that I might have found a solution to our domestic situation.'

'No! I won't discuss it and I will *never* apologise.'

'You *will* discuss it and there's no need to apologise, not to me at any rate. In fact, I believe *I'm* the one who owes you an apology.'

'What?' Her face swung sharply towards him.

'For being a blind, insensitive fool.'

'A blind, insensitive… I don't understand.'

'No, I'm not making myself particularly clear, am I? All right, let me put it this way. The moment we get back to Falconmore Hall we're going to sit down in my library and work out how much income you and your daughters need every year. Then we're going to double it and make it official. After that we'll decide where you want to live. Not in the hall or in the Dower House. London, perhaps? Or Derbyshire, if you prefer?'

'London?' Sylvia sounded breathless. 'Do you mean it?'

'Wholeheartedly. I should have thought of it sooner.'

'But what made you think of it now?'

'I didn't. It was Miss Fairclough, your *usurper*, who suggested that perhaps you were feeling insecure about the future.'

'Oh.'

'She even thought that your jealous behaviour might stem less from a desire to marry me than a fear of being homeless?'

There was a telling pause. 'And what did you say?'

'*I* said that I had every intention of taking care of you and your daughters for the rest of your lives. Frankly I thought it was offensive to imply otherwise. She countered by suggesting that, offensive or not, I put it in writing.'

'I see. That was…perceptive of her.'

'Indeed. Thoughtful, too.'

'Yes.'

'Deserving of an apology even?'

'I… Yes.'

'Excellent. So London it is. I'll send word for the house to be made ready. There should be room for all of us there when we come to town, too.' He rubbed his hands together with satisfaction. 'I think Magnus would have approved of this arrangement, don't you?'

There was a lengthy silence, long enough to make him turn his head. When he did he could see that her eyes were bright in the gloom of the carriage, as if there were real tears sparkling inside of them.

'Sylvia?'

'I did love Magnus you know, very much, but I've been so angry at him, too. He should never have tried jumping that fence.'

'No, he shouldn't have.'

'I felt as if he'd abandoned me.' Her voice sounded small. 'I never meant to disrespect his memory either, but I didn't know what else to do. I had to take care of my girls and I thought...'

'I know.' For the first time in almost a year, Cassius put an arm around her shoulders, letting her sob quietly into his jacket. 'Perhaps it's time for us both to stop dwelling on the past? Perhaps it's time to look to the future instead?'

'I'd like that.' Sylvia gave a loud sniff. 'And I *will* apologise. I'll speak to Miss Fairclough and set everything right, I promise.'

'Thank you. In that case, I wonder if Isolde and Hermione might like to be bridesmaids?'

Chapter Twelve

This couldn't be right.

Millie stared at her white-satin-and-organza-swathed reflection in the bedroom mirror, battling with the ominous conviction that something was about to go wrong. If her life at the Foundation had taught her anything it was that life wasn't fair, especially for women. Errors in judgement, particularly those involving men, had to be paid for. *Any* deviation, however small or unintentional, from the path of virtue would inevitably be punished. *That* was how the world worked and how it had always worked. And yet, not only had she deviated from the path and *not* been punished, but here she was, dressed like the Queen herself, about to marry a kind, handsome, intelligent and apparently sane marquess. She felt as if the whole world had turned on its head. Surely *something* was about to go wrong.

Unless… She pursed her lips at her reflection. Maybe this *was* a kind of punishment, marriage to a man who claimed to be incapable of love. Not that she loved him, at least not yet, but he struck her as the kind of man it would be all too possible to fall in love with. What would her life be like then, trapped in a one-sided marriage? On the other hand, maybe one side was better than no side at all? And if he really *was* incapable of love, then it wasn't his fault. In which case, all she could do was guard her own heart and not let herself yearn for any more than he could give. Then they might *get along together*, after all...

'Dearest?' Her mother's head appeared around the edge of the bedroom door. 'Oh, Millie, you look lovely. Five days' worth of sewing well spent, I think. You've always been so clever with a needle.'

'You and Alexandra helped.'

'We only followed your instructions. It looks wonderful. Your father would have been so proud.' She held out a small bouquet tied with white ribbon. 'I've brought you some myrtle. It stands for love.'

'Love?' Millie's hand faltered in mid-air. 'But this isn't a love match, Mama.'

'No, but *I* love you so *I'm* giving it to you. I carried one just like it on my wedding day.'

'Oh.' She reached for it eagerly this time. 'Thank you, Mama. Do you think Lottie will be very upset that I haven't written to her? Only I don't want her travelling if she's still feeling unwell and it all feels strange enough. I'd prefer to have as few witnesses as possible.'

'I'm sure she'll understand once you explain that, but...' her mother looked anxious '...there was another reason I came up here.'

'What's that?'

'You have a visitor.'

'Now? But we have to leave in ten minutes. Who would call now?'

'Me!' Sylvia swept into the room suddenly, looking her usual pulchritudinous self in lavender silk. 'I'm so sorry to barge in on you like this, but I was afraid if your mother told you who it was then you'd refuse to see me. Which I wouldn't blame you for, by the way, but I've come to throw myself on your mercy and apologise.'

'You have?' Millie looked from Sylvia to her mother and then back again in amazement.

'Yes. I've behaved terribly towards you. Worse than terribly, *abominably*. I've come to ask your forgiveness.'

'Oh.'

'But not just that. I need to thank you, too. Cassius told me what you said the other evening and it was true, all of it. How did you know?'

'Well…' Millie lifted her shoulders. 'To be honest, it was just common sense.'

'To another woman, yes, but to a *man*? It's like common sense is another language. I've so much wanted to tell him myself, but I didn't know how.'

'Millie?' Her mother looked confused. 'Is everything all right?'

'It's all absolutely wonderful.' Sylvia spun towards her, smiling radiantly. 'Cassius is going to open up the town house in London and I'm going to live there, out of everyone's hair so to speak, but we're all going to be the best of friends from now on.' She turned back towards Millie. 'You *will* be my friend, won't you?'

'I'd like that.'

'And you *will* forgive me?'

'Of course.'

'Thank you.' Sylvia looked visibly relieved. 'And as an additional thank you, I'll leave today.'

'So soon?'

'Yes, although I won't go straight to London. I've been invited to stay with a friend, Lady Vanessa Fentree, for a few days. I don't suppose you know her?'

'Ye—es. We've met, but please don't feel you have to leave straight away.'

'Oh, but you and Cassius need time to get to know each other and you don't want me and the girls, never mind my old aunt, getting under your feet.' She paused and then peeked up through her lashes. 'Speaking of which, Cassius thought you might let Isolde and Hermione be bridesmaids?'

'I'd be honoured.'

'Thank goodness! Because I've already raided the hothouse to make them flower crowns. They're downstairs now, entertaining Lord and Lady Malverly and looking perfectly adorable.' She grasped Millie's hands. 'I've left you a wedding present back at the hall, too. Several presents actually. I hope you won't be offended, but I noticed your gown the other day looked a bit faded and since Cassius has given me enough money for a new wardrobe in London, I've left you a few of my old ones, just until you can get to town and order more. You might need to adjust them a bit, but we're about the same height.'

'Oh.' Millie looked at her mother in consternation. 'I don't know what to say.'

'Say that you'll accept them as an apology. It would make me feel a thousand times better. And I have to say you look perfectly beautiful today.'

'Do you really think so?' Millie peered anxiously over her shoulder at her reflection.

'Yes! Don't you like it?'

'It's just my hair… I wanted to do something more interesting with it.'

'Let me see.' Sylvia tipped her head to one side and scrutinised her face. 'What about barley curls at the sides? Here, just over your ears?'

'But we need to leave soon.'

'Oh, don't worry about that. I told Cassius I was coming to visit you and he knows I'm always late wherever I go.' She put her hands on Millie's shoulders, pushing her down on to the stool in front of the dressing table. 'Now we'll need pins and a curling iron.'

'I really don't think…'

'Trust me.' Sylvia's eyes met hers in the mirror. 'If there's one subject I know about, it's hair. When I'm finished, the most honourable Lord Falconmore won't know what hit him.'

Cassius gave one last wave to their assembled families and then climbed into the carriage beside Millie. It had been a long day. Long, tense and unexpectedly stressful. Waiting for any bride was surely nerve-racking enough. Waiting for a bride with martyrish tendencies and a long list of reasons why she ought *not* to marry him was nerve-shredding. He'd felt physically drained by the time she'd finally appeared at the church door, almost twenty minutes late, preceded by two little girls who looked as if they'd had the entire contents of a flower-erbed flung over them.

Not that he'd spared many glances for the brides-maids. His eyes had gone straight to Millie, a vision in white on George's arm, clasping a far more discreet bouquet of winter foliage with pink-topped stems. Her face was covered by a gauzy veil, but he could still see the auburn glow of her hair beneath, twisted into ringlets on either side of her head.

The ceremony itself had gone smoothly, though he'd only finally relaxed once the gold wedding band was on her finger. It had been a small and intimate affair with only Sylvia and her daughters, Mrs Moore, Millie's mother and the Malverlys as witnesses. They'd returned to the Malverlys' house afterwards for a long wedding breakfast, followed by a leisurely, albeit somewhat chilly walk through the village, something he'd insisted on to lay all the gossip to rest once and for all. That had been followed by another light meal, a few more toasts, and then they'd climbed into the carriage, ready to return to Falconmore Hall.

So that, as they said, was that. His conscience had been appeased and overall he felt satisfied as well as relieved. Not just because she'd showed up and he didn't have another thing to feel guilty about, but because he'd fulfilled one of the two key tasks that were expected of him as a marquess. He was married. Now all he had to do was beget an heir and society would consider his job done. Which led his thoughts in a straight line to their wedding night.

He studied his bride out of the corner of his eye. The light outside was already fading, casting the carriage into semi-darkness, but he could still see her profile. Her gaze was fixed straight ahead, as if the cushion opposite were of some immense interest, and she was sitting very upright, almost impossibly straight-backed with her small hands clenched tight in her lap. He had no doubt that the knuckles beneath her gloves were white. Briefly, he considered taking hold of one of her hands and then discarded the idea. Touching her hands would only encourage him to think about touching other parts of her and, given the circumstances, he probably ought to put all thoughts of their wedding night firmly out of his mind. It had only been just over a week since they'd first met and there was no need to rush. Which the rational part of his brain knew even if the rest of his body was tempted to ignore it.

If only she'd worn some kind of sack to their wedding instead of looking so stunning in her tight-fitting, yet somehow still modest, white gown. Now his imagination was running riot. Even the scent of orange blossoms was driving him to distraction. Considering how little interest he'd felt in the opposite sex for the past year, the feeling took him by surprise.

But it was better to wait. Any disruption to his everyday routine tended to make his moods more erratic. He'd slept reasonably well for the past few nights, but the last thing he wanted was for his nightmares to come back and frighten her. It was one thing for her to hear him break a bottle downstairs, another thing entirely for her to be in the same bed when he woke up shouting. It would probably be best if they slept in separate rooms for a while. Besides, no doubt she'd found their wedding day as trying as he had. The best, most gentlemanly thing he could do was to leave her alone. For a few nights anyhow. And there were plenty of things he could do that evening to distract himself. Play billiards, read a book, go over Linton's accounts. Because what bridegroom *wouldn't* want to study land management on his wedding day? Maybe he could go for a walk instead? At least that would expend some energy.

Or perhaps he could just talk to her?

He leaned forward, making a show of peering outside. 'It's amazing, isn't it?'

'What?' She looked from him to the window and back again.

'The sky hasn't fallen, after all. Now that you're a marchioness, I mean.'

She pursed her lips. 'It's not a joke.'

'It's true, though. Or are you going to tell me you feel like a different person now that you're Lady Falconmore?'

'I'm not sure who I am any more.'

'You're Millie.'

'Am I?' There was a plaintive note in her voice. 'Because ever since that night we met I've felt…divided. Torn. It's hard to explain.'

'Try anyway.'

She glanced at him dubiously for a moment and then sat up even straighter. 'It's just that when I left London I was Amelia Fairclough. I *knew* who I was and what my purpose was. Then that night at Lady Fentree's, I felt so sick of everything. I told myself it was the people around me, but mostly I think it was of myself. It was like something inside me rebelled. I wanted to be my *old* self, the person I was before my father died, someone adventurous and daring.'

'I remember. You said that you felt trapped, that you were tired of everyone expecting you to be virtuous and self-sacrificing all the time.'

She looked surprised. 'You remember that?'

'Of course. If I recall correctly, you said that you'd become someone you didn't want to be.'

'Yes, but I still knew I had to go back. Being Millie was only supposed to be for one night. Then I met you and…'

'And?' he prompted her as her brow crumpled.

'I never imagined that there would be any consequences. Then when you came to propose, I *tried* being Amelia again, but you called me Millie and…' She gave a self-conscious shrug. 'I know I'm not explaining this very well. Everything happened so fast that I got confused, but *she's* the one who accepted your proposal. Millie, not Amelia.'

'I see. That's why you were so upset at me for calling you Miss Fairclough the other day?'

'Yes. Miss Fairclough is Amelia. It just felt wrong.'

'Ah. So now you're Millie?'

'I think so. Yes. But maybe I shouldn't be.'

'Why not? Weren't you happy that night you rebelled?'

'Until I almost froze to death, you mean?' She gave a barbed smile. 'Yes, I was.'

'Then why would you want to go back to being Amelia again?'

'Because I was only happy as Millie because I decided to be reckless and selfish that night. I can't live my whole life like that.'

'A lot of people do.'

'But *I* can't! I'm used to having a purpose in life.'

'And you think a marchioness can't have purpose?'

'It's not that. It's just a big change and it doesn't make any sense either. I did something wrong, sinful even, and it feels like I've been rewarded.'

'Sinful?' Despite his earlier resolve, he reached for one of her hands and folded his own around it. 'My memory may be flawed, but I don't remember anything particularly sinful about that evening.'

Her gaze flickered to his mouth and then away again. 'We kissed.'

'We did, but surely a kiss isn't so very wrong?'

'For an engaged couple, no, but if that maid hadn't seen me leaving then we would never have seen each other again.' The flush of her cheeks was visible even in the darkness. 'I kissed you thinking that I'd never see you again.'

'Ah, so you're *afraid* of remaining Millie? You think she might lead you into a life of debauchery and vice?'

'Now you're making fun of me.'

'No, I'm not. I just don't understand why an intelligent woman is so afraid of happiness. And I vehemently disagree with the part about your being selfish. You didn't *just* think of yourself that night. You came to rescue me with an umbrella, remember?'

'Yes, but...'

'*And* you listened when I told you about Edward.'

'Ye—es.'

'*And* you tried to comfort me, too.' He rubbed his thumb slowly across the palm of her glove. 'I wouldn't call any of that selfish.'

She didn't answer for a moment. 'I still don't know who I am.'

He tipped his head back, resting it on the cushion behind them. 'Do you realise that over the past few days you've tried every possible way to dissuade me from marrying you? You've said that you'd prefer to marry someone else, that you don't belong at Falconmore Hall, that you don't want to ruin my life, that you don't deserve to be a marchioness and that I must be in love with Sylvia. Did I miss anything?'

'I was trying to help you, to ease your conscience.'

'*Or* you were trying to punish yourself.' He stopped rubbing her hand and gripped it instead. 'I believe that if you could, you would have sacrificed yourself to public opinion and been a social pariah for the rest of your days. The only reason you didn't is because I said that it would damage my reputation if you refused. So you sacrificed yourself by agreeing to marry me, for *my* sake, instead. Only since most people wouldn't consider becoming a marchioness a punishment, you still feel guilty about one night of *extremely* mild sin. Maybe marriage to me doesn't feel like enough of a self-sacrifice. Which I'm pleased to know, by the way.'

She jerked her hand away. 'Stop it.'

'I'm not trying to upset you. All I'm saying is that it doesn't have to be a choice between self-sacrificing or selfish. Most of us find a path between the two. You're a good person. You've done good here already.'

'I have?' Her forehead creased in surprise.

'For Sylvia.'

'Oh…yes, she said you spoke to her.'

'And as it turned out you were right about everything.' He lowered his head towards hers. 'For which you have my eternal gratitude.'

'She said she's going to stay with the Fentrees for a few days.'

He laughed. 'Problem solved.'

'I'm not sure it's very gentlemanly to call her a problem, but, yes, I suppose it is.'

'All thanks to you. So perhaps you ought to stop thinking about who you are and whether or not you deserve to be happy and just relax for a few days. Maybe then it will all seem clearer.'

'Maybe.'

'When had you intended to go back to London?'

'In another week, just after Christmas.'

'All right then, why not consider the time in between as a holiday? A honeymoon, if you will? Don't think or worry about whether you're Millie or Amelia, just...' he spread his hands out *'...be.'*

She sighed softly. 'That actually sounds like a wonderful idea.'

'Don't sound so surprised.' He reached for her hand again, gratified that this time she didn't pull it away. 'In the meantime, I'm still calling you Millie. I met her first.'

Chapter Thirteen

'You're awake early.' Cassius glanced up in surprise as his new wife entered the dining room. It was just past seven o'clock, a good two hours before Sylvia usually made an appearance.

'Am I?' Millie made her way to the table, smiling at the footman who pulled a chair out for her. 'We start earlier at the Foundation, but please don't let me disturb you.'

'Disturb away.' Cassius folded his newspaper and tossed it on to the table, taken aback by a buoyant sensation in his chest as if his heart had actually just leapt to see her. She looked bright-eyed, fresh-faced and pretty. Unlike some people, she clearly hadn't spent the night tossing and turning. 'How did you sleep?'

'Very well, thank you, after I'd finished exploring. I've never had a bedroom to myself before, let alone a dressing room and private drawing room.'

'But comfortable, I hope?'

'Very. It's not Sylvia's old room, I take it?'

'How did you guess?' He made a wry face. 'No, your room is adjacent to mine. They're officially guest rooms, but it didn't seem appropriate for me to use the master chamber while Sylvia was still in residence. Her rooms are a little more pink, I believe.'

'In that case I'd better stay where I am.' She lifted a hand to her head. 'Otherwise I'd clash horribly.'

He smiled, taking the opportunity to let his eyes travel over her hair. The ringlets were gone this morning, but instead of her usual severe bun the sides were twisted into plaits that looped back over her ears and then coiled together loosely at the back of her head. The softer style made her look even prettier, damn it.

'Is that a new dress?' He cleared his throat, aware that he was staring.

'No, it was one of Sylvia's. She left me a few gowns as a wedding gift and I thought I should probably start dressing the part of a marchioness.' She ran a hand over the bodice. 'Do you like it?'

'It's very pretty, only...' he paused, distracted by the position of her hand, and wondering how to ask the question without actually referencing his cousin-in-law's expansive cleavage '...I wouldn't have thought that you and Sylvia were the same size.'

'No.' She gave a knowing laugh. 'We're definitely not, but I made a few adjustments last night.'

'Last night?' His eyebrows shot up. 'You weren't tired after such a long day?'

'Ye—es, but I wasn't sure whether or not I ought to stay up.' She busied herself with the sugar bowl. 'That is, whether or not you'd want me to?'

'Ah.' He felt his stomach plummet, uncertain about how to answer. Given that he'd spent a large portion of the night throwing longing glances at the door that connected their adjoining apartments, the fact that she'd been sewing on the other side felt somewhat mortifying. 'We never discussed our sleeping arrangements, did we?'

'No.'

'I thought you would want some time to settle in.'

'I see. That was very thoughtful of you.'

'Which isn't to say that I didn't want to visit you last night…'

'Oh.'

'Only I wasn't sure how you'd feel about it.'

'Ah.'

He waited the length of several heartbeats. 'How did, *do*, you feel about it?'

He thought he heard a soft intake of breath while she stirred her tea. 'I'm your wife. I understand that I have certain…duties.'

Duties. He winced. If ever a word contained less enthusiasm, he'd yet to hear it.

'I suppose your mother told you what to expect?'

'Yes.' She started to rearrange her cutlery. 'And I've heard gossip at the Foundation.'

'Ah.' He didn't think his stomach could sink any lower. Given the nature of the Foundation, he doubted much of that gossip would have been very encouraging. No wonder she called it a duty. She'd probably been waiting in a state of nervous dread for most of the previous evening. It was hard to imagine their wedding night going any worse even if they *hadn't* been in separate rooms.

'Well then…' He decided to change the subject. 'What would you like to do this morning? I'm entirely at your disposal.'

'I thought I ought to speak to your housekeeper about the ball. We don't have much time to plan.'

'Good point. I'll join you.'

'Actually I'd like to do it myself, if you don't mind? I have a lot of questions about…' she gestured around the room '…well, all of this.'

'If that's what you want.'

'But I'll need to write invitations afterwards. I'll need your help with those.'

He drained the last of his coffee. 'Or I could take you to some of the farms on the estate and we can issue invitations in person? It's a beautiful day for a ride and that way you'll know a few faces at the ball.'

'That sounds like a lovely idea, but I'm afraid I can't ride.' She looked apologetic. 'I've tried to learn a few times, but horses always seemed to sense that I'm nervous.'

'Then that's something we can work on next summer. In the meantime, how about I call for a barouche? Then you can relax and look around while I drive?'

'That sounds perfect.'

'Good. Come to my library when you're ready. If we leave by ten we should have about six hours of daylight left.'

'Six hours?' She looked startled. 'How long will visiting take?'

'Probably longer. Trust me, you're going to be bombarded with questions.'

'That's not very reassuring.' Her green eyes turned anxious. 'Maybe it's not such a good idea, after all.'

'But I'll be right by your side.' He gestured to her plate. 'By the way, I wouldn't eat too big a breakfast if I were you.'

'Why not?'
'You'll see.'

An hour and a half later Millie knocked on the library door, waited for Cassius's answering call from within, then twisted the handle and caught her breath on the threshold. The view before her was literally, figuratively and every other way breathtaking. Row upon row of shelves crammed with books and ornaments stretched from floor to ceiling on two of the walls while another was taken up with a large brass fireplace, on either side of which stood a collection of tanned leather armchairs, facing each other across an Aubusson rug. The rest of the floor was covered in a maroon-coloured carpet that gave the room an overwhelmingly warm ambience. It even smelled cosy, of coal and coffee and books.

She walked in a few steps and turned around slowly on the spot, not wanting to miss anything. 'I think this might be the most perfect room I've ever seen.'

'I've always thought so, too.' Cassius stood up from behind a walnut and leather-topped desk, smiling as if he were genuinely pleased to see her. 'Although I was slightly frightened of it, too, as a boy. If I was summoned here, then it usually meant I was in trouble.'

'Oh, dear. Was that often?'

'No more than for your average hellion.'

'Why didn't you show me this on our tour?' She gave him an arch look. 'Then I would have married you no matter what.'

'If only I'd known.' He laughed and then looked faintly sheepish. 'I'm afraid I wasn't in the right frame of mind the other day. I didn't want to show it to you like that.'

'I see.' She let her gaze drift over the stuccoed ceiling and back to his face. 'Is it all right for me to be here now?'

'Now you're more than welcome.'

'Good.' She gave a wide smile. 'Because I'd much prefer spending my evenings here than in the drawing room.'

'Then we shall. Pick an armchair and make it your own. I might even tolerate an embroidery chest in here. Now…' he came around the side of the desk and offered an arm '…are you ready to make some calls?'

'For everyone to gape at me, you mean?'

'That, too, but then I think it would be hard *not* to look at you today.' His gaze slid appreciatively over her green day gown. 'That dress never suited Sylvia half so well.'

'Now I know you're exaggerating.'

'Not at all. It brings out your eyes.'

'Oh. Thank you.'

She smiled shyly and laid her fingers on his bicep, feeling it flex slightly as they walked side by side out into the hall. There they paused briefly to put on coats and hats before going outside to where a barouche led by two grey horses stood waiting.

'How did you and Mrs Turner get on?' he asked, handing her up on to the bench before taking his own seat. 'Have you worked out all the details for the ball?'

'Some of them.' She felt a tingling sensation in her lower body as the length of his thigh pressed lightly against hers, but she could hardly move away without making it obvious and she wasn't sure she wanted to anyway. The solid pressure of his body, not to mention his body heat, felt surprisingly pleasant. 'We've decided on next Thursday. That way the staff can have their party the following evening.'

'That sounds good to me.'

'Then Christmas Eve is the day after that.' She glanced sideways, wondering how he'd react to her next idea. 'I thought it would be nice if we gave the staff a few days off as a present?'

'All of them?'

'Yes. Maybe not all at once, but since we've already agreed to have Christmas dinner at the Malverlys, it would be perfect timing. We could manage with a reduced staff for a few days, couldn't we?'

'I should think so.'

'Then do you agree?'

'Why not? Since it's Christmas.' He threw her a smile. 'I think my staff are going to be very pleased I married you.'

She smiled back, though the words made her feel somewhat unsettled, too. Never mind his staff, how did *he* feel about marrying her? He'd been in a reasonably cheerful mood since their wedding the day before, but that was probably just due to her being a weight off his conscience. He was being very kind, too, but not particularly husbandly. He hadn't even kissed her since they'd sealed their vows with a brief, almost chaste peck on the lips, and as for their wedding night... Her cheeks flushed at the memory. She hadn't realised that when he'd bade her goodnight outside her new bedroom door that he'd *really* meant it. After the way he'd kissed her those other times she'd expected... Well, she wasn't sure what he'd expected, but she'd been curious to find out. She definitely hadn't anticipated feeling quite so disappointed by his non-appearance…

She twisted her face away to hide her red cheeks. The air was cold and crisp, though the blue sky more than made up for it. Most of the snow had gone, but there were still traces here and there, stray piles in north-facing spots where the sun couldn't reach and melt them, making the landscape seem to glisten in places. There were swans out on the lake, too, adding to the sparkling effect. They squawked loudly as the barouche rolled by, down the main drive for half a mile before turning off on to a smaller track.

'The hall looks beautiful from here.' She looked back over her shoulder, admiring the way the pallid winter sunshine reflected off the grey stone.

'It does, although sometimes I wish they hadn't knocked down the original house. It was built in the sixteenth century, all red brick and low arches. The pictures I've seen look rather grand, but my uncle wanted something modern.'

'Is that how long your family's been here, since Tudor times?'

'Apparently so. Legend has it that one of our ancestors did something incredibly brave and Queen Elizabeth gave him this land as a reward. Of course, no one can actually say what the incredibly brave thing was, but that might be for the best. Magnus and I always suspected piracy.'

'An acquaintance of Sir Francis Drake, then?'

'Quite possibly.' He leaned back on the bench, stretching one arm out casually behind her while the other held on to the reins. 'What about your family? You told me that your mother's father was an inventor, but you haven't said anything about your father's family.'

'No. You're right, I haven't.' She felt a stab of anxiety. 'Perhaps I should have said something before the wedding, but it's not easy to talk about. They were very rich and seemingly respectable, but their money came from the Americas. From trading in people.'

'Slavery?' His expression sobered instantly.

'Yes. My father was horrified when he came of age and discovered the truth about his family's fortune. He tried to persuade them to give it up and support the abolition movement instead, but there was a big falling out and they disowned him. Alexandra was the only member of his family who didn't.'

'I see.'

'He and my mother both lobbied for a change to the law, but the Abolition Act wasn't passed until the year after he died. I wish he could have lived to see it.'

'He sounds like a good man.'

'He was. I still miss him even now. Every day.'

'I miss mine every day, too. It's been twenty-seven years since he died, but some people never leave us, do they?'

'No.' She swallowed. 'No, they don't.'

'I wish I could have asked your father's permission for your hand. I'd have liked to have known whether he thought I might deserve it.'

'I think so.' She murmured the words without thinking, tensing as his head twisted towards her.

'You do?'

'Yes.' She gave a small shrug, keeping her gaze fixed on the horizon where a herd of red deer were gathered beneath an oak tree. No matter what their relationship was, or more accurately wasn't, she had no doubt that he was a good man. He certainly had a conscience. Their marriage alone was proof of that. And she had a feeling her father *would* have liked him.

'How many farms are there on the estate?' She cleared her throat, very aware of his eyes still watching her.

'Twenty-eight, although some are bigger than others. We'll start with the closest.'

'*Twenty-eight?* Surely we can't visit them all?'

'No, they're too spread out anyway, but we'll make a start and then send messages to the ones we don't get to today.'

'Oh.' She looked relieved. 'I thought it would be nice if we invited everyone. Whole families, I mean, the children as well as the adults if they're old enough to dance. Then it would be more of a party than a ball.'

'A party?' She sensed rather than saw his raised eyebrow. 'I'm starting to think that you're something of a revolutionary, Lady Falconmore. Giving servants days off and inviting children to parties? You'll be telling me to hand out presents next.'

'Oh! Presents!' She clapped her hands together. 'Do you think there's time to arrange that?'

'I'm sure we can arrange something.'

'And we'll need holly to decorate the house. As well as laurel, ivy and mistletoe if we can find any.' She swivelled around, eyeing the back of the barouche speculatively. 'I think we should be able to get quite a lot in here.'

'That would be a good idea if only I'd thought to bring some shears.'

'Oh…' She felt crestfallen. 'I didn't think of that.'

'But I'm sure we can borrow some. If there's one thing farmers have plenty of, it's tools.' He grinned and then gestured towards a large stone house up ahead. 'This is Home Farm, the biggest on the estate, as the incumbents will no doubt tell you. They don't like to let anyone forget it. It's entirely likely that Mrs Petch will expect you to curtsy to *her*.'

'Oh, dear.' Millie looked towards the house with trepidation. 'Do you think they will have heard all the gossip about us?'

'I'll be amazed if they haven't.'

'So they'll know *why* we had to get married.' She almost groaned aloud.

'They'll think they do.' Cassius nudged his shoulder against hers. 'So why don't we confound them?'

'What do you mean?' She caught her breath, her chest tightening at the contact. A leg was one thing, but the whole of one side of her body was now pressed against him. And she still didn't want to move away!

'Have I told you how beautiful you look today, darling?'

'You mentioned my dress.' She blinked, the low tone of his voice making her feel even more breathless.

'Not your dress. *You*.'

'Me?'

'Yes. You look radiant. All vibrant and…green.' He tipped his head sideways, his blue eyes capturing hers. 'Like spring.'

'But it's winter.'

'Winter still holds the promise of spring.'

'I don't understand.' She licked her lips. 'What are you talking about?'

He made a tsking sound. 'There's no need to sound

quite so shocked. It's a perfectly harmless and entirely accurate compliment. But I think what you meant to reply is that I look very handsome, too.'

'Well, yes, you do, but I don't understand what this has to do with confounding anyone.'

'Don't you?' He laughed. 'You can call me darling if you like. Or sweetheart if you prefer. Honeysuckle even.'

'Honeysuckle?'

'Honeycomb?'

'But...' she was starting to wonder if he'd been drinking '...why?'

'To confound the gossips!' He drew the trap to a halt. 'People may *think* they know why we got married. They might even be right, but that doesn't mean we have to go along with their version of events. Surely it's far more romantic to let everyone think we're in love.'

She gave a small start at the word. 'You mean pretend to be in love? Wouldn't that be dishonest?'

'Perhaps, but I prefer to keep my private business private. Or would you prefer for everyone to be studying us and wondering if we secretly resent each other?' He jumped down and came around to her side of the barouche, offering a hand to help her descend. 'Besides, it might be fun.'

'You have a point.' A frisson of warmth shot up her arm as his fingers closed around hers. 'So we're in love, then?'

'Deeply and passionately.'

'After just over a week?'

'But *what* a week.' He grinned, turning the frisson into a raging torrent, so potent it was as though she'd just been scorched.

She felt her pulse flutter and then accelerate rapidly, not just at the grin, but at the implication behind it. She seemed to feel his words, too, deep down in the pit of her stomach. Deeper even, in some previously unknown part of her body that seemed to be quivering with excitement. No, she corrected herself, quivering wasn't a strong enough word. Throbbing felt more accurate. She laid her spare hand on her stomach, trying to quell the sensation with a series of deep breaths.

'Very well then, *honeysuckle*, but I'm still not sure I approve.' She started to move away, but he tightened his grip on her hand, tugging her back towards him.

'Wh-what are you doing?' She felt her cheeks blossom with colour as he slowly unpeeled one of her gloves and pressed his lips to the inside of her wrist.

'We're being watched,' he murmured softly, the warmth of his breath raising goosebumps on her skin and making the throbbing intensify again.

'Oh.' She glanced across at the farmhouse. If she wasn't mistaken, a couple of faces immediately jumped away from a window. 'You're right.'

'Then let's give them something new to talk about. Are you ready?' His lips lingered against her skin as he looked up at her, the blue of his eyes an almost perfect match with the sky beyond.

'To be in love?' Somehow she forced herself to answer in a calm voice. 'I think so.'

Chapter Fourteen

'Delicious.' Millie set her empty plate on the parlour table beside her. Cassius certainly hadn't been exaggerating about her not needing a big breakfast. At this rate she wouldn't have any room left for dinner either. In the space of four hours, she'd consumed two pieces of plum cake, two ginger biscuits, a buttered tea cake and three mince pies. Not to mention eight cups of tea. The combination was starting to make her feel somewhat queasy.

'Thank you, Lady Falconmore.' Her hostess, Mrs Shepherdson, beamed with pride. 'My youngest made the mince pies this year, didn't you, Sophie?'

'Well, it was delectable. Perfectly balanced.' Millie smiled at the girl standing beside her mother's chair. She looked to be about thirteen, with copper-blonde hair and a shy, pleasant face. 'In return, I hope you'll be able to come to the ball, too? The whole family is welcome.'

'Can I?' The girl's eyes slid towards her mother. 'Please, Mama?'

'You certainly can.' Mrs Shepherdson nodded her

approval and then turned back to Millie. 'We're so flat-tered by your visit, Lady Falconmore. We didn't expect it so soon after your marriage.' She shuffled forward with a look of barely concealed curiosity. It was be-coming familiar, the same expression Millie had seen in every house they'd visited. 'Everyone was *so* sur-prised by the news, especially when we heard you only arrived in Rayleigh just over a week ago.'

'Yes, I confess I was somewhat surprised myself.'

'It must have been a whirlwind romance, then?'

'Very much so.' After eight almost identical con-versations, the answers, which she preferred to think of as exaggerations rather than lies, slid off her tongue like honey. 'I'm still feeling quite dizzy.'

'But you know I'll always be here to catch you, my darling.' Cassius chose that moment to enter the kitchen, accompanied by Mr Shepherdson. 'Although I'd call it more of a hurricane than a whirlwind, but then what's the point of waiting when you've met the perfect woman?'

'Not to mention the perfect man.' Millie batted her eyelashes in a way that she hoped conveyed an appro-priate level of devotion.

'What was the wedding like?' Mrs Shepherdson's eyes lit up eagerly. 'We heard you wore a white dress like the Queen.'

'She did,' Cassius answered for her. 'She looked so radiant I was almost blinded. I barely noticed any-one else.'

'How wonderful.' Mrs Shepherdson and Sophie sighed together.

'Of course, in my eyes she becomes more and more radiant every da—'

'But we look forward to seeing you at the ball,' Millie interjected quickly. 'I do so want it to be a success.'

'We wouldn't miss it for the world, my lady.'

'Excellent.' Cassius made a formal bow. 'In that case, I hope that both you and your daughter will agree to save me a dance.'

'Oh!' Mrs Shepherdson laid a hand on her chest. 'We'd be honoured, sir.'

Millie took hold of his arm, smiling at the flurry of giggles behind them as they walked back out into the yard.

'You know at this rate you'll be dancing all night,' she pretended to remonstrate as they climbed back up on to the barouche. 'You've promised to dance with every woman we've seen today.'

'Have I?'

'Yes, and there were seven daughters at the last farm!'

'Well then, we'll just ask the musicians to play for as long as it takes.' He picked up the reins with a flourish. 'And don't think you'll escape their fate either. It's custom for the lord and lady to open the ball.'

'I suppose if I must.' She heaved an exaggerated sigh and waved back at the house. 'Especially since we're in love. Although I think you might be overdoing the pretence slightly. *Blinded by radiance? More and more every day?*'

'I thought it was poetic.'

'Except that we only got married yesterday.'

'Oh, yes, so we did.' He laughed. 'You're coping very well with all that tea and cake, by the way.'

'Don't remind me.' She put her hand on her stomach as the barouche lurched forward. 'Any more and I might burst.'

'*I* could do with a cup of tea right about now. The men just want to clap me on the back and offer me brandy. Maybe we should swap places?'

'No, thank you. But maybe we could take a break from visiting and look for some holly instead? I need a walk before I even *look* at another mince pie.'

'Good idea. There's a wood right along here.' He swayed briefly against her as they turned a corner, making that side of her body come alive again. 'You know you don't have to eat all the cake. You could just refuse it.'

'But that would be rude.'

'Marchionesses are allowed to be rude. Didn't you know?'

'Well, this one isn't.'

'You really are a revolutionary, aren't you?' He smiled at her. 'I'm starting to wonder what I've let myself in for.'

Cassius tugged on the rim of his top hat, shielding his eyes from the low sun. What *had* he let himself in for? The moment the words had left his mouth he'd felt a jolt of surprise. Just a few days ago he'd resolved to put distance between them and yet here he was, riding about his estate, pretending to dote on his new wife. Why? What on earth had made him suggest such a thing? Why propose that they ride about the estate together *at all*? Of course it had only been good manners to show her around, but he could have found an easier, less time-absorbing way to do it. Instead, he'd actually *wanted* to spend the day with her!

On the other hand, after three glasses of brandy—he'd refused the others on the grounds of safety—perhaps now wasn't the best time to think about his motivations. Besides, he didn't want to spoil the undeniable fact that he was enjoying himself, as if he were on holiday, too. Playing the part of adoring husband had proven surprisingly entertaining and, despite Millie's accusations, he hadn't exaggerated that much at all. She *had* looked radiant on their wedding day and even more so today, especially when she'd been pretending to dote on him, too. And now the sunshine was bringing out the various red shades of her hair, from cherry to burgundy, all combining together to make one rich auburn hue. Even her eyes had a hint of amber about them, he noticed, a copper ring around the pupil before it blended into green. She looked so warm and vibrant that it took no effort at all to believe that he was in love with her. In fact, it was alarmingly easy. Natural almost.

'Over there.' He directed the trap to the side of the road and gestured into the wood. 'If I'm not mistaken, that's a holly tree.'

'You're right.' She jumped down almost the moment they stopped. 'We'll need a few long branches so that I can arrange it over the windows.'

'How many windows are you planning to decorate?'

'As many as I can in the ballroom. Then we'll need to make wreaths for the doors, too. I want the whole house to look festive.'

He climbed down from the trap and folded his arms sternly. 'You know, they warned me this would happen.'

'Who warned you about what?'

'Marriage. People warned me it would be just like the army and I'd end up following orders again.' He lowered his brows for a moment, then pulled a pair of shears from the back of the barouche. 'Fortunately, Shepherdson lent me these.'

'Can I help?' Millie stood to one side as he strode up to the holly tree.

'No, you can stand back and admire my manly prowess. And no picking up branches either. You look far too *radiant* to get covered in scratches.'

She laughed, watching as he cut down a few boughs and then piled them on to the back of the barouche.

'There.' He rubbed his sleeve over his face when he was finished. 'I'll send some of the stable boys out tomorrow to get more. If that's acceptable for your plans?'

'It is, thank you. Oh, look!' She pointed towards a ditch by the side of the track. 'There's still some snow over there. It's such a shame the rest melted so quickly.'

'So there is. Which reminds me…' he strode straight towards it '…I owe you a debt.'

'You do?'

'I'm afraid so.' He picked up a clump of snow and shaped it into a ball with his hands. 'One of honour, otherwise I wouldn't dream of doing anything so unchivalrous.'

'You wouldn't!' Her eyes jumped from his hands to his face with a look of alarm.

'I'm afraid that I would. Although as a gentleman I'm prepared to give you a ten-second head start. One…'

'Cassius!'

'Two. I suggest you start running. Three…'

'Beast!' She bent down, scooping up her own snowball before running headlong into the trees.

'Four…' He laughed and started after her. 'Ten!'

'Cheat!'

'You might want to get it over with.' He slowed his footsteps as she dived behind a large oak. 'I promise to be gentle.'

'Never!' She bobbed out again almost instantly, flinging her arm back and knocking his top hat to the ground with her snowball.

'Nice aim.' He darted around the trunk, just in time to see her skirts whisk away again. 'But you're out of ammunition.'

'There are other things I can throw!'

'Twigs and acorns?'

'Something like that.' There was a strange scraping sound from the other side of the tree.

'Do you remember that I said I have a twin brother?'

'Yes.' He glanced down at his snowball. It was starting to melt in his hands.

'Well, when we were children I was determined to do everything he could.'

'Really?' He circled his way stealthily around the thick trunk. 'And what exactly did you get up to?'

'Oh, the usual things…'

He jerked his head up as her voice came from a different direction all of a sudden, just in time to catch a glimpse of her standing on a branch before a flurry of leaves tumbled into his face. 'Climbing trees, for example.'

'You win.' He ruffled his hands through his hair, laughing when he'd finished shaking out the last of the dried leaves. 'I've only water left anyway.'

She laughed, too, and then jumped down to the

ground, proffering a hand for him to shake. 'Are we friends again? Do you concede defeat?'

'I do.' He took her hand, though the moment their fingers touched he realised it was a mistake. Or if not a mistake then a miscalculation. There was nothing remotely friendly about the way his blood surged in response to the feel of her body, even separated by two layers of glove.

'Well then...' her lashes fluttered and lowered '...we ought to move on to the next farm before it gets dark.'

'True.' He started to let her go and then changed his mind, lifting her up into his arms impetuously and heading back towards the snow instead. 'On the other hand...'

'What? No!' She started to wriggle frantically as she realised where they were going.

'Debt of honour, remember?' He stopped beside the pile of snow. 'Although I suppose I could take something else in exchange.'

'What?'

He pretended to think for a moment. 'I might accept a kiss.'

'Oh.' Her body stiffened in his arms, though she stopped struggling. 'But I don't see any mistletoe.'

'Apparently it's not necessary.'

'So if I kiss you, you'll let me go?' Her eyes widened with a searching look.

'It's worth a try.'

'Well then, I don't suppose I have any choice,' she murmured softly as she lifted her head up, tipped it back and then pressed her lips against his with a sweetness that took his breath away. Fortunately, it was only a few seconds before it came back again, along with an

overwhelming impulse to kiss her back. His body re-
sponded even faster, a wave of heat flooding his veins
as he tightened his hold around her. A few moments
later her arms wound their way around his neck, pulling her small breasts tight against his chest in a way
that made him wonder if a snow bed was aptly named,
after all. How comfortable would it really be for re-
clining on, he asked himself, or for doing other things,
too? Because he was decidedly tempted to find out.

'Lord Falconmore!' The sound of his name being
called from the direction of the wood brought him back
to his senses. Barely.

'What?' He wasn't sure if he put her down or if she
actually jumped out of his arms. Either way, he found
himself muffling several choice swear words while she
quickly adjusted the position of her bonnet.

'I saw you stopping your barouche like you said you
might, my lord.' It was Shepherdson himself, accompanied by two boys, emerging out of the undergrowth.
'We've come to help gather some holly.'

'Thank you.' Cassius forced a smile through gritted teeth. He could hardly fault the man for coming to
assist, even if his timing left a great deal to be desired.

'We can bring it all up to the house in a cart tomorrow, too, if you like?'

'That would be a great help.' He nodded and then
threw an apologetic glance towards Millie. 'I'm sorry.'

'Is the debt repaid, then?' she asked the question
softly, her cheeks an extremely becoming shade of
pink.

'That might be something we need to discuss later
in more detail.' His voice sounded huskier than he'd
intended. 'And in private.'

Chapter Fifteen

'It's getting dark already.' Cassius pointed towards the east, to where the sky was already turning a forbidding shade of grey. He didn't particularly need to say it aloud since they both had eyes in their heads, but he needed to break the silence somehow. They were the first words either of them had spoken since they'd left Shepherdson and his two sons. 'We'd better get back to the hall.'

'You're probably right.' She gave a small shiver. 'The temperature's dropping already.'

'Here.' He reached under the bench and pulled out a blanket, draping it gently over her knees. 'How is your stomach feeling?'

'Mmm?' She sounded distracted. 'Oh, much better, thank you, although I don't think I'll need any dinner.'

'Still bursting with cake?'

'I'm feeling better, but I don't think I'll be hungry again for a week. I enjoyed myself today, though.'

'So did I.' He resisted the urge to tuck the blanket more closely around her. The feeling of her legs beneath the fabric had already made his pulse quicken. 'I don't remember the last time I laughed so much.'

'I'm not sure that's much of a compliment when you were pretending to be in love.'

'Ah, but that was the enjoyable part.'

'Oh.' She pressed her lips together for a moment as if she were considering saying something. 'About what I said this morning…about our sleeping arrangements and it being a duty.'

'Yes?'

'I didn't mean to imply anything unpleasant about the idea.'

'I see.' He was aware of a tightening sensation in his body, as if all his nerves were standing to attention. 'Theoretically speaking, then, if we were to—'

'Yes.' She didn't wait for him to finish the sentence. *'Yes?'*

'Yes.'

'Millie, I'm not certain we're talking about the same thing.'

'We are.'

'Ah. Well then…good.' He picked up the reins, suddenly eager to get back to the hall as quickly as possible. 'If you're certain?'

'I am.'

'Well then, I just have one small matter to discuss with Linton when we get back and then… You're sure you don't want any dinner?'

'Definitely not, thank you.'

'All right. Then perhaps it will be an early night for both of us?'

Millie sat up in bed, waiting. Her maids—for some reason she had two of them—had finally left and not a moment too soon. She'd been unlaced, undressed, unbraided, washed, brushed, re-braided and then dressed all over again in a frilly lace concoction of a nightgown that made her feel somewhat ridiculous. Apparently a marchioness was expected to dress for an audience, even in bed.

What now? she wondered, plucking at the bedsheets with her fingers. Now that she'd agreed to go through with this—now that she'd actually suggested it, although she could still hardly believe the audacity of her own words—she wasn't sure what to do next. There were candles on either side of the bed, but as to whether she was expected to keep them burning, she had no idea. It felt bizarre to just sit there waiting. Surely she ought to get up and *do* something? If only to distract herself from her nerves…

She tossed the covers back and swung her legs over the side of the bed, intending to start work on another of Sylvia's gowns when she heard a light knock on the door of her dressing room and Cassius appeared on the threshold.

'Forgive my tardiness.' He was wearing a russet-coloured dressing gown, his blond hair swept away from his face. 'Linton has the worst timing. He wanted to discuss a new drainage scheme.'

'That sounds important.'

'Not tonight it isn't.' He smiled, his teeth flashing white in the half-darkness. 'He's an excellent manager, but somewhat lacking in imagination. I very nearly had to fire the man.'

'Well, I hope that you didn't.' She curled her legs back on to the bed and tugged the covers up to her chin.

'Cold again?' He closed the dressing-room door with

his foot, a hint of a smile playing about his lips, and she lifted her chin, sensing that he was mocking her.

'No, but you haven't seen what I'm wearing.'

'I caught a glimpse. It looked elaborate.'

'Let's just say I hope you like lace.'

'I like *you*. Fabric has nothing to do with it.' He gave a slow smile and then gestured towards the fireplace. 'This is just like old times, though I'm afraid I didn't bring any port. Would you care for anything to drink? Some wine, perhaps? I promise not to smash any bottles.'

'No, thank you.' She smiled back, aware that he was trying to put her at ease. If only that were possible...

'Are you nervous?' He sat down on the opposite side of the bed and looked at her, his gaze unexpectedly tender.

'No.' She shook her head quickly. *Too* quickly as the room seemed to heat up suddenly, the air between them thick with tension.

'No? Because you look like you're about to face a firing squad. If you've changed your mind...?'

'I haven't.' She gave another, even more vigorous shake. 'I just want to get it over with.'

'Ah.'

She winced. 'That came out wrong. I didn't mean...'

'You mean you want to know exactly what you've let yourself in for?' He leaned closer, lowering his voice as if someone might overhear them.

'Yes. I suppose I'm curious.' She sank her teeth into her bottom lip worriedly. 'Is that bad?'

'I think it's natural. I can tell you if you like or we can do this the old-fashioned way and I'll show you?'

'I think…' she hesitated momentarily '…if you show me.'

'All right then.' He stood up, untying his dressing gown and tossing it aside before sliding beneath the covers. 'Come here.'

She shuffled cautiously towards him as he held out an arm, holding her breath as her head came to rest against his shoulder.

'There.' He curled his arm around her and pressed his mouth into her hair. 'That's not so bad, is it?'

'No.' She tilted her head slightly to look into his face. 'But we haven't…'

'One step at a time. If we rush, then it really might be as bad as you seem to expect.'

'Oh.'

'You know, my aunt used to say that if something was worth doing then it was worth doing properly.' He laughed softly. 'Of course she probably had a different context in mind, but trust me, some things are worth taking their time over.'

'I suppose so, but all those things I overheard…they didn't explain what *I* ought to do.'

'Whatever you feel like doing. We could just kiss for a while? We've done that before.'

He lowered his head as he spoke, claiming her mouth before she could think of a protest, his lips warm and soft and infinitely gentle as if he were *still* offering her a chance to change her mind. Instead she kissed him back, mirroring each movement even when his tongue slipped between her lips, possessing the whole of her mouth. The longer they kissed the more possessive it became. Deeper and hotter, as if her body were heating up from the inside. She didn't protest even when one of his hands slid downwards, gently stroking and then cupping one of her breasts.

'How bad was that?' He came up for air finally, his eyes smouldering.

'It…wasn't…bad.' She closed her eyes, breathing the words between gasps.

'I'm pleased to hear it.' He touched his lips briefly back to hers and slid his hand over her stomach. 'And now?'

'Not…bad.'

'Even better.' He kissed her cheek this time, then her chin and neck, trailing a path of kisses over her throat and down to the soft curve of her shoulders. 'Trust me, Millie.'

'Cassius?' She inhaled sharply as he moved lower, kissing her breasts through the fabric of her nightgown. She was vaguely aware of his fingers tugging at the edge of the fabric, too, pulling it up around her thighs as his mouth drifted even further down…

'*Cassius!*' She repeated his name, more urgently this time, grasping at his shoulders and holding tight. 'What are you doing?'

'Trying to help you relax.' He lifted his head. 'Although judging by your expression, I'm not succeeding very well.'

'You're kissing my stomach.'

'I noticed.'

'Oh.' She licked her lips. 'I just didn't expect you to kiss me there.'

'You might be surprised by where I want to kiss you.' He put a hand on either side of her waist and climbed back up the bed, arching his body over hers. 'But if you don't like it…'

'I didn't say that. I just didn't expect it.'

'Millie.' He lowered his face, brushing his lips lightly against hers. 'I won't do anything you don't want me to. If you want me to stop, you only have to say so. I would never hurt you intentionally.'

'Intentionally?' She swallowed. 'You mean it *might* hurt?'

'At first. So I understand, anyway.' He gave a self-deprecating smile. 'I don't make a habit of deflowering maidens.'

'Good.' She laughed despite herself. 'That makes you sound like a villain.'

'Oh, I'm sure I could be quite villainous with you, too.' He rolled to one side, propping himself up on one elbow as he toyed with the fabric of her nightgown. 'This garment really doesn't seem like you. Another gift from Sylvia?'

'I think so.'

'Do you mind if we remove it?'

'No—o, but then you'll see me.'

'That's the point.' He glanced downwards. 'You can already see me.'

'That's different.'

'Why? We'll both be naked. It only seems fair.'

She considered the point silently for a moment before wriggling further down beneath the bedcovers, dragging the nightgown over her head while her body remained covered.

'Impressive.' His lips twitched at the corners. 'Now about your braid.'

'You want me to undo it?'

'If you don't mind. I haven't seen your hair loose since the first night we met.'

'That seems like such a long time ago.' She reached behind her, removing the tie from her hair and letting it slowly unravel. 'So much has happened.'

'I have to keep reminding myself it's been little more than a week. *There.*' He spread the long tresses out around her head and buried his face in them, breathing deeply. 'Orange blossom, I knew it.'

'What?'

'You feel like silk and smell like orange blossom.'

'It's my soap.'

'It suits you.' He caressed her jaw and throat with his fingertips. 'From now on, you shouldn't wear anything to bed except that scent. Now, do you trust me?'

'Yes.'

'Good. Where were we?'

She gasped as he leant over her, the muscles of his chest pressing hard against her breasts. His skin felt warm and smooth and wonderfully soft. It made her want to touch him all over, even if she didn't have the nerve yet to do so. Instead she kissed him again, trying not to stiffen as his fingers slid between her legs, moving in slow circles that felt surprisingly, shockingly good. Relaxing even. Despite herself, she felt the tension in her muscles start to ebb away, as if she were sinking into the bed itself. Before she knew it, her body was moving of its own accord, undulating with the teasing rhythm of his fingers.

'Cassius?'

'Yes?'

She opened her eyes, surprised to realise she'd murmured his name aloud. 'Nothing.'

'Do you want me to stop?' There was an edge of tension in his voice.

'No.'

'Thank goodness.' He nudged her thighs apart with his legs. 'Don't stop what you were doing.'

'What was I doing?'

'You were moving your hips.' His fingers continued to tease her. 'Just like that.'

'This?'

'Perfect.' He buried his face in her neck. 'How does it feel now?'

'Good.' She frowned slightly. 'Wet.'

'That's a good sign.' He moved his hand away and lowered his body over hers, pressing his lips to her throat. 'Forgive me.'

'Forgive wha—? Oh!' She uttered a small cry as he entered her, every muscle tightening in surprise. There was pain, too, a slight tearing sensation before he slid past it and deeper inside her body.

'Millie?' His breath was warm against her ear.

She didn't answer, moving her hips to see if it made the position any more comfortable. It didn't, though the sensation was interesting, causing a familiar tingling in her abdomen. Cassius gave a low moan in the back of his throat, one of his hands tugging the bedcovers aside while the other held his weight off her. She didn't protest. At this point she didn't care how much he could see of her body. All she could think of was the feeling of his body inside hers. She tried clenching and unclenching her muscles. It felt so strange and intimate and the pain was diminishing…

'Millie?' He repeated her name, though his voice sounded strained, as if he were speaking through clenched teeth.

'Mmm?'

'Are you all right?' He lifted his head, holding on to her gaze as he slowly began to withdraw and then apparently changed his mind, pushing inwards again.

'Yes.' She took a deep breath and shifted beneath him, tilting her hips upwards this time. The pain was definitely receding now, replaced by a feeling of slickness. Every time he slid inside her it seemed to become easier, natural almost, as if they were meant to be joined together.

'Just tell me if...' His voice trailed away as he groaned and pressed his forehead to hers, starting to move faster. She moved with him, lifting one of her legs and coiling it tentatively around his waist. Somehow the position made her feel better so she did the same with the other, arching her back and rolling beneath him as the tingling sensation in the pit of her stomach built to an ache. It was almost unbearable now, so intense that she thought they might have to stop after all, until a wave of sensation seemed to rush through her body all at once, making her cry out and shudder at the same time. He must have felt it, too, because he gave an answering cry as his body convulsed and then pressed down on top of her.

They lay like that for a few moments, both of them breathing heavily before he rolled to one side, drawing her into the crook of his arm and tugging the bedcovers up over their damp bodies. She twisted her head, allowing his lips to claim one last kiss, before laying it on his chest and falling fast asleep.

Chapter Sixteen

'Good morning.' Cassius reached a hand out, hooking it around Millie's waist and pulling her back as she started to roll away. It was the first time she'd moved since he'd been watching her and he didn't want to let her go. Somehow just looking at her, his senses engulfed by her orange blossom scent and the warm, steady pulse of her body, made him feel calm inside.

'Cassius?' Her eyes flew open at the sound of his voice. 'What are you…? Oh!' Her look of shock turned to one of sudden recollection. 'Good morning.'

'How did you sleep?' He smiled lazily.

'Very well, thank you. I forgot that we…that is, I only just woke up.'

'I know.' He let his gaze drift from her face to her shoulders, the only exposed parts of her body he could see. The rest was covered with a bedsheet, though he could still see the outline of her figure and remember how it looked *and* felt. She was lithesome and slender, not particularly curvaceous, though the small curves she had were in all the right places. Eminently kissable places, too, if he could only get at them… Their night together had been even more satisfying than he'd expected. Once she'd begun to relax, she'd been positively abandoned.

'Couldn't you sleep?' A look of anxiety crossed her face.

'Actually I slept very well. I just woke early. How do you feel?'

'A little sore.'

'Next time should be less painful.'

'You were right, though. The pain passed quickly and the rest was quite…'

'Pain*less*?'

'Yes. And pleasurable, too.' She smiled shyly. 'Is that how it's supposed to be?'

'That's exactly how it's supposed to be. For a first time, I'd say we excelled ourselves.' He trailed his fingers gently along the side of her face, over the rounded curve of her cheek and the straight line of her nose. Except it wasn't an entirely straight line, he noticed. There was a slight bump in the middle. Somehow that made it even more adorable.

'Do you think—?'

She stopped at the sound of a tap on the door followed by the almost immediate appearance of a maid carrying a tray. The girl took two steps into the room and then froze in horror at the sight of them.

'Oh, my lady…my lord… I'm sorry.'

'No apology necessary.' Cassius sat up and gestured at the tray. 'Is that hot chocolate?'

'Yes, my lord.'

'In that case you can leave it and tell Cook we won't be down for breakfast for another hour. *At least.*'

'Yes, my lord. I will, my lord.' The flustered girl put the steaming hot cup on the bedside table and fled.

'Do you know, I think she was surprised to find me still here. We've managed to scandalise our own staff.' Cassius looked back down at Millie and grinned. 'Were you just hiding beneath the covers?'

'I might have been.' She heaved herself up beside him. 'Why is nothing we do ever private?'

'I'm afraid that's the price of being the Marquess and Marchioness of Falconmore. At least we're married now.'

'I suppose so and I *do* want my hot chocolate.'

'Here.' He picked up the cup and handed it to her. 'You need to rebuild your strength.'

'I'm not ill. Or broken.'

'That's a relief. If you were, then I'd have to stay away from you for a while and I'm not sure I'm capable of that, especially now I know what I'd be missing.'

She gave him a quizzical look as she took a small sip of chocolate. 'You're in a good mood.'

'I wonder why?'

'I didn't know if you'd still be here when I woke up either. Only I remember what you told me about your nightmares. You said you didn't want anyone to hear if you shouted out in your sleep.'

'Ah.' He pushed a hand through his hair. 'To be honest, I *did* intend to leave, only I fell asleep, without any nightmares I might add, and then when I woke you looked so peaceful I wanted to keep looking at you.' He frowned at his own admission. 'Does it bother you that I'm still here?'

'No. My parents always shared a bedroom.' She looked awkward suddenly, a faint blush suffusing her cheeks. 'Not that I'm saying we *should* share a room, but…'

'But we could,' he concluded for her. 'Although I can't promise not to have nightmares.'

'But if you do, then I would be here to talk, just like last time. If you want to, that is.'

'Thank you.' He pressed a kiss to the end of her nose. 'Am I allowed a sip of that?'

She opened her mouth, looking from him to her cup and then back again. 'You know sleeping here is one thing. Drinking my chocolate is quite another. Fortunately for you, I'm in a good mood, too.'

'Then I'm doubly grateful.' He swallowed a mouthful and licked his lips appreciatively. 'I might have to consider changing from coffee. This could be our new morning ritual, hot chocolates in bed.'

'That sounds very decadent.'

'Another good reason.' He passed the cup back and lay down, folding his arms behind his head and grinning as she tucked the bedclothes tighter around her. 'If you're still trying to protect your modesty, then I wouldn't bother. I saw everything there was to see last night.'

'Cassius!'

'Although I wouldn't mind seeing it again.' He smiled wickedly and then dipped his head beneath the covers.

'What are you…?' She gave a small shriek. 'Stop it or I'll spill the chocolate!'

'Then you'd better drink up and join me.' He laughed, waiting until he heard her put the cup aside before grabbing her waist and pulling her down beside him. 'It's quite cosy under here. Like a tent.'

'We should be getting out of bed, not back inside it.'

'Nice try.' He brought his mouth down on hers, savouring the sweet trace of chocolate on her tongue. 'But you heard what I said. No breakfast for at least another hour. Now how do you think we should pass the time?'

'I'm sure I have no idea.'

'None at all?' He smoothed a hand over one of her breasts, gently caressing the nipple between his fingertips and smiling as she let out a gasp. 'Fortunately, I have several.'

'Lady Falconmore…? Lady Falconmore?'

Millie started at the sound of the housekeeper's voice. She'd been so engrossed in her memories of the previous night *and* that morning she'd completely forgotten she wasn't alone.

'Excuse me, Mrs Turner.' She smiled apologetically and started down the ladder she'd been using to fasten a bough of holly over one of the ballroom windows. 'I was daydreaming.'

'Of course, my lady. I just asked if you thought we might need any more vases?'

'How many do we have now?' She counted the ones set out on a table below. 'Twenty. That's one for each table. Perfect.'

'Very good.' Mrs Turner nodded approvingly. 'We can fill them with flowers from the hothouse on the day.'

'Yes, but only in red, white and green. We want to keep the same colour scheme.'

'It's going to look lovely, my lady. And the staff

are all excited about the party below stairs, too. Not to mention having a few days off.'

'I'm glad. Will you be going away to visit family?'

'Bless you, no.' The housekeeper shook her head. 'I don't have much family, only a brother in Surrey and I doubt he'd recognise me these days. No, I'm perfectly content staying here with Mr Kendrew. We'll keep each other company.'

'As long as you're happy to stay.' Millie glanced at the housekeeper curiously. 'Are you and Mr Kendrew good friends?'

'We've got to know each other over the years.' If she wasn't mistaken, Mrs Turner's cheeks turned a duskier shade as she spoke. 'But we know the rules, my lady. We would never break them.'

'What rules?'

'About…family matters. Staff aren't allowed to marry or we lose our positions, we know that.'

'But that's ridiculous!' Millie put her hands on her hips indignantly. 'Who on earth would make up such a rule?'

'It's just the way things are, my lady. It always has been.'

'Well, it shouldn't be. Do you and Mr Kendrew want to marry?'

'We haven't talked about it.' Mrs Turner looked flustered. 'What with it not being allowed.'

'Well, if you think that you might then you *should* talk about it. As soon as possible.'

'But Lord Falconmore…'

'Lord Falconmore what?' Cassius came striding into the ballroom suddenly, looking windblown and yet even more handsome than he'd been in her daydreams.

'Lord Falconmore will approve of the decorations, I'm sure,' Millie answered as a flash of panic shot across the housekeeper's face. 'How was your ride?'

'Bracing. It's turned colder again. To be honest, I'm glad to be back inside.'

'And what do you think of my flower arranging?' She gestured towards the bough above the door.

'I think that may be a misnomer. I can't see any flowers.'

'Branch arranging, then. It *is* winter.'

'In that case I think it's excellent.' He caught her about the waist as Mrs Turner bobbed a curtsy and hurried away. 'What was that all about? You weren't really talking about decorations just then, were you?'

'How do you know?' She peered up at him shyly, the pressure of his hands on her waist making her heart jump and then flutter. She could feel the heavy thrum of his heartbeat, too, through her gown, not to mention his body heat, as hot, hotter even, than hers.

'Because Mrs Turner looked as if she were about to have a fit of the vapours.'

'She's far too sensible a woman to do any such thing.' Millie smiled at the image. 'She was just telling me about a rule that says staff can't marry.'

'And?'

She put her hands on her hips again. 'Then it's true?'

'Of course. It's true everywhere.' He paused. 'Everywhere except the Fairclough Foundation, presumably?'

'You presume correctly. What right do we have to tell people who they can and can't marry?'

'Don't tell me this conversation is directly appertaining to Mrs Turner somehow?'

'Yes, and Mr Kendrew if you must know.'

'Kendrew?' He let out a low whistle. 'Well, blow me down. The old hound…'

'He is *not* a hound and I've said that they're free to marry if they want.' She narrowed her eyes. 'Unless you disagree?'

'Something tells me that's a trick question.' He pulled her hands from her sides and curved them around him instead. 'No, far be it from me to interfere. If Kendrew wants to shackle himself into the oppressive bonds of matrimony then—ow!'

'Oops.' Millie gave a look of feigned innocence. 'Did my foot slip?'

'Right against my ankle, as it happens.'

'How careless of me. Only I thought perhaps you enjoyed *some* aspects of marriage?'

'I do, only not everyone can be as fortunate as me. Some men get through their entire lives with their ankles unscathed.' He laughed and then pulled an envelope from his jacket pocket. 'Fortunately, I bring a peace offering. This was waiting for you in the hall.'

'That's Alexandra's writing.' She took it and broke the seal eagerly, scanning the contents with a growing sense of dismay. 'Oh, no.'

'What's the matter?' Cassius's expression turned serious at once. 'Has something happened?'

'Not yet, but it's going to.' She looked at him in horror. 'She's invited me to tea tomorrow!'

'Monstrous!' He lifted an eyebrow. 'And that would be terrible because…'

'Because it's not just *me* she's invited. She says there'll be "a handful of other guests" so that she can reintroduce me as Lady Falconmore.'

'Ah.'

'She says she wants to do it while my mother's still visiting.'

'Ah.'

'What should I do?'

'What do you want to do?'

'Go upstairs and hide under the bedcovers again?'

There was a flash of heat in his eyes. 'In that case I'd be more than happy to keep you company, but…'

'You think I should go?'

'I think that your cousin might be right and it's a good idea to do it sooner rather than later. And a handful of guests doesn't sound too intimidating. I'll come with you, if you want?'

'No.' She smiled and shook her head. 'Thank you, but I think this is something I need to face on my own. I just don't know if I'm ready.'

'Your cousin thinks you are.'

'She hasn't seen me since the wedding.'

'Well, I have…' his gaze dipped '…quite a lot of you, too, and you don't have anything to worry about. Just be yourself and you'll be wonderful.'

'Do you really think so?' She felt her breasts tighten as his gaze lingered over them briefly.

'I do, but if you'd like to hide under the covers *today*…?'

'It's the middle of the afternoon!' She felt obliged to make some kind of protest. 'And we didn't get out of bed until noon.'

'Really? It feels like an age ago.'

'What about all the decorating?'

'If I'm not mistaken, we have another four days to finish. Not to mention a houseful of staff.'

'Then what will everyone think?'

'That we're newlyweds. And you know…' his hand moved caressingly over her lower back '…it might take your mind off tomorrow.'

She looked at the letter again and grimaced. 'I'm not sure anything will be able do that.'

'Challenge accepted.' He pressed his face into her neck. 'At the very least you can let me try.'

'I suppose we could just go and lie down.' She caught her breath and then tipped her head backwards as his lips nuzzled her earlobe. 'Just for a while.'

'Good.' There was a definite smile in his voice. 'And for the record, I'll consider myself a sorry excuse for a husband if you so much as *think* about afternoon tea for the rest of the day…'

Chapter Seventeen

Millie climbed the steps to the Malverlys' front door with a growing sense of unease. The last time she'd attended a social event in the area she'd been an unmarried Miss, an insignificant, impoverished nobody in the eyes of society. Now she was a wife and a member of the aristocracy to boot, with no clear idea about how a marchioness ought to behave. She could only be herself, like Cassius had said, and hope for the best.

Cassius... Just the thought of him made her body tingle and her pulse start to flutter erratically. After spending a large part of the previous afternoon locked in their bedchamber, they'd retired early again after dinner. Which was really quite shocking, she thought, pausing briefly on the steps to regain her composure, the things they'd done there even more so. If she hadn't been on holiday and specifically *not* thinking about who she was and how she ought to behave, then she might have been somewhat mortified. Not by the actions themselves—on the contrary, those had been unexpectedly and intensely enjoyable—but at her own enthusiastic participation in them. She'd never imagined that her body could feel so many thrilling sensations. Or that married life could be quite so stirring...

'Lady Falconmore.' Alexandra's butler opened the door, taking her outer garments and bowing so formally that she half-wondered if he didn't recognise her.

'Millie!' Thankfully her mother did, rising from a chair to greet her with a look that expressed both welcome and warning, before pressing a kiss to her cheek. 'Courage, dear.'

'I'll try,' Millie whispered back, her stomach lurching with panic as she entered the drawing room. It was a long, *very long* way from the 'handful of guests' Alexandra had referred to. In fact, it was packed almost to bursting with well-dressed, mostly middle-aged ladies, all of whom were studying her as if she were some kind of scientific exhibit. One even had a lorgnette raised to her eye. And there, in prime position beside the fireplace, sat Lady Fentree and her daughter Vanessa.

One of Cassius's more virulent epithets popped loudly into her head.

'Lady Falconmore, dear.' Alexandra stood up and approached them, her expression suggesting she knew *exactly* what Millie was thinking. 'Do come and sit down. I believe you've already been introduced to everyone.'

'I think so.' She took her cousin's arm, smiling nervously around at the assembled gathering. 'Good afternoon.'

'Lady Falconmore, how pleasant it is to see you again.' Lady Fentree's smile was positively fawning. There was certainly no hint of the antipathy she'd displayed at their last parting. As Millie remembered it, that conversation had ended with a distinctly *un*pleasant dismissal. *'I very much doubt that our paths will cross again'* had been the exact words, but it seemed Lady Fentree had a short memory. Either that or she didn't want to get on the wrong side of a marchioness. But good manners were good manners...

'Lady Fentree. How delightful to see you again, too,' she lied, taking a seat on a small sofa.

'I can't tell you how delighted we all are that you're staying here in the country, even if it means losing dear Sylvia.'

'Thank you.' She glanced around, searching for a friendly face. 'Is Sylvia here?'

'Unfortunately not. She came down with a nasty cold the day after she arrived at our house,' Lady Vanessa answered, shooting Millie a look that suggested she held *her* responsible. Evidently the daughter was less forgiving than her mother. 'She sends her regrets.'

'That's a shame. Please do give her my best wishes.'

'Of course we were shocked when she confirmed some of the wilder rumours we'd heard about your marriage,' Lady Vanessa continued as if she hadn't spoken. 'But it seems to have worked out very well. For you anyway.'

'Yes.' Millie exchanged a glance with Alexandra. Of course it was inevitable that the story of how she and Cassius had spent a night together in the gatehouse would have reached the Fentrees' ears, too. No doubt such a pointed remark was revenge for her having removed such an eligible bachelor from the marriage market. Everyone in the room, her family excepted, was probably thinking the same thing, that she'd trapped him. As she effectively had.

'Lord and Lady Falconmore are throwing their first ball in a few days.' Alexandra came to her rescue.

'Really?' Lady Vanessa's lips pursed as if she were wondering where her invitation had got to.

'Yes, but only a small one for the families who live on the estate.'

'What a charming notion.' Lady Fentree smiled obsequiously. 'Well, in that case I'll dare to hope that you might throw another for the whole county quite soon. To celebrate your wedding, perhaps?'

'Perhaps.' Millie strove to repress a look of horror. 'I'll mention the idea to Cassi—Lord Falconmore.'

'Well then.' Alexandra looked satisfied. 'Time for tea, I think.'

'Lord Malverly to see you, sir.' Kendrew appeared, as usual, out of thin air.

'Malverly?' Cassius closed his book of accounts with an enthusiastic snap. He hadn't been paying a great deal of attention to the rows of numbers anyhow, not when his mind was preoccupied with the memory of a certain slim-hipped, auburn-haired beauty lying naked across a bed. The image was as rousing as it was poignant, making him feel oddly emotional. 'Show him in.'

He stood up and crossed the room just in time to greet the older man at the door. 'Lord Malverly, to what do I owe the honour?'

'Refuge! I've been chased out of my own house, don't you know?' George Malverly shook his head in an aggrieved fashion. 'Too many women disturbing my peace. It's a sorry state of affairs when a man can't hear himself think in his own library.'

'Then you're welcome to take solace in mine.' Cassius gestured towards one of the armchairs by the fireplace. 'Care for a drink?'

'I'd like nothing more, but unfortunately I have an ulterior motive for being here.'

'What's that, sir?'

'Aye, well...' Malverly threw a longing glance towards the fireplace and then clasped his hands behind his back. 'Some voices are impossible *not* to recognise, that old cat Lady Fentree's being one of them.'

'Fentree?' Cassius arched an eyebrow. '*She's* at your house?'

'Indeed. No doubt my wife thinks she's helping, but it strikes me that Millie ought to have been warned.'

'You think Lady Fentree might insult her?'

'If she doesn't, her daughter will. A chip off the old block, that one, and some claws are sharper than others.' Malverly gave him a pointed look. 'I won't beat about the bush, Falconmore. I don't like to interfere, especially considering the potential risk to myself if my wife finds out, but I've always had a soft spot for Millie. You might want to consider a rescue mission. If she's not a damsel in distress already, then she soon will be.'

'I'm on my way.' Cassius was already striding back to the door. 'In the meantime, you're welcome to stay here.'

'No, I'd better come, too.' The old Viscount trailed behind him with a hangdog expression. 'With any luck, Alexandra won't have noticed I've been gone. But if she has and she asks, we bumped into each other on the road.'

'Duly noted. I owe you a favour, Lord Malverly.'

* * *

It was half an hour before Cassius dismounted in front of Malverly House. Which meant it must have been over an hour since Millie had arrived and no doubt been subjected to all manner of questions and insinuations about their marriage. Her mother and cousin were there to defend her, at least, but the very thought of her having to deal with such behaviour infuriated him. He adjusted his cravat, straightened his jacket and took a deep breath. Walking into the middle of a ladies' afternoon tea party seemed like a fresh kind of torture, but if Millie could face it then so could he. No matter what she'd said about doing it alone, he *needed* to be there, not just to rescue her, but to put a stop to the gossip once and for all. And after their tour of the farms, he knew exactly how to do it...

'Best of luck.' George Malverly gave him a friendly pat on the shoulder and then turned in the opposite direction. 'Rather you than me.'

'Where are you going?' Cassius looked around as he pulled on the doorbell.

'Back entrance. Don't want to be spotted together, eh?'

Fortunately, he didn't have to wait long for the door to be answered. The butler stood aside at once, accepting his top hat as if it were some kind of trophy before leading him straight to the drawing room.

'Lord Falconmore.'

The butler's announcement caused a shocked silence to descend over the scene. It would have been easy, Cassius thought, to hear a pin drop. Except that he didn't have a pin and neither did anyone else apparently. The hush was almost deafening.

'Good afternoon, ladies.' He made a low bow, his eyes searching the room for Millie. 'I hope you don't mind my intrusion?'

'Of course not.' Alexandra was the first to recover her wits, springing to her feet as if she'd just sat on something hot. 'Do come in and join us. I'm sure Mrs Cooper will gladly move so that you can sit next to Lady Falconmore.'

'Thank you.' He looked quickly in the direction indicated, his heart skipping a beat and then performing some kind of disorientating somersault in his chest as his eyes connected with Millie's. She was gazing at him with an expression of unconcealed amazement.

'Millie.' He found himself standing in front of her before he'd even made a conscious decision to start walking.

'Cassius.' Her voice was as amazed as her expression. 'I didn't expect you to join us.'

'I didn't intend to, but I enjoyed myself so much making calls with you around the estate the other day that I thought it might be fun to do it again.' He lifted an eyebrow. 'If that's acceptable to you, that is?'

'Oh.' Her eyes flashed with understanding and humour. 'Well, then…' She patted the recently vacated space on the sofa beside her. 'You'd better sit down, *darling.*'

'Thank you…' he gave a quick wink *'…honeycomb.'*

'Lord Falconmore, it's been so long since I've had the pleasure.' Lady Fentree leaned so far forward in her chair opposite that he had a momentary fear she was about to fall out of it. Which was especially alarming since that would force him to catch her. 'You've been quite a stranger this past year.'

'Indeed.' His fingers touched lightly against Millie's on the sofa, sending a thrill shooting up his arm. 'I'm afraid that the estate has kept me quite busy.'

'Of course. There must have been a great deal to attend to after your cousin's death, but I hope your presence here today signals a change?'

'Ah.' He smiled as Millie's fingers closed around his. 'As to that, what can I say except that I missed my wife? I find even an hour without her company far too long to bear.'

'An hour?' Lady Fentree looked taken aback.

'I missed you, too, darling.' Millie turned her face towards him, her green eyes glowing with a look of such genuine-looking tenderness that he felt the breath stall in his throat.

'You did?' He coughed the words out, actively trying to remember how to breathe. It seemed impossible that five words and one pair of eyes could have such an extraordinary effect, especially when they were playacting, and yet he was feeling decidedly light-headed.

'Well,' Lady Alexandra interrupted, 'I suppose we have to make allowances for newlyweds. Would anyone care for another cup of tea? Lord Falconmore, can I tempt you?'

'Thank you.' He finally succeeded in regaining some control over his senses, dragging his gaze away from Millie's with an effort. After all, he had a job to do, he reminded himself. He was there to put a stop to any gossip once and for all and he was going to do it properly. Thoroughly. With his wife beside him and her hand entwined in his as if they belonged together. By the time he was done, not one single person in the room would suspect their marriage to be anything other than a love match. Even if it wasn't and could never be, no matter how much he was starting to wish otherwise. Not unless his heart managed to open itself to the possibility of loving someone again. Which was surely impossible, wasn't it?

Cassius waited until the front door closed behind them before heaving a sigh of satisfaction.

'Well, I think we can call that a succ—' He didn't get any further as Millie flung her arms around his neck, embracing him fervently.

'You didn't mind my intrusion, then?' he asked in surprise, dodging his head to one side as the rim of her bonnet threatened to poke him in the eye.

'Not at all.' She pulled back slightly to beam at him. 'Your timing was perfect and you were wonderful. Although I don't know how you managed to keep a straight face.'

'At which part?' He knitted his brows. He didn't remember having said anything particularly comical.

'When you described our first meeting for a start. You called me a vision of loveliness.'

'You were.'

'My nose was bright red and I was dripping wet!'

'But still lovely.' He felt unjustly accused. 'I remember the moment I opened the door quite clearly. I thought you were the prettiest snowman I'd ever seen.'

'*Then* you said you've always had a weakness for red-haired women.'

'True again.'

'*Really?*'

'Really.' He threaded an arm around her waist. 'Although in the interests of marital harmony, I refuse to provide further details. What a man gets up to in his misspent youth isn't something he generally admits to his wife.'

'Oh.' Her eyes widened. 'Well then, what about the part when you said you'd spent your whole life waiting for a woman like me?'

'Did I say that?' He stalled, momentarily stumped for an answer. He could hardly blame brandy for his eloquence this time. The words had simply come naturally. Sincerely, too. 'Well, maybe not my whole life. I was far more interested in cricket when I was a boy.' He gave a small shrug. 'Perhaps I deserve a kiss for my gallantry, too?'

'Later.' She threw a glance at the drawing room window. 'Right now we're making a public spectacle of ourselves again.'

'All the better.' He caught at her hand, holding her back as she made to descend the steps. 'And no pecks on the cheek. Let's do it properly.'

'Cassius...' She started to speak and then stopped as his mouth touched against hers, her breath catching and then releasing on a moan that made all his limbs feel heavy and his blood surge with desire.

'There.' He wrapped his arms around the base of her spine, holding her tightly against him. 'If that doesn't convince people I'm in love with you, nothing will.'

And there was no play-acting about it.

Chapter Eighteen

Perfect. Millie added one last sprig of holly to a vase and looked around the supper room with a combined sense of satisfaction and pleasure. It was ready. The tables and chairs were all informally set out, a line of sofas had been placed along one wall for those who found the ballroom too hot or crowded, and there was a piano in one corner for singing Christmas carols. That was another important task out of the way. Now she just had a dress to take care of.

'Cassius!' she called out as she caught a glimpse of him in the corridor.

'Millie?' He swung around and came back towards her at once. 'I was heading to the ballroom to find you.'

'I'm just finishing up here.'

'What is all this?' He looked confused by the sight of so many tables.

'This is the fourth—or is it fifth?—drawing room, now the supper room.' She lifted an eyebrow. 'Or did you expect us to eat in the ballroom?'

'To be honest, I never thought of it.' He threw her an apologetic look. 'I'm afraid that when I asked you to help arrange a ball, I underestimated the amount of work involved.'

'Yes, you did. As if marrying you wasn't enough.' She gave him a teasing look, though he didn't seem amused.

'This really hasn't been much of a holiday for you, has it?' He wrapped his arms around her. 'You know you don't have to work so hard.'

'I know, but I want everything to be perfect.'

'Are you sure? Because there are plenty of people already seeing to that. The whole house is buzzing with activity. I don't want you working just because you think you ought to.'

'I'm not. I'm enjoying myself.'

'Good.' He sounded appeased. 'Because this is still our honeymoon, remember? You're allowed to relax and sit down for an afternoon at least.'

'Everything's about ready in here anyway.' She laid her head against his shoulder with a sigh of contentment. The supper room was finished, the ballroom was *almost* finished, the last of the invitations had been accepted, and she was clasped tight in her husband's warm and comfortable arms. She felt really and truly happy. Which for some reason provoked a new sense of disquiet. How could she of all people be happy as a marchioness?

'Begging your pardon, my lord, my lady?' A maid's voice interrupted them. 'But there's a visitor to see you, Lady Falconmore.'

'To see me?' Millie lifted her head in surprise. Judging by the maid's expression it obviously wasn't her mother or Alexandra.

'It's a gentleman from London, my lady. He says his name is Mr Griffiths.'

'Gilbert?' She caught her breath at the same moment as she felt Cassius's hand tighten around her waist. 'Here?'

The maid nodded anxiously. 'Mr Kendrew was downstairs so I showed the gentleman into the drawing room. I hope I did the right thing?'

'Yes, you did, thank you... Catherine, isn't it? Please tell him I'll be there shortly.' She looked back at Cassius with consternation. 'This is awful. I was supposed to be considering Gilbert's proposal, not marrying someone else in the meantime! What on earth can he be doing here?'

'Did you write to tell him about our marriage?'

'No. I thought it would be better to tell him in person after Christmas. I never imagined he'd find out on his own.'

'Well, if he's here then someone must have told him.' Cassius looked stern. 'Do you want me to speak to him?'

'No.' She shook her head quickly. 'I owe him an explanation. It might be better if I do it on my own.'

'I helped yesterday.'

'You did and I'm grateful, but yesterday was different. Gilbert's a friend.'

'As you wish.' He looked decidedly unhappy with her answer. She had the distinct impression that he didn't want to let go of her waist either, though he finally did. 'In that case, I'll be in the library if you need me.'

'Thank you.' She made her way quickly through the house, past footmen carrying chairs and housemaids draping tinsel over every available surface. Now that she knew Gilbert was there she wanted to see him as soon as possible to explain her behaviour, although *how* she was going to do that was another matter... If only she'd sent him a letter, after all!

'Gilbert?' She didn't hesitate on the threshold of the drawing room, hurrying across to where he was standing by the fireplace.

'Amelia.' He looked up at the sound of her voice, his expression doleful. 'You're here then?'

'Yes.' She didn't know what else to say, struck with an acute pang of guilt. He looked exactly the way she remembered him, tall and austerely handsome, dressed in muted colours with his black hair cut just a little too neatly.

'So you really are married? I told myself I wouldn't believe it until I saw you with my own eyes.'

'I am, but it's not what you think. That is, it *is* what you think, but I was going to tell you, Gilbert, I promise. Only I wanted to tell you in person, not by letter. I thought it would be better that way, but...' She raised her hands to her cheeks. 'How did you find out?'

'The Vicar of Rayleigh is a friend of my father's. He heard you lived in the same area of London as us and mentioned your wedding in his Christmas missive. He wondered if we were acquainted. Needless to say we were shocked.'

'Yes. Of course.'

'Naturally I thought there must have been some kind of mistake so I came here to discover the truth.' His gaze settled sombrely upon hers. 'But here you are.'

'Oh, Gilbert.' She felt tears prick the backs of her

eyes. 'I'm so sorry. If I'd thought for one second you might find out by accident…'

'I know.' He lifted a hand to forestall her. 'I know *you*, Amelia. I wish I hadn't found out like that, but I know you would never hurt me deliberately. I know you're not the kind of woman to be swayed by titles or fortune either, so I came to ask why. *Why* did you marry him? And why so quickly? I thought you were considering my offer?'

'I was! I swear I was. Only I made a foolish decision to walk home in the snow by myself one night and got myself into a compromising situation and…well, then we *had* to get married.'

'*Had* to?' He frowned. 'So it wasn't by choice?'

'Ye—es. Or at least I decided that it would be for the best. There was so much gossip, it wouldn't have been fair to accept your proposal afterwards.'

'I still wish that you'd come to me.' He sounded reproachful. 'I hate to think of you being forced into anything.'

'But it all worked out for the best.' She smiled. 'I'm happy, truly I am, Gilbert. It was a strange beginning, but it turns out that Cassius and I are well suited, after all.'

'Do you care for him?'

'Yes.' She didn't baulk at the question. The answer was so blindingly obvious, even if after only a week it seemed incredible. She *did* care for him. More than that, she *loved* him, but Gilbert wasn't the man she wanted to tell first. 'Very much.'

'Well then.' His scowl slid gradually into a smile. 'In that case, I wish you joy.'

'Really? Do you forgive me?'

'I do.' His expression turned sheepish. 'While we were apart I started to wonder about some of the things you said when I proposed.'

'What did I say?'

'That we weren't in love.' He reached for her hands and squeezed them. 'I believe at the time I told you an emotional attachment didn't matter, but now I think perhaps I was mistaken. Not that I would have withdrawn my offer, but perhaps you were right.'

'There's no perhaps about it. Now you're free to find a wife you really care about.' She hugged him impulsively. 'You're a good man, Gilbert. You deserve to be truly happy.'

'Thank you.' He wrapped his arms lightly around her, as if he were embarrassed. 'I hope we can always remain friends, although I suppose I'll have to call you Lady Falconmore from now on.'

'Don't be silly. And we'll still see each other often, I hope.'

'I hope so, too, but… Amelia?' He dropped his hands abruptly.

'Yes?'

'Perhaps, in the meantime, you'll be so good as to introduce your husband?'

'Of course. He's in his library, but I'll go and fetch him.'

'Actually I believe he's somewhat closer than that.'

'What?' She pulled her hands away from his shoulders, turning around to find Cassius standing right behind her, arms folded and looking distinctly unhappy. 'Oh! I didn't hear you come in.'

'Evidently.'

'Cassius…' she blinked at his harsh tone '…this is

my dear friend, Mr Gilbert Griffiths. Gilbert, this is my husband, Lord Falconmore.'

'Mr Griffiths.' Cassius held a hand out. 'An honour to meet you.'

'Lord Falconmore. The honour is all mine.'

Millie shifted from one foot to the other, looking between the two men as they exchanged pleasantries. If pleasantries was the right word for it, which she rather thought it wasn't. Instead, they seemed to be sizing each other up, both their stances rigid with tension.

'I've just been explaining to Gilbert what happened.' She hoped that her voice didn't sound as flustered to them as it did to her. 'About our marriage and why we had to go through with it.'

'Quite.' Cassius's voice had a distinct and somewhat discomforting edge.

'But it's all right. Gilbert understands and he's forgiven me so there's no need to worry, after all. Isn't that wonderful?' She was aware that she was floundering. 'Shall I call for some tea?'

'Thank you, but I ought to be going.' Gilbert took a step towards the door. 'It's been a long day and you seem to be very busy here.'

'Oh…yes.' There was a load thud from the hallway as if to emphasise the point. 'You'll have to forgive all the commotion. We're holding a ball soon.'

'A ball?' He lifted an eyebrow.

'Yes. It's for everyone on the estate. You should come!' she said before she could think better of it, feeling somewhat relieved when he shook his head.

'Thank you, but I should be getting back to London.'

'Surely you're not travelling home tonight?'

'No. I've taken a room at the inn in Rayleigh and

the Malverlys have been kind enough to invite me for dinner this evening. Naturally I called at their house first to pay my respects to your mother and...well, to discover whether I'd been misinformed.'

'Oh.' She darted a quick glance at Cassius, though both his stance and stare were unrelenting. 'In that case, thank you for coming and letting me explain. I hope that we'll meet again soon.'

'Indeed.' He made a formal bow. 'Lord Falconmore.'

'Mr Griffiths.' Cassius bowed in return, his manner relaxing slightly. 'Have a safe journey.'

'Thank you.' Gilbert gave her one last smile. 'Goodbye, Amelia. It's been good to see you.'

'Goodbye...' Millie waited until the door had closed fully behind him before turning towards her now thunderous-looking husband. 'Well, thank goodness for that. He seems to be...'

'*"Why we had to go through with it"*?' Cassius's voice was like cut glass, sharp and brittle.

'What?'

'That was what you said, wasn't it? *"Why we had to go through with it."*'

'Yes, but it's true! And I didn't mean it in a bad way.' She put her hands on her hips, annoyed by the fearsome way he was glaring at her. 'And you said you'd be in the library!'

'I thought you might need some help.'

'To do what? I told you I wanted to talk to Gilbert by myself.'

'It didn't look much like talking.' His tone turned accusing.

'Because he was so understanding. I've treated him shabbily, but he forgave me at once.'

'No wonder when you had your arms wrapped around him.'

'Cassius!' She tipped her head to one side and peered closer. 'Are you jealous?'

'Are you surprised?'

'You *are* jealous!'

He folded his arms again. 'I just entered my own drawing room to find my wife in the embrace of another man, the man she was thinking of marrying when we met, to be exact! I believe jealousy is an understandable response.'

'But you *know* I didn't want to marry him!'

'Do I? Because your actions today would seem to suggest otherwise.'

'Just because I hugged him?' She gave an incredulous laugh. 'Now you're being ridiculous as well as overreacting. I told you from the start that he's more like a brother to me. I could never think of him in the same way I think of you.'

'Never?' Blue eyes narrowed intently. 'You're certain?'

'Positive.' She slid her hands up over his shoulders, silencing any further protests with her lips.

'There's no need to be jealous.' She pulled away again after a few moments. 'Not even a tiny bit.'

His expression wavered and then relented finally. 'No regrets, then?'

'None at all. I'm happy. Which you would have heard me tell Gilbert if you'd only arrived a few seconds sooner. That and I hoped he might be as happy as I am, too, some day.'

She pressed her lips back to his with a smile. It was on the very tip of her tongue to mention love, but something stopped her. The realisation of how she felt was still new to her and it was so soon after their marriage. Besides, what if he didn't *want* her to say it? Despite their newfound intimacy they hadn't talked about their feelings at all. According to him, he wasn't even capable of love, even if he was clearly capable of jealousy. An unwanted declaration could ruin everything. Worse, it might make him feel uncomfortable around her. No, they were happy as they were. Surely *that* was enough?

'All right.' He looked appeased and mildly shamefaced. 'Then I admit I *was* a little jealous. You never told me how good looking he was.'

'Oh, yes, he's very handsome.' She couldn't resist a mischievous smile. 'Didn't I mention that?'

'No.' His eyes narrowed again. 'You didn't.'

'Half the girls in his parish are besotted. They'll be pleased to hear he's eligible again.'

'Indeed.'

'Lottie says he looks like a neat-looking Byron. She thinks someone ought to ruffle him up some day.'

'Just as long as that someone isn't you.'

'Oh, it won't be. I was never a great admirer of Byron.'

He gave her a suspicious look. 'Who *do* you admire, then?'

'Are there any tortured blond poets?' She looped her arms around his waist and placed her cheek to his chest. 'One of those, definitely.'

Chapter Nineteen

There was a sound of shouting. Of metal and gunfire, too, interspersed with shrieks and epithets.

Cassius felt a weight pressing down on his chest, so heavy that it was becoming difficult to breathe. There was a pain in his stomach, too, he realised, a searing, burning sensation as if his insides were being torn apart. Even his heartbeat was painful, thudding like a drum against his ribcage though the sound was drowned out by the tumult all around him. He looked down and saw a red patch on his skin, a bright crimson stain that seemed to get bigger and bigger as he watched, spreading across his stomach like a puddle. It was only then that he noticed the tear in his flesh, the jagged cut slicing all the way across his torso.

A wave of panic crashed over him, accompanied by a jolt of surprise. This was new, not how the dream usually went, yet it felt more real and terrifying than ever. His whole body was drenched in sweat and blood and he was shaking as if he were red hot and icy cold at the same time.

'Cassius!' A hand touched his shoulder.

'No!' He lurched forward, sitting bolt upright and clamping a hand to his stomach as he looked around the room. It was dark and mercifully silent. The pain and the blood were gone, as was the jagged cut, but the sweat and panic were still there. 'Millie?'

'It's all right.' She sat up beside him, her voice soft and soothing. 'It was a dream.'

'Millie.' He repeated her name with a sigh of relief, running his fingers through hair that felt plastered to his head. 'I'm sorry for waking you.'

'Don't be sorry.' She moved her hand lightly across his shoulder blades. 'You couldn't help it. Is there anything I can do?'

'No.' His throat felt dry and hoarse. 'Just be here.'

'Then I'm here.' She shuffled closer, placing her chin on his shoulder and wrapping her other arm around his upper body. 'Were you dreaming about the past?'

He nodded. 'Was I shouting?'

'Mumbling. You were moving around a lot, too, clutching your stomach.'

'I remember.' He winced as fragments of the dream came back to him. 'But it was different this time.'

'What do you mean?'

'It wasn't my usual dream. This time *I* was the one who was wounded. In the past, it's always been Edward.'

'Was he there?'

'I don't know. I heard shouts, but I didn't see anyone else.'

She rubbed a hand down his side, over the damp skin. 'You're not injured. It's over now.'

'You don't understand.' He twisted to face her. 'In

all the other dreams I *wanted* it to be me who was injured. I *wanted* the pain. I should have been pleased
that it was me this time, but I wasn't. I changed my
mind. I wanted to live.'

'But isn't that a good thing?'

'Not at the expense of Edward.' He shook his head
vehemently.

'Cassius.' Her voice was soft and tender. 'Just because you want to live now doesn't mean you wanted
him to suffer.'

'Doesn't it?'

'No.' She reached up and cradled his face between
her hands. 'What happened to Edward was a tragedy,
but it wasn't your fault. You were under attack and
Edward chose to save you. Neither of you could have
known what the consequences would be, but you need
to stop punishing yourself for surviving.'

'Is that what you think I'm doing?'

'Maybe.' She slid her fingers up into his hair. 'It's
not a criticism. I know that you can't just stop feeling
guilty, but you don't have to suffer like this for ever.
If the situation *had* been reversed and you'd saved Edward, what would you tell him to do now?'

'To get on with his life. I know. I want to, but…'

'It doesn't make you ungrateful or mean that you've
forgotten him if you do.'

He dragged in a breath and lay down again, pulling
her with him. 'I remember what you said about wounds
that can't be seen and how they need time to heal, too.
This whole past year it's felt like mine's been fester-
ing. Then you came along, cleaned the wound out and
changed all the bandages. I'm tired of living in the
past, but it feels wrong to want a future when Edward

and Magnus don't have one. Everything I have now is because of them.'

'Not everything.' She laid a hand gently on his chest. 'But it's not wrong. It's natural to want to move on. Maybe this is your mind trying to tell you that.'

He stared at the ceiling, thinking over his own words. He *did* want a future. More specifically, he wanted a future with her. He wanted to let go of the past and feel something other than guilt and regret. He wanted to live, to love, to... The last idea stopped him in his tracks. *He wanted to do what?*

'Cassius?' Millie lifted her head. 'Your heart is racing.'

'It's nothing.' He drew her down again. 'Try to get back to sleep.'

'Just remember you're not alone. I'm here if you need me.'

'I know.' He pressed a kiss on to the top of her head and wrapped his arm tight around her. She was right, he *wasn't* alone any more. The realisation buoyed his spirits, making him feel almost optimistic again. Millie was with him, beside him, half on top of him, in fact, her auburn hair spilling across his chest like a silken blanket. He hadn't exaggerated. Meeting her had changed everything. How was it possible that his heart could have healed itself in so short a time? And yet somehow, amazingly, it had.

He closed his eyes though he didn't sleep, waiting until her breathing had steadied before rolling her gently to one side and then climbing out of bed. With his eyes accustomed to the darkness, he retrieved his clothing and pulled it on, closing the door to the bedroom softly behind him.

The corridors were all swathed in darkness, but he found his way by memory, down the stairs, out of the front door and on to the steps outside. Then he stopped, drawing in deep mouthfuls of air until his lungs felt clean again. There was no hint of dawn yet, but the moon and stars still cast enough light for him to make his way safely down to the lake.

The night-time world was still and soundless, save for the occasional screech of an owl in the distance. It was all so peaceful that it was hard to imagine any other way. Hard to believe, too, that he'd once lived among hundreds of men, amid the tumult and clamour of an army camp, in constant fear for his life, for the lives of his friends, too. Afghanistan and India seemed a long way and a whole lifetime ago, though the memories held as much power as ever.

He stopped and crouched down by the edge of the lake. It looked black as ink, and so smooth that he could see the reflection of the stars above. He'd come here often when he'd first arrived home, before he'd discovered the gatehouse, trying to escape from his dreams. He'd walked and walked until he'd been exhausted, then sat beside the lake, watching his breath emerge in white plumes as it was now. This time, however, he *wanted* to think about his dream, about what Millie had said about it being his mind's way of trying to move on. Was it possible?

He picked up a stone and weighed it in his hand. His best friend had been laid beneath a stone, too, a headstone, far away from the home and people he loved, but Millie was right, the Edward he'd known wouldn't have wanted him to blame himself, or carry the burden of guilt for ever. He would have wanted him to move on.

'Forgive me.' He closed his fingers around the rough surface of the stone and then drew his arm back, hurling it out into the middle of the lake. The splash sounded unnaturally loud in the stillness, disturbing a family of swans in the reeds. There was a flurry of movement and then small waves started to appear across the water, spreading outwards until the whole surface seemed to ripple and reverberate. One stone, capable of changing everything.

He put a hand on his knee and pushed himself back to his feet. He didn't know if his heart was properly healed or not, but he knew what he had to do, what Edward would have wanted him to do. And he had to do it today.

'Cassius?' Millie opened her eyes as a hand touched her cheek. 'What time is it?'

'Still early.' He stroked a lock of hair out of her face. 'But I have to go. There's something important I've been putting off, but it's time to stop hiding.'

'Should I come with you?' She struggled up on to her elbows, trying to blink her way back to consciousness.

'No.' He shook his head, his gaze tender though a small frown puckered his brow. 'I'll need to ride hard to get there and back before the ball, but I'll return in time, I promise.'

'If you're sure?' She tilted her head to one side uncertainly, fighting the urge to rub her fingers across his forehead, to kiss his brow and soothe away the lines.

'I am. Now try to get back to sleep. You've had a disturbed night and you'll need all your strength for dancing later.'

She flushed at the words. His nightmare had only been the first disturbance of the night. She'd woken up again when he'd slid back into bed some time in the early hours, his face so cold that she'd guessed he'd been outside, though she hadn't had a chance to ask him as he'd started to kiss her, pulling her into his arms with such urgency that she hadn't even tried to resist. He'd needed her and she'd given herself to him willingly, surrendering to his touch as his mouth had covered almost every inch of her skin with hot, open-mouthed kisses.

Their coupling had been fierce and yet somehow even more intimate than before. She'd found herself on her side, then on top of him, then beneath him again, their bodies building to a climax together. Afterwards, they'd remained as they were, one of his arms clamping her tightly against his chest. It had been impossible for her to go back to sleep that way, but she hadn't wanted to wake him again and so she'd just lain there, moving in time with the steady rhythm of his breathing, until he'd finally rolled on to one side and she'd been free.

She'd curled up beside him then, burrowing beneath the blankets with a feeling of intense satisfaction. It still felt strange to be so physically close to someone and yet it hadn't felt wrong. Instead it had felt as though she were in the right place somehow, the place where she belonged. Which was doubly strange since she'd always thought of the Foundation as that. If Gilbert's visit had shown her anything, however, it was that she'd made the right decision. She belonged here with Cassius, the man she could no longer deny that she loved even if he couldn't love her. Perhaps intimacy and friendship would be enough for them to be happy, but what he'd said about his dreams made her feel hopeful, too. If his dreams were changing, then perhaps he was finally coming to terms with his past and finding a way to move on. She wouldn't ask for more than he could give, but perhaps there was hope for them—for love—after all.

Perhaps.

Cassius walked along a narrow gravel path to the front door of the cottage, lifted the knocker and then let it fall before he could change his mind. It was a pretty house, two floors of red brick elaborately draped in ivy, with a winter-flowering clematis trailing over the porch, just the way Edward had described it to him during those last few days when his mind had been wandering back to England and the woman he loved. He hadn't understood the depth of his friend's emotion at the time, but now... Now, to his shame, he understood his visit was a long time overdue.

'Oh!' The maid who opened the door looked taken aback to find a gentleman on the doorstep.

'Good morning.' Cassius removed his hat. 'I'd like to speak with Miss Barrow if she's at home, please?'

'Yes, sir.' The maid appeared too flustered to go and check whether her mistress was at home or not, showing him straight through to a cosy-looking parlour.

'I'll go and fetch her.'

'Thank you.'

He waited by the fireplace, studying a collection of small porcelain ornaments on the mantelpiece. Pastoral figurines mostly, milkmaids and shepherdesses and even a couple of wood nymphs. He frowned, wondering if Edward had ever stood in this same spot, looking at these same figures...

'Can I help you?' A soft voice jolted him back to the present. He turned around to see two women standing in the doorway, one young and slender with wavy chestnut hair swept up into a chignon, the other an older, slightly less slender copy. Mother and daughter, he presumed.

'Forgive my intrusion.' He bowed. 'My name is Cassius Whitlock. Do I have the honour of speaking to Miss Lucy Barrow?'

'Whitlock?' The younger woman's face blanched as he spoke, one hand reaching out to steady herself on the doorframe.

'Forgive me.' Cassius hurried forward, though fortunately she regained her balance quickly. 'I didn't mean to startle you. I should have sent word ahead, but to be honest, I didn't know I was coming myself until a few hours ago.'

'It's all right. You're very welcome here.' She turned to the older woman with a strained-looking smile. 'Mama, if you don't mind, I'd like a few minutes alone with Lord Falconmore.'

'Are you sure?' The other woman cast a wary glance in his direction. 'Perhaps I ought to stay as chaperon?'

'Under normal circumstances I would agree, but these aren't normal circumstances. Please, Mama.'

'You know who I am.' Cassius lifted an eyebrow as the mother departed, grumbling.

'Oh, yes. Falconmore Hall isn't so far away. We heard what happened to your cousin and then when you came back...well, I recognised your name.' She gestured towards a chair. 'Please, won't you sit?'

'Thank you.' He waited until she took a seat herself before doing the same. 'You're right, it isn't far, though I'm afraid that makes my behaviour even worse.'

'How so?'

'In not visiting you until now.'

Her hands twitched and then wound themselves into the folds of her skirts. 'You sent me a very kind letter.'

'It wasn't enough. It wasn't worthy of Edward either. A true friend would have come in person. Only I didn't know what to say. I felt so guilty.' He ran a hand around the back of his neck. 'I tried to think up a speech during the ride over here, but no words seemed good enough. You already know what happened to Edward. I wouldn't blame you for resenting me, hating me even. All I can say is that I'm sorry. He was my best friend in the world and I would have died to protect him, but he did it for me instead. He was a brave, good, honourable man and his last words and thoughts were of you. I know because I sat by his bedside and listened. Never doubt how much he loved you, Miss Barrow, because he did, very much. He survived longer than the doctors thought possible because he was so determined to come back to you. I wish I could have saved him the way he saved me.' His voice cracked and he clenched his jaw, staring at the floor while he tried to regain control.

'He told me about you, too.' Cassius almost jumped out of his chair as a small hand closed over his. 'In his letters, he called you his best friend, too. He said that he'd asked you to be best man at our wedding. It was supposed to be last summer.'

'I'm sorry I couldn't bring him home.'

'So am I.' Her eyes glistened with tears. 'But you

tried and you're here now. By your own definition that makes you a true friend.'

He let out a long, shuddering breath. 'You're very forgiving, Miss Barrow.'

'It's taken me a long time to be so. When I first heard about what had happened to Edward, I was not so calm. If you'd come then…' she made an apologetic gesture '…it might not have helped either of us. Even now there are times…' She dragged a hand across her cheek and gave a ragged laugh. 'I didn't think I had tears left to shed.'

'I understand.'

'I know. Of all people, I know you do. The pain is always there, but most days I can close it away in a box. In here.' She tapped her chest. 'That's where he'll always be. Only I try not to open the lid too often.'

'I'm so sorry, Miss Barrow. You must hate me.'

She smiled sadly. 'I could never hate you, Lord Falconmore. You were his best friend. Only I have to ask, why visit me now?'

'I suppose because I've realised I can't hide any more. That's what I've been doing, hoping that all the horror and guilt might just go away on its own. Instead I just gave myself something else to feel guilty about. I should have come to visit you straight away. That's what Edward would have wanted, but I put my own feelings first. I thought of him as *my* friend, but I didn't appreciate your feelings enough. I didn't understand love and what that meant before.'

'But you do now?'

'I think so.' He nodded and cleared his throat. 'I married recently. It wasn't a love match at the time, but…'

'Now you've fallen in love with her?'

'Yes. She's made me want to come out of hiding again.' He grimaced. 'I'm sorry. I don't mean to upset you…'

'You're not. Just because I lost Edward doesn't mean I can't be happy for others.' She smiled. 'I'm truly happy for you, Lord Falconmore.'

'Thank you.' He felt a lump swell in his throat. 'In my letter I asked if there was anything you needed, anything I could do to help you?'

'Yes, it was a kind offer, but I have everything I need.'

'Edward would have wanted me to take care of you.'

'That sounds like him.' She laughed softly. 'Then if there's anything I need, I'll ask. I promise.'

'Good. In that case, perhaps you might allow me to visit again with my wife? I believe she'd like to make your acquaintance, too.'

'I'd like that very much.' She met his gaze steadily, her own expressing a deep well of feeling. 'Thank you for coming, Lord Falconmore. It makes me feel better to think that Edward died for a reason. For a friend. It means it wasn't all just a waste. And for what it's worth, he would have been happy for you, too.'

Chapter Twenty

'You're back.' Millie laid her sewing aside as Cassius entered the library. 'I was starting to worry.'

'I'm sorry.' He came straight to her chair, crouching down and gathering her into his arms. 'I went to visit Edward's fiancée, Miss Barrow.'

'Oh.' She placed her hands on his shoulders and looked into his face anxiously. Despite running through a thousand different scenarios in her mind, that one had never occurred to her. More than anything at that moment, however, she was simply relieved to see him. His quiet intensity that morning had alarmed her. 'How did it go?'

'It wasn't easy, but it went better than I'd expected. I thought she would hate me, but she didn't. It was good to talk to someone else about Edward. Someone who loved him, too.'

'I'm glad.'

'I asked if I might take you with me to visit next time.'

'Oh? What did she say?'

'That she'd like it very much. And I think you'll like

her, too. She was just as Edward described—*"Eyes like cornflower, hair like hazel, a smile like the first hint of sunshine in spring."'* He smiled sadly. 'I think they were very much in love.'

'What a terrible waste.'

'Yes.' He cleared his throat and glanced at the pile of fabric beside her. 'What's that?'

'My gown for tonight.'

'Your gown?' He frowned. 'I thought I told you to buy one.'

'And I told you I like sewing. This one of Sylvia's hardly needed mending at all and the silk is exquisite.'

'What would you do with your time if you didn't have some project or other to work on?' His smile tempered the words. 'Am I allowed to see it properly?'

'Here. It's just finished.' She stood up and held the fabric in front of her. The dress was pale blue and shoulderless with short lace sleeves and a triangular-shaped bodice that tapered down to a point just below the waist. From there, dozens of pleats spread outwards into a wide skirt embroidered with tiny white flowers.

'I thought they looked a bit like snow.' She gestured at the pattern.

'They do.' His smile widened. 'You'll be the belle of the ball, Lady Falconmore, but that's enough work for now. You don't want to wear yourself out.'

'Says the man who's been up since dawn.'

'Touché.' He made a face. 'But I'm glad that I went. It was something I should have done a long time ago.'

'Forgive the intrusion, my lord.' Kendrew appeared in the doorway suddenly. 'But the musicians have just arrived.'

'Excellent. Tell Mrs Turner to feed them, will you, please, Kendrew?'

'I'll see to it straight away, sir.'

'Something's wrong.' Millie murmured as the butler departed again.

'What do you mean?' Cassius looked at her with immediate concern.

'Something's the matter with Kendrew. Mrs Turner, too. They've both been acting oddly since yesterday evening. I'm worried they've had some kind of argument.'

'In that case it's none of our business.'

'It is if I caused it.'

'How would you have done that?'

'Because I said they could get married.' She bit down on her bottom lip. 'Maybe I shouldn't have said anything.'

'I'm sure they'll sort it out between themselves.'

'Or maybe you could talk to Kendrew?' She looked at her husband hopefully.

'I really don't think—'

'He's such a stickler for tradition, after all. Maybe he thinks it's still against the rules to get married? Maybe he needs to hear it from you rather than me?'

'Maybe he doesn't want to get married at all.'

'You could find out?'

Cassius groaned and ran a hand over his face. 'It's not the kind of thing Kendrew and I discuss.'

'But you could do it for me?'

He rolled his eyes. 'Why do I get the impression I don't really have a choice?'

'Because you're a good husband?' She smiled coyly. 'And I'll make it up to you.'

'Well, that sounds promising at least. Do you have any particular method of compensation in mind?'

'A few ideas.' She walked her fingers one by one up his waistcoat and shirt-front.

'All right, you've convinced me. I'll *try to* speak to him, but I'm not promising anything.'

'Thank you.' She pressed a kiss on his cheek at the same moment as there was a loud thud and then raised voices in the hall.

'It's here!' She jumped away from him with a gasp of excitement and rushed to the door.

'What's here?' Cassius followed after her. 'I thought we were discussing my compensation?'

'Later.' Millie flung the door open to reveal half-a-dozen men carrying a towering pine tree through the hallway. 'The finishing touch has arrived.'

'*That's* what you call a finishing touch?' He came to stand beside her, folding his arms with a look of bemusement.

'Yes. They say Prince Albert put one up in the drawing room of Windsor Castle last year.'

'Well, I suppose if it's good enough for the Queen.' He lifted an eyebrow. 'Where exactly is it going?'

'Right over there.' She gestured to a space beside the stairs. 'So all of the guests will see it as they enter. It's supposed to be decorated with candles, but with so many people coming Mrs Turner and I thought it would be safer to use ribbons and gingerbread men instead. Then we'll have bowls underneath filled with nuts and sugared plums so everyone can take a treat. Now we just need to decorate it.'

'When you say *we*…?'

'I mean you and me. It's *our* tree.'

'I suppose so. Well, if it delays my talk with Kendrew... First things first, we'll need some rope to tie it to the banisters. Guests tend not to appreciate trees falling on them.'

'And I'll go and fetch the gingerbread men.' Millie darted off towards the back stairs. 'Cook and I baked them this morning.'

'You've been baking, *too*?'

'I like baking.'

'Of course you do.' Cassius removed his jacket and rolled his shirt sleeves up. 'While you're there, tell her to get some mulled wine ready, too. When we're done with this, we're all going to need some.'

'Do you have a moment, Kendrew?' Cassius called his butler into the library when the tree was finally finished, resplendent in red ribbons, gingerbread and sweets wrapped in tissue paper.

'Of course, my lord. Lady Falconmore indicated there was a matter you wished to discuss.'

'Yes, she told *me* that, too.' He rolled his sleeves back down as he walked to his desk, trying to adopt a detached, businesslike demeanour. 'You know I wouldn't normally consider it my place to interfere with personal matters, but I need to ask you a question. To be clear, however, you're in no way obligated to answer. Please feel at liberty to walk out at any point.'

'I would never do such a thing, sir.'

'That's what I was afraid of. All right then.' He cleared his throat and rubbed his hands together. 'Lady Falconmore has brought it to my attention that you and Mrs Turner might be interested in forming a union of your own?'

For the first time in memory, his butler's impassive expression actually wavered. He looked rather like a landed trout, Cassius thought, opening and closing his mouth soundlessly.

'I'll be blunt,' he said hurriedly. 'Do you *want* to marry Mrs Turner, Kendrew?'

'It's not a question of want, sir.'

'Isn't it?'

'No.' The butler recovered enough to draw himself up to his full height. 'Marriage between servants has never been allowed at Falconmore Hall.'

'Maybe not in the past, but it's a new era, Kendrew. My wife is quite adamant about that fact.'

'Indeed, and while I wouldn't dream of criticising Lady Falconmore, her ways are…*new* here. Personally I do not believe such a union would be appropriate.'

'Appropriate be damned! Do you want to marry the woman or not?'

'I confess that Mrs Turner and I have discussed the matter.'

'And?'

'And she understands the way of things like I do. Any change to established habits now would set a bad example for the rest of the staff. It would encourage licentious behaviour. After some, ah, discussion, she and I were in full agreement on that point.'

'Really?' Cassius lifted an eyebrow. 'Because my wife was afraid the two of you might have quarrelled.'

'Women are prone to their foibles, sir.'

'But you do have an attachment to Mrs Turner?'

'We've worked together for a number of years, sir. I admit to having a certain fondness for her, yes.'

'And she has a fondness for you, too?'

'She suggested as much.'

'Then for pity's sake, man, marry her! Set as bad an example as you like.'

'Lord Falconmore!' The butler's shocked tone was compounded by a look of horror.

'Kendrew.' Cassius pushed himself up off his desk and folded his arms behind his back. 'Are you suggesting that Lady Falconmore and *I* set a bad example?'

'Of course not, sir. I would never…'

'But *we're* married.'

'This is your house, sir.'

'Yes, but by your logic our union must already be encouraging intimacies among the staff. It's a wonder the footmen aren't flinging themselves at the housemaids already. Therefore your refusal to marry Mrs Turner is a slight against ourselves.'

'I don't…' The butler looked distinctly confused.

'More than that, I believe that your *not* marrying Mrs Turner at this point would seriously grieve Lady Falconmore and if she is aggrieved then I am aggrieved. Do you understand me, Kendrew?'

'I believe so, sir.'

'Excellent. In that case, *if* you and Mrs Turner are so minded, I suggest that you put any scruples about staff morale aside and marry forthwith. Let the consequences be what they may. Now go and propose or I'll never hear the end of it.'

'I'm afraid it may be too late for that, sir.' Kendrew's pained expression was back. 'Despite our being in complete agreement, Mrs Turner seemed rather upset after our last conference.'

'Then go and put things right. Grovel if you have to.'

'Very good, sir.' Kendrew started to turn and then

stopped. 'Pardon me for asking, but how exactly does one grovel? What should I say?'

'Well…' Cassius rubbed a hand over his forehead. 'Just tell her the truth. Tell her how you feel and say that you made a mistake before, but that you'll make it up to her every day for the rest of your life if she'll let you. Tell her you'll crawl over hot coals if she asks it. Tell her that she's made every day since you met seem brighter and more vibrant. Tell her that she's changed your whole life and way of thinking and that you can't live without her.'

'I see.' Kendrew looked as if he'd just eaten something sour. 'Perhaps just the part about making a mistake.'

'Perhaps.' Cassius tipped his head. 'Only make it heartfelt, Kendrew.'

'I'll do my best, sir.'

Cassius watched his butler depart, the echo of his own words running through his mind. *Tell her the truth, tell her how you feel, tell her you can't live without her…* Why was he giving Kendrew advice that he wasn't following himself? Why wasn't *he* telling the woman he loved that he loved her? Why wasn't he telling her he'd made a mistake and then thanking her for helping him to heal? Even if he still had a long way to go, why *wasn't* he offering his newly mended heart?

He would, right after their ball. Tonight.

Chapter Twenty-One

As ballrooms went, Cassius had to admit, it was impressive. In fact, from his vantage point in the doorway, it was breathtaking. There were candles in all of the wall sconces, as well as in three crystal chandeliers overhead, the light from which was reflected not just in the mirrors, but in the polished oak-and-mahogany floor itself, making the whole room seem to glow with golden vibrancy. Every window was hung with boughs of laurel and holly, all tied together with bows of gold ribbon, while red flowers from the hothouses were arranged in tall vases set out at intervals around the side of the room. It was even better than he'd expected. And it was all thanks to Millie.

'Well?' She sounded nervous. 'What do you think?'

'Honestly?' He tore his gaze away from the decorations to look at her. She looked exquisite, the pale shade of her gown making her auburn hair stand out even more dramatically. 'I didn't think it would be possible for anything to outshine you tonight, but you may have succeeded with this. Not that I doubted your abilities for a second, but you've worked wonders.'

'Do you really think so?'

'I think you have a talent for decorating. It's like a winter wonderland.'

'That's what I hoped for. I almost wish it *would* snow again, except that it might stop people getting here.'

'Maybe just a dusting?' He curved an arm around her waist, tugging her close. 'You've done a wonderful job, Millie. You were clearly born to be a marchioness.'

'I don't know about that.' A small furrow creased her brow.

'Well, I do. Now I hope you remember what I said about the opening dance?'

'I'd be delighted, Lord Falconmore.' The furrow faded again. 'I enjoy dancing.'

'Really? Was there much call for it at your Foundation?'

'Not a lot, but we visited the local assembly rooms occasionally.'

'Is that so? And who exactly did you dance with? Bearing in mind that if you say the name Gilbert I will go into a sulk.'

'All right then—' she gave him an arch look '—I won't *say* it.'

'Were there any other suitors I should know about?'

She pursed her lips and tapped her chin as if she were trying to remember. 'A few, but I forget their names.'

'Hmm.' He tightened his grip on her waist possessively. 'It's bad enough that I'm going to have to watch you dance with half the estate tonight. Just remember that your first dance is with me. *And* waltzes. You can polka or gallop with anyone else, but I refuse to share you for waltzing. You're going to attract far too many admiring glances as it is.'

'You know, if you're not careful I won't point out where we're standing.'

'Where are we…?' He glanced around and then upwards. 'Mistletoe?'

'I thought we ought to have some somewhere.'

'So you thought over the entrance to the ballroom itself?'

'In plain view to avoid any private nonsense, as Mrs Turner put it.'

'*Private nonsense?* I like the sound of that.' He bent his head to kiss her, smiling at the way her lips clung softly to his. It felt good to kiss her, just as good as it had the last time and the time before that. He would have thought the novelty might have worn off by now, but apparently it wasn't fading any time soon.

'Oh.' She pulled away suddenly, sounding faintly breathless. 'That sounds like wheels outside. I suppose we ought to go and greet our first guests.'

'Pity.' He smiled into her eyes. 'I'd rather stand here all night. Now that I've got you under the mistletoe I can't quite remember why we're bothering with all this disruption.'

'As a Christmas present for all your tenants.'

'*Our* tenants, but, yes, that was it.'

'I just hope I've remembered people's names.'

'They won't mind if you haven't. It was a lot to learn all at once. Don't be nervous.'

'Nervous? I'm terrified. I wish Mother and Alexandra were coming. Mother's note was very strange. She just said that they were indisposed, without any details. I wonder if they've all caught Sylvia's cold?'

'Perhaps. In any case, there's no need to be terrified. You look wonderful, you are wonderful and you'll *be* wonderful. Just remind me to bring that mistletoe upstairs later. We could do with a sprig of it over the bed, don't you think?'

'I can't remember the last time I enjoyed myself so much.' Mrs Shepherdson could hardly contain her enthusiasm when Millie stopped to ask how her evening was going. 'Everyone's saying the same thing.'

'I'm so pleased.' Millie smiled at the elderly woman standing beside her. 'I don't believe that we've met?'

'Oh, pardon my manners, Lady Falconmore. This is my mother-in-law, Mrs Agnes Shepherdson.'

'How do you do, Mrs Shepherdson?'

'Very well, my lady. Forgive my not curtsying, but my old bones won't allow it these days.' The woman gave her a toothless grin. 'I'm just entertaining myself by watching your husband. *Such* a handsome man.'

'Mother!' Mrs Shepherdson looked horrified. 'I'm sorry, my lady.'

'It's all right. He is very handsome, isn't he?' Millie glanced across the room to where Cassius was dancing with one of the Petch girls. Having offered to dance with just about every woman on the estate, he'd barely had a chance to rest all evening, but he was smiling, too. He looked positively carefree, chatting and joking to put his young partner at ease. As she watched he looked up suddenly, as if sensing her scrutiny, and his smile spread even wider. Wider than she'd ever seen it. So wide that she felt a tremor of warmth sweep all the way from the top of her head to the tips of her toes.

'I remember the first time I came to a ball here.' The older woman gave her a small nudge, much to her daughter-in-law's obvious horror. 'I was sixteen years old and I hardly dared speak to a soul. I hid behind my mother's skirts for most of the evening.'

'Oh, dear. No dancing, then?'

'Eventually.' The old woman chuckled. 'A young man from one of the farms took pity on me. We ended up dancing two sets before he asked if he might call on me the next day.'

'Really? And how did you answer?'

'Oh, I said yes. Or I mumbled it anyway. We got married ten months later.'

'How lovely.'

'We were happily married for sixty-eight years, until he was buried last autumn. Altogether, we had seven children, thirteen grandchildren and nineteen great-grandchildren. So far.'

'Sixty-eight years? So that makes you...'

'Eighty-four.' The elder Mrs Shepherdson heaved a sigh. 'I'm afraid that my dancing days are over.'

'I think mine are finished for tonight, too.' Millie smiled sympathetically, glancing down at the pair of green slippers poking out from beneath her voluminous skirts. Fortunately, it had turned out that she and Sylvia had the same shoe size. 'My feet are exhausted.'

'But you looked so lovely opening the ball with Lord Falconmore,' the younger Mrs Shepherdson commented wistfully. 'Waltzing is *so* romantic and the way he was looking at you...well, you should have heard the sighs.'

Millie felt herself flush. She *hadn't* heard the sighs, but then she'd been too busy gazing at Cassius, too. The look in his eyes had made it difficult to remember the steps.

'Sometimes it only takes a few days to fall in love.' The old woman nudged her again. 'That's what I said when we first heard the news of your marriage and everyone said…'

'Mother!' her daughter-in-law interjected quickly, her tone scandalised. 'I'm sure nobody said anything they shouldn't have.'

'It's all right.' Millie lifted a placatory hand. 'Our wedding *did* happen rather quickly. I'm sure there were a lot of rumours.'

'Oh, yes. Some people thought—'

'Mother!'

'However, Lord Falconmore and I are very happy.'

'That's obvious, my lady. Nobody looking at the two of you could think otherwise. And we're all very pleased by the fact, too.'

'Thank you. In that case, I hope you enjoy the rest of the evening. I hope to visit your farm again soon.'

'We'd be honoured, my lady.'

Millie inclined her head and then moved away quickly before the elder Mrs Shepherdson could tell her anything else about what people thought, making her way around the edge of the room towards the door. It would be time for supper soon and she wanted to make sure the food was on its way…

'Lady Falconmore?' A man in a glossy black superfine dress coat and matching black cravat stepped in front of her suddenly, sweeping into an elaborately low bow.

'Lord Falconmore.' She curtsied back. 'How are your feet?'

'Holding up very well, thank you. I trust that you're enjoying the evening's entertainment?'

'Very much. I've just been asking everyone else the same question. Fortunately, they all assure me they are.'

'I'm delighted to hear it. Now, if you'll do me the honour?'

'Again? We've already danced three times. Won't people talk?'

'Undoubtedly, but we've weathered enough gossip already. A little more can't hurt. Besides...' he held a hand out '...it's another waltz.'

'What a surprise.' She smiled, marvelling anew at how handsome, sardonic almost, he looked all in black. 'Anyone would think the musicians are being instructed to play them, but who would do such a thing? Still, I suppose it means I don't have a choice.' She folded her fingers around his as they walked into the centre of the dance floor. 'Mrs Shepherdson's mother-in-law kept trying to tell me what people *have* been saying and Mrs Shepherdson kept stopping her.'

He placed his other hand on her back. 'It's not hard to guess. I should imagine most people here think you're with child already.'

'What?' She almost forgot to move her feet in surprise. 'But we only met two weeks ago!'

'True.'

'You mean they think *that's* why we had to get married? Because of that night in the gatehouse? They think that we...?'

'Got carried away?' His lips twitched. 'Something like that. You have to admit, nightmares and frozen digits aside, it was quite romantic.'

'I admit no such thing!' She batted at his chest, resenting his obvious amusement. 'I would never have behaved in such a way!'

'You and I know that. Other people have lurid imaginations.'

'But what if I really *am* with child now?' She darted a quick look around and lowered her voice. Given the amount of time they'd spent in bed together over the past week, it was hardly outside the realms of possibility. 'Then they'll think they were right!'

'Does it matter?'

'It does to me!'

'Ah.' He looked as if he were trying to suppress another smile. 'I'm afraid it may be a little too late to do anything about that.'

'Not necessarily.' She lifted her chin. 'We ought to stop doing anything to make a baby, just in case.'

'Anything?'

'For at least a month!'

'A *month*?' He let out a low whistle and then lowered his head, brushing his lips lightly across her brow. 'If that's what you want. Only you might have to keep reminding me. I'm finding it somewhat hard to keep my hands off you these days.'

'This isn't a joke!'

'Absolutely not, although we should probably start discussing baby names. How about Aloysius for a boy and Esmerelda for a girl?'

'We'll do no such thing!' She pulled her hand away from his shoulder and clamped it over his mouth. 'If anyone overhears us they'll really think it's... *Cassius!*' She let out an unladylike yelp, pulling her hand away again as his tongue darted across the backs of her fingers.

'Yes?' His expression was a picture of innocence.

'You're incorrigible!'

'I'm enjoying myself.' Blue eyes glinted with amusement.

'Stop laughing.'

'I didn't make a sound!'

'I can see it in your face.'

'But it's so difficult not to. You look even prettier when you're indignant. Which makes you irresistibly attractive right now.'

'Don't be silly.'

'I'm not. I've lost count of the number of times I've been congratulated on my good fortune this evening. Sophie Shepherdson told me she wants to be just like you when she grows up and her mother says you're glowing.'

'Only because we're *pretending* to be in love!'

'Are we?' The pupils of his eyes seemed to widen as they bored into hers. 'It's strange, but I feel like I'm hardly pretending any more.'

Millie caught her breath, the words spinning around her head. Her feet didn't feel tired any more. She was barely aware of them, in fact. She felt as if her whole being was focused on the points where they touched, on his hands, one of them clasped tight in her own, the other splayed out across her back, warming her skin even through her gown and corset. There were only a few couples left on the dance floor, most having already danced themselves out, giving the impression that they had the whole room to themselves. Somehow it felt that way, too, as if the rest of the world didn't exist and there was only the two of them, gliding effortlessly around the floor.

And he was *hardly pretending* to be in love any more. And neither was she... Which meant that they were really and truly in love... Didn't it?

Chapter Twenty-Two

'Why exactly are we up so early?' Cassius stretched his arms above his head at the breakfast table.

'It's eleven o'clock.' Millie stifled a yawn. 'Although you're right, it doesn't feel as if we got much sleep.'

'What time *did* we go to bed in the end?'

'Around three o'clock. The Petches were the last to leave.'

'And then you kept me awake for another hour.'

She put down her butter knife with a clatter. '*I* kept *you* awake?'

'Yes.' He gave a nonchalant grin. 'I told you not to look so irresistible. If you'd only looked haggard, then we might have gone straight to sleep.' He let his gaze dip lazily over the front of her gown and then winked. 'I thought we were stopping all that for a month anyway.'

'We are. Only last night I forgot.' She shot him an accusatory look. 'And I notice you didn't remind me.'

'There's only so much you can expect of a man. Besides, I chose to believe you were joking about all that. I still do. However, there *was* something I wanted to talk to you about last night actually. Perhaps you'd care for a stroll on the terrace after breakfast instead?' He picked up his cup of hot chocolate as if he were making a toast. 'In the meantime, I think that we can call the ball a great success. You're the toast of the county.'

'Oh, dear, that reminds me. Lady Fentree wants us to throw a party for the local gentry.'

'Lady Fentree can go hang. We'll do what we want.'

She smiled and picked up her knife again, feeling a warm glow at the words. *What we want*, as if they were a real husband and wife...

'Lady Falconmore.' Kendrew entered the room bearing a small tray. 'A letter came for you this morning, my lady.'

'Thank you.' Millie smiled up at the butler, waiting until he'd left again before leaning towards Cassius. 'Did you speak to him about Mrs Turner?'

'I did.'

'And?'

'And we'll see. I've told him it's permitted, but the rest is up to him. With any luck the staff party tonight should do the trick.'

'I do hope so.' She tore open the letter. 'I'd hate to think... Oh!'

'Millie?' Cassius darted around the table as she pressed a hand to her mouth. 'What's the matter?'

'My sister Lottie...' She pulled her hand away again. 'She's in Rayleigh!'

'What's wrong with that? I thought you said she was coming for Christmas?'

'Yes, but she's not alone. She's here with a fiancé! She's getting married!'

'Oh.' He went back to his own chair, relieved. 'Well,

that's not so bad either, surely? This is the little sister who had a cold?'

'That's what she told us when we left London.'

'And now she has a fiancé?' His lips curved. 'Then maybe she wasn't so sick, after all? Do you know the man?'

'Yes, or at least I used to. His name is Jasper King and he owns an engineering company. Silas was an apprentice for him for a few years before he went to America.' She shook her head in bewilderment. 'I just don't know what to think. How on earth could she even have met him again, let alone get engaged? We've only been away for two weeks.'

'But a lot can happen in two weeks. No doubt she's thinking the same thing about us.'

'Yes, I suppose we might both have some explaining to do.' She pushed her chair back and stood up. 'Do you mind if I go and see her?'

'Of course not. I'll even accompany you, if you've no objections?'

'None at all. I'd like you to meet her, only you should know...' She paused awkwardly. 'Lottie can be very forthright. She doesn't believe in withholding her opinions.'

'It must be a Fairclough trait, but I'm sure I can cope. I'm looking forward to meeting her.'

Millie leaned forward impatiently in the carriage as it rolled towards Rayleigh. Despite what she'd told Cassius, she was feeling somewhat anxious about introducing him to Lottie. There was so much to tell and to explain—to hear, too, apparently.

'I wouldn't be surprised if we get more snow in the

next couple of days.' Cassius reached for one of her hands, pulling it across on to his knee.

'Just as long as I get to see Lottie first.' She tipped her head so that it rested on his shoulder. 'I don't know why I'm so nervous.'

'Are you worried about what she'll think about us?'

'I suppose so.' She frowned. Why *was* she so worried? She and Lottie were close enough that she could tell her anything, but the truth was that she didn't know *what exactly* to say about her marriage, at least not yet. No matter how close she'd felt to Cassius the previous evening, neither of them had declared their feelings yet. She didn't doubt her own, but what if she'd misinterpreted his words? She stole a discreet glance towards him. He was looking out of the window, though his fingers were absently stroking the back of her glove. She wondered if he was aware that he was doing it. For a man who claimed he wasn't capable of love, he was surprisingly *loving*. What he'd said the previous evening about not being able to keep his hands off her was true, too. When they were in the same room, he was always finding reasons to touch her, to put an arm around her waist or to stroke her cheek. Not that she objected, only it didn't *seem* like the behaviour of a man who couldn't love… She only wished that she could have a few more days alone with him. Somehow Lottie's arrival signalled an end to their honeymoon and something about that alarmed her even more. She actually had the bizarre impression that the carriage walls were closing around her.

'Here we are.' Cassius twisted his head towards her and she gave a guilty start, realising that she'd been staring.

'So we are.' She felt butterflies start to flutter and then flap wildly in her stomach as she looked out at the Malverlys' house. 'That was quick.'

'Would you like me to wait outside for a few minutes? I can pretend to examine the axles or something.'

'No.' She smiled at the image. 'You're my husband. You should come with me.'

'All right, but if you change your mind and want some time alone just give me a signal. Tug on your left earlobe.'

'Just my left? I'll try to remember.'

The front door opened to admit them, though Millie had barely taken two steps into the hall before Lottie came flying out of the drawing room and flung her arms around her.

'You came!'

'Of course I came.' Millie staggered briefly and then hugged her sister back. 'As soon as I got Mother's note. When did you arrive?'

'Yesterday afternoon, but Mama said you were holding a ball so we didn't want to disturb you. That's why she sent that bizarre message about being indisposed. I knew you wouldn't believe it for a second, but it was the best we could think of.' Lottie paused for breath. 'How did it go?'

'Very well, but never mind that.' Millie extricated herself from her sister's embrace long enough to pull off her bonnet and cape. 'Mama's note said that you were engaged?'

'And you're *married* to a marquess! I can't tell you how surprised I was when she told me. And here I was thinking I was going to be the one to shock you!' Lottie laughed and then looked expectantly past her. 'You must be my new brother.'

'Otherwise known as Cassius.' He took her hand and kissed it. 'And you must be Lottie. Millie's told me so much about you.'

'Oh, dear.' Lottie rolled her eyes dramatically. 'That sounds ominous.'

'Not at all. It's a great pleasure to meet you.'

Millie looked between the two of them with a growing sense of agitation. It wasn't jealousy, she was certain of that, more like discomfort, though she couldn't quite put her finger on why.

'Mama's note mentioned something about trouble at the Foundation, too,' she said, trying to distract herself.

'Oh, yes, it's all quite shocking, but Jasper and I will tell you all about that later.' Lottie caught hold of her arm and dragged her into the drawing room. 'First we have some more, even better news.'

'What else can there be?'

'Can I tell her, Mama?'

'Go ahead.' Their mother stood up from her seat by the fireplace, her face already beaming.

'A letter from Silas!' Lottie burst out excitedly. 'It arrived here this morning! He thinks his letters to the Foundation have been going astray somehow so he wrote to Alexandra instead.'

'Silas?' Millie felt her stomach lurch with relief. 'You mean he's all right?'

'Even better than that! He says he's about to make his fortune and he's on his way home!'

'Oh!' Millie clasped her hands together, all her discomfiture forgotten. 'You're right, that *is* wonderful!'

'And just in time for Christmas,' Lottie declared happily. 'We'll all be together again soon.'

'Speaking of *together*...' their mother interrupted gently '...allow me to make some introductions. Lord Falconmore, this is my daughter's fiancé, Mr Jasper King. Jasper, you remember Millie?'

'Of course. It's a pleasure to see you again, Lady Falconmore.' A familiar, dark-haired gentleman stood up and walked towards them. He had a slight limp, Millie noticed, one she didn't remember from their previous meetings, though his smile was as charming as ever.

'Mr King.' She offered him her hand. 'Congratulations. I'm delighted for you and Lottie.'

'Thank you. I'm quite pleased myself.' He threw an affectionate glance towards her sister before turning towards Cassius. 'Lord Falconmore, I'm honoured to make your acquaintance.'

'As am I to make yours.' Cassius shook his hand enthusiastically. 'Especially since we're going to be family.'

'Then you must call me Jasper. I expect Charlotte's already told you about our recent adventures?'

'No, actually...' Lottie laughed as she threaded an arm through his '...but only because I haven't had a chance yet. Now sit down and I'll tell you everything.'

'Now it's your turn!' Lottie grabbed hold of Millie's elbow as they made their way upstairs. 'Tell me what happened.'

'What do you mean?' Millie twisted towards her sister in surprise. 'I thought you said you had something to show me in your bedroom?'

'Oh, that was just an excuse to get you alone. If

anyone asks, I have a new bonnet or something.' Lottie waved a hand dismissively and then pulled her into an alcove on the landing. 'I want to know what's been going on.'

'Hasn't Mother told you?'

'She's told me the official version, but I want to hear the details from you. He's *very* handsome. If it wasn't for Jasper, I could be quite jealous. Is it true that you turned up on his doorstep in a snowstorm?'

'Ye—es, but nothing untoward happened. It was all perfectly respectable.'

'You don't have to tell *me* that.' Lottie gave a snort. 'If anyone can be trusted to do the right thing then it's you, but what was a marquess doing in his gatehouse in the first place?'

'It's complicated. He wanted to be alone.'

'Then what were you doing out in a snowstorm?'

'I was being adventurous.'

'*You?*'

'Yes.' Millie lifted her chin. 'I *can* be sometimes, you know.'

'I know you used to be.' Lottie gave her an approving look. 'So he was feeling reclusive and you were feeling adventurous and he ended up offering you shelter?'

'Yes. The snow was so heavy that I couldn't go anywhere else so we were trapped together overnight. Unfortunately a maid saw me leaving the next morning and we were compromised.'

'So he was forced to propose?'

'Yes.'

'And that's it? Nothing else happened at all?' Lottie made a clucking sound. 'No, of course not, silly question.'

Millie's chin jutted higher. 'Actually he kissed me.'

'I knew it!' Lottie's eyes lit up. 'What was it like? Was it very romantic? I won't tell anyone, I promise.'

'It was…good.'

'Good?'

'Very good.'

'But how did it happen?'

'Well, I told him that Gilbert had never kissed me and then…' she felt her cheeks start to burn '…he asked me if I'd like to be kissed just to see what it was like and…well, I agreed.'

'You *told* him about Gilbert?'

'Yes. Why is that a surprise?'

'Well, that's not like you for a start. You wouldn't even speak to Mama and me about him.'

'I know, I'm sorry. It just seemed easier to speak with someone who didn't know him and I felt comfortable with Cassius. It's ironic really. He told me I shouldn't feel compelled to marry anyone and then ended up having to marry me himself.'

'I'm sorry that you were forced into it. I thought with me marrying Jasper *I* could be the one to take care of you and Mama for a change.'

'It's all right.' Millie smiled reassuringly. 'I do like Cassius. He's kind and thoughtful and decent. There's no need to worry about me, truly.'

'All right. If you like him, then so do I. And so does Jasper, I can tell.'

'But there's one thing I don't understand. How did you and Jasper meet again? Was it by chance?'

'Not exactly. It was a bit of a madcap scheme to be honest.' Lottie looked faintly shame-faced. 'The truth is, I went to find him for you.'

'For me? What do you mean?'

'Well, I knew you were on the verge of marrying Gilbert just to protect Mama and me. Not that I didn't like Gilbert, but I knew you weren't in love with him. Then I remembered how much you liked Jasper when you danced with him that time.'

'What ti—?' Millie's jaw dropped. 'Lottie, that was eight years ago!'

'Yes, well, I just agreed it was mad. Anyway, I went off to find him.'

'I thought you said you were sick when we left?'

'I *did* have a small cold. Only I might have exaggerated a little.'

'*Lottie!*' Millie exclaimed in consternation. 'You didn't!'

'I did it for you.'

'Did Mama know about this?'

'Oh, no, she would never have agreed.' Lottie shrugged. 'Anyway, Jasper and I met and one thing led to another and, well, here we are. And it turned out that you didn't need my help in finding an alternative husband, after all. So it's all worked out for the best, hasn't it?'

'Yes.' Millie reached out a hand and drew it slowly along the banister. 'I admit I had reservations about our marriage at first, but now…well, I'm happy.'

'It's true. You *do* seem happy.'

'You say that like it's a bad thing.'

'No, but considering it wasn't a love match…' Lottie gave her a shrewd look. 'Isn't it strange, though? Two weeks ago, we were worried about being homeless and now I'm engaged and you're a marchioness!

It seems too incredible to be true. I actually wondered if I ought to curtsy when I saw you.'

'Stop it, Lottie.'

'But you seem so different already! Holding balls, wearing silk gowns…' Lottie rubbed her fingers admiringly over the bodice of Millie's green-muslin day dress. 'Which looks beautiful by the way. You're even wearing your hair looser.'

'Ye—es…' Millie raised a hand to her head self-consciously. 'But I'm still the same person underneath.'

'Oh, I know. There's just a lot to catch up with, but I suppose a lot of things will be changing now so we'll just have to get used to it. There's the Foundation for a start. Mama's going to have a hard time finding someone to replace you.'

'I suppose so…' Millie felt a pang of guilt '…but I can still help.'

'Not when you're living here, you can't, although you could be a patron or something. But I can help more and, now Silas is coming home, we'll work something out. We'll *definitely* need a new embroidery-and-crochet teacher, though. I'm hopeless at anything like that.'

'Yes, but…'

'Of course you'll have to come back to say a proper goodbye. Everyone's going to miss you so much.'

'I'll miss them, too.'

'Not that they won't all be thrilled. A marchioness…' Lottie grinned and then started back downstairs. 'Who would ever have thought it?'

Millie waited a few seconds and then followed. The drawing room was filled with cheerful voices and happy chatter, but she felt detached from the scene suddenly, as if a glass window had descended between her and the other inhabitants. She wished that she'd never gone upstairs with Lottie at all. Not that her sister had meant to upset her, she knew, but their conversation had left her feeling uncomfortable. She and Cassius had agreed to stay for dinner, but now she had no appetite for food *or* conversation. Had she really changed so much in two weeks? Lottie's observations bothered her. Not to mention what she'd said about the Foundation...

She took a seat by the window. Somehow the realisation that she wasn't going back to London hadn't fully sunk in before. She'd been so busy enjoying her honeymoon and planning the ball that she'd deliberately *not* thought about the future, but Lottie was right. Her mother would have twice as much to do from now on and she'd only be a visitor to the Foundation. It wasn't her home any more. Home was here, with Cassius, the husband she loved, who might or might not love her back.

She glanced towards him. He was deep in conversation with Jasper, his expression smiling and animated. The sight filled her with a confusing blend of yearning and guilt. She *wanted* him to love her and yet if he did then she'd have everything she ever, *could ever*, have wanted. She'd be really and truly happy. But what about duty and sacrifice? What about her role as little mother at the Foundation? What about her father's legacy? How could she live with herself if she just abandoned all of those things? Her transformation from Amelia into Millie would be complete.

The honeymoon was definitely over.

Chapter Twenty-Three

'Are you sure you're feeling all right? You look pale.'

Cassius unwound his cravat and tossed it carelessly across a chair. It was the third time he'd asked the question since they'd left the Malverlys, the third time, too, that he'd received a placid nod and strained smile in reply. He hadn't truly expected the answer to be anything different even though something was very clearly *not* all right.

They'd come straight up to their chamber on their return home that evening, not wanting to interfere with the party going on below-stairs. Millie had thanked the maid who'd brought up a tray of wine and biscuits and then dismissed her for the evening, much to the girl's evident relief. Now she was simply standing by the window, her posture stiff, lace net curtains swept back in one hand as she stared out into the gathering darkness over the lake.

He made a move towards her and then stopped, something in her body language warning him not to go any closer. After the intimacy of the ball, the sense of distance between them felt strange. Last night he'd almost told her he loved her. He'd *meant* to tell her, only the hour had been so late and she'd fallen asleep after their lovemaking. Now he wished he'd woken her up and told her anyway, unable to shake the uncomfortable feeling that he'd missed his chance. *Something* had happened during the course of the afternoon, nothing obvious or dramatic and yet something that had caused the bright, happy, albeit somewhat nervous, woman he'd accompanied that morning to transform into a monosyllabic wraith, as if some light inside her had suddenly, for some inexplicable reason, gone out. Now that he thought about it, it had been after she'd gone upstairs with Lottie, though surely her sister wouldn't have said anything to upset her? Whatever the cause, she'd seemed to withdraw deeper and further inside herself on the carriage ride home, turning her head so that he couldn't see her face.

At this point it was clear that whatever the matter was, she wasn't going to tell him.

'Your sister and Mr King seem very happy.' He decided to try a new subject instead, removing his jacket and depositing it on top of his cravat.

'Yes.' That subject at least provoked a small smile. 'Jasper was always very pleasant. I'm happy for both of them.'

'Your sister says that they're planning to wed soon.'

'Yes.'

'And that she asked you to be her matron of honour.'

'Yes.'

'Would you care for some wine?' He gestured towards the tray, struggling to think of anything else to say.

'No.' She moved away from the window, her expression guarded. 'Thank you, but I thought I might just read tonight.'

'Then I'll join you.'

'To be honest, I don't think I would be very good company.' She glanced at his waistcoat as it fell on top of his jacket. 'If you don't mind, I think I'd like an evening on my own.'

'I see. As you wish.' He fought the urge to argue. Since their first night together, he'd come to think of her room as his, too. *Their room*, in fact. Except that now she was effectively throwing him out. 'In that case, I'll see you in the morning.'

'Goodnight, Cassius.'

'Goodnight, Millie.'

He made an awkward bow and went to his own chamber instead.

'Good morning, sir.' Kendrew, for once, made a somewhat elaborate show of announcing his presence, closing the library door with an audible click behind him and then clearing his throat.

'Good morning.' Cassius leaned back in his chair and steepled his fingers beneath his chin, regarding his butler enquiringly. 'How was the party?'

'I believe the staff enjoyed it a great deal, sir. The presents were particularly well received.'

'Good, and what about you? Did you enjoy it? Anything of note to tell me, Kendrew?'

'As a matter of fact…' The butler's throat appeared to need clearing again. 'There *is* something, sir.'

'Really?'

'Regarding myself and Mrs Turner.'

'Yes?'

'She's done me the great honour of agreeing to become my wife.'

Cassius stood up, smiling for the first time that day. 'She forgave you, then?'

'Eventually. I'm sorry to say it required a substantial amount of grovelling.'

'Good for you. Out of interest, did you use any of the phrases I suggested?'

'One of them, although I'd prefer not to say which.'

'Then don't. Let me congratulate you instead, Kendrew. I hope the two of you will be very happy together.'

'I hope so, too, sir. It's something of a change at my time of life.'

'But a positive one, I'm sure.' He reached for his butler's hand and pumped it up and down vigorously. 'Have you told Lady Falconmore the news yet?'

'Mrs Turner has just gone to inform her, sir, although I understand Lady Falconmore is still in her chamber.'

'I believe so.' Cassius tried not to flinch at the statement. After waking up alone and decidedly *un*rested in his own bed that morning, he'd briefly considered going through to see her and then discarded the idea, uncertain about what to say if she *still* didn't want to talk to him. He could only hope that she'd tell him what the matter was in her own time, though waiting made him feel somewhat queasy. On the other hand, now there was some good news to discuss with her...

'My lord?' Kendrew's voice jolted him back to the present.

'Forgive me, I was just thinking...' he shook the butler's hand one last time '...about your wedding gift!

I insist on your taking a honeymoon. Anywhere you like.'

'A honeymoon?' Kendrew's expression was horrified. 'You mean *more* time off, sir?'

'Exactly. How about the seaside? Bournemouth or Brighton, perhaps?'

'I'll have to discuss it with Mrs Turner, although surely you couldn't manage without both of us?'

'We'd muddle through somehow.' Cassius flung open the library door. 'It's a new era, Kendrew. Christmas presents are just the start. I intend for us all to take as many holidays and be as happy as we can from now on. Those are the new house rules.'

'If that's *really* what you want, sir.'

'It is. More importantly, it's what my wife wants. Ah, the bride herself.' Cassius smiled at the sight of his housekeeper traversing the hallway. 'Felicitations to you, too, Mrs Turner.'

'Thank you, my lord.' She looked startled as he pressed a kiss to her cheek.

'Now go and celebrate!' He started eagerly towards the staircase. 'I don't want to see either of you for the rest of the day. Until Boxing Day, in fact!'

He took the stairs two at a time, giving a cursory knock on their—*her*—door before pushing it open.

'Millie?' At first glimpse, the room appeared to be empty. He was about to leave again when he noticed her standing beside the window, staring out. It was the exact same spot where she'd stood the previous evening, as if nothing had changed. He felt his heart plummet, but he still had to try to talk to her.

'There you are.' He advanced slowly. 'Shall we celebrate?'

'Celebrate?' She looked towards him and then away again quickly, her voice sounding strange.

'About Kendrew and Mrs Turner. I thought she'd been to see you?'

'Oh, that. Yes, she did.'

'That?' He stopped. 'I thought you'd be more excited, especially since it was your doing.'

'I only told them that marriage was allowed.'

'But if it hadn't been for you then they'd probably never have thought of it. I certainly wouldn't have. Give yourself a little credit.'

'I suppose…'

'Millie.' He touched a finger to her chin, turning her face towards him as her voice trailed away. 'Will you tell me what's happened?'

'Nothing's happened. I'm just…' She gave her head a small shake. 'I don't know what I am, but seeing Lottie again, and getting news of Silas… There's been a lot to take in.'

'But it was all good news, wasn't it?'

'Yes.' She drew her brows together as if she were concentrating on finding the right words. 'I just didn't appreciate how much was going to change in my life. I suppose I'm feeling a bit confused about who I am.'

'I thought we agreed you wouldn't think about any of that until after Christmas?'

'It's Christmas Eve. That's close enough.'

'Is there anything I can do to help?'

'No.' She shook her head quickly. 'I just need to think.'

'Maybe there's one thing I can do.' He looked at her thoughtfully for a moment and then steered her towards a chair by the fireplace. 'Just wait here and don't move until I come back.'

'Why? What are you going to do?'

'Wait and see. I *was* going to wait until tonight to give you your Christmas present, but maybe now is the right moment.'

'Cassius?'

He ignored her questioning look, running headlong down the stairs, out to the stables and then back again with a wooden box.

'Here you go.' He deposited the box on the carpet, relieved to find that she'd stayed where he'd left her. 'Only don't try to pick it up. It's heavy.'

'But what is…?' She stopped mid-question at the sound of a faint *meow*, her eyes widening in surprise as she reached down and tore off the lid. Four green eyes in a pair of grey-and-white faces stared back.

'Cats?' Her expression seemed dazed.

'Orestes and Electra!' he announced, crouching beside the box to watch her reaction. 'They're brother and sister.'

'You got me two cats?'

'You said it was what you'd always wanted.' He frowned. 'Aren't you pleased?'

'Of course I am!' She seemed to come back to herself suddenly, reaching down and scooping them into her lap. 'But where did they come from?'

'When we did our tour of the estate the other day Mr Petch happened to mention they'd had a litter of kittens and were still looking for homes for a few.' He grinned. 'I sent a couple of the stable boys over to collect them this morning.'

'They're adorable. Oh, yes, you are, aren't you?'

She gave a delighted laugh, rubbing her hands over a pair of grey heads while the recipients purred approvingly. 'And they have white socks! Oh, they're lovely, Cassius, thank you.'

'I'm glad you approve. Now all we need is a *chaise longue*, a box of macaroons and then you can lie around and read novels all day. Just for one day, of course.'

'Oh…yes.' Her smile faltered. 'I said that, didn't I?'

'I want to give you your perfect day, Millie.' He tickled one of the kittens under the chin, letting it curl its tiny paw around the rest of his hand. 'I want to give you everything you've ever wanted.'

'I don't expect anything else, Cassius.'

'But I want to give it to you.' He took a deep breath and then ploughed on. 'You've given me so much already. When we first met, I thought all I wanted to do was to hide from the world and be left alone. I thought that I was broken and beyond saving, that I had no joy or love left in me. You've shown me I was wrong. I've only been half-alive for the past year, but you've made me feel as if I can get better in time. You've made me *feel* again. And I don't want to be alone any more. I want to be with you. Not because we were compromised, but because you're the kindest, most caring, most determined, most alarmingly hard-working person I've ever met and I love you.'

'You love me?' She seemed to go very still all of a sudden.

'Yes. I don't expect you to say it in return. It's not what we agreed when we married, but I want to say it anyway. I love you. I'm *in* love with you and I'll do whatever it takes, wait as long as it takes…'

'No.' She picked up each of the cats in turn and placed them back in the box. 'No.'

'What?'

'I can't.' She stood up although she didn't look at him. 'This is wrong.'

'Wrong?' He felt as if his blood had just turned to ice. 'What do you mean?'

'It was a mistake. All of it. It started with a mistake and it's led to more and more mistakes. You can't be in love with me.'

'Do you think I'm lying?'

'No.' She stole a fleeting glance at his face. 'But you have to go. Take the cats, too. I can't keep them.'

'Millie?' He reached for her, but she darted quickly out of his reach, her face ashen.

'Just go! *Please!*'

Chapter Twenty-Four

'Millie!' Five people shot up from the table in unison as she burst into the Malverlys' dining room, three of them exclaiming her name.

'Darling?' Her mother was the first to reach her, closely followed by Alexandra and Lottie. 'What's happened? What's the matter?'

'I've left Cassius!'

'You've done what?' A pair of arms wrapped comfortingly around her. 'And you're frozen! Surely you didn't walk here?'

'Yes, but I'm not cold.'

She laid her head on her mother's shoulder. It was true, she didn't feel remotely chilly at all. On the contrary, she felt far too hot. After scribbling a hasty note she'd fled from her chamber at Falconmore Hall only a couple of minutes after Cassius had left, pausing only to put on a cloak and bonnet before running out of the house and almost the entire way back to the village. She'd had no choice. Those three words, *I love you*, should have been everything she'd wanted to hear, but instead they'd had the opposite effect. For one brief moment her heart had glowed at the words, but then her skin had turned cold, as if she'd just been scorched and frozen at the same time. It had been too much to bear, too much happiness and guilt joined together in one terrible moment. All she'd known was that it was impossible, that she couldn't be Millie, the impulsive, adventurous side of her character who lived only for herself and her desires. It was the opposite of everything she'd been for the past ten years. How could she just walk away from Amelia?

'I think a walk around the village may be in order, wouldn't you say, King?' George made a beeline for the door.

'Good idea.' Jasper followed a few steps behind, throwing Lottie a speaking glance as he went. 'We'll take our time.'

'Now tell me what's happened.' Her mother drew her towards a chair. 'Why have you left Cassius?'

'Because he said he loves me!' Millie looked at each of her female relatives in turn and then dissolved into tears.

'He said…' Her mother looked from Alexandra to Lottie and then back to her again. 'I don't understand, dear. Why would his saying he loves you make you want to leave him?'

'Because it's wrong!' she heard herself wail. 'I should never have agreed to marry him in the first place. It was all a mistake. I *can't* be a marchioness. I *can't* live in a big house and have thirty servants at my beck and call. I thought I could learn, but I can't. I'm Amelia, not Millie, and I belong at the Foundation.' She clutched at her mother's hand. 'I want to go back to London, Mama. You'll take me back with you, won't you?'

'Of course, if you really want to go, but...'

'Nonsense.' Alexandra drew up a chair beside her and sat down. 'You're not going anywhere. It's about time something like this happened.'

Millie looked up at her incredulously. 'You think this is a *good* thing?'

'Yes, actually. A young woman ought to cry sometimes, especially over a young man, and you, my dear, went straight from childhood to middle age with nothing in between. I take this as a very good sign. In my experience there's only one thing that makes a person behave quite so foolishly or dramatically. You're in love, too.'

Millie stared at her cousin, dumbstruck for a few seconds before flinging her hands up over her face and bursting into a fresh bout of tears. '*I know!* But I shouldn't be. We weren't *supposed* to fall in love. He said that he couldn't love anyone so I tried not to think about it at first, but then I couldn't help myself. And now it's too late and we love each other and he gave me *two cats!*'

'Dearest.' Her mother touched a hand to her cheek. 'I think perhaps you're not thinking clearly. Arranging a ball at such short notice must have been quite exhausting. Perhaps you're just overwrought?'

'That's another thing!' Millie shot upright again. 'I don't get overwrought! I don't even cry! Lottie's right, I've changed. I've become a bad person.'

'What?' Lottie looked startled. 'I never said you were a bad person.'

'But I *have* changed!'

'Yes, but I meant your clothes and hair and the fact that you were smiling. None of those things make you a bad person.'

'But they do!' she wailed. 'They do because they're all about me! I have a big house, beautiful clothes, a husband I love who loves me, too, and two cats! It's all too perfect!' She heaved another sob. 'It can't be right!'

'Well…' Alexandra shook her head '…if you want my opinion, bearing in mind that I intend to give it anyway, this is what comes of being *too* virtuous. You think that you don't deserve to be happy unless you're miserable.'

'I do not!'

'Oh, I don't mean *miserable* miserable. I mean that you can't be happy unless you're being selfless, too. But you can do good in the world and still enjoy yourself once in a while.'

'I've done nothing *but* enjoy myself for this whole past week and it *can't* be right for me to have so much. It feels selfish.'

'I doubt you could be selfish if you tried. Unless, of course, you abandoned a man who says he loves you just because you think that being happy is wrong. What about *his* happiness? How do you think he's feeling now?'

Millie shuddered at the memory. 'When I told him our marriage was a mistake it was like I'd stabbed him in the heart, but I didn't know what else to say. I had to get away. Oh, dear, I'm afraid I hurt him very badly.'

'Very likely.' Alexandra pursed her lips.

'But not deliberately.' Her mother put a comforting hand on her knee. 'And hopefully not irreparably. I think perhaps you panicked, dearest. Alexandra's right, you're so used to thinking about other people that you don't know how to think about yourself, but being happy doesn't make you selfish.'

'But to have so much…'

'Tell me this, do you think you could be happy *without* Cassius?'

'No…' She sniffed and rubbed a hand over her nose. 'I told you, I love him.'

'What about the house and the clothes and even the cats? What if you lost all of those things, but still had Cassius? Could you be happy then?'

'Ye—es. As long as the cats went to a good home.'

'Naturally.' Her mother smiled. 'But I think then we can conclude that Cassius is the determining factor. You haven't become materialistic or selfish, you've just happened to fall in love with a marquess who comes with a big house and cats. But you might just have to forgive him for those shortcomings. Nobody's perfect.'

'So you don't think it would be wrong or wicked of me?'

'I think that denying love would be wrong.'

'What about the Foundation? I'm *the little mother*.'

'We'll manage.'

'But it's Father's legacy. I need to uphold it.'

'No, dearest, your father's legacy is you and Lottie and Silas, wherever you are and whatever you do. The Foundation was his work. He was proud of it, but his family was his life. The way to uphold his legacy is to find your own path and be happy.' Her mother touched a finger to her butterfly brooch. 'Do you remember what he used to tell you and Lottie about this?'

'Yes.' Millie gave a loud sniff. 'He said these were

what we'd grow into one day, when our wings were fully grown.'

'Exactly. Now I think they're ready, don't you?'

'But you need me...'

'Actually, my dear, you're dismissed.'

'What?' Millie blinked in surprise.

'You're dismissed from your post at the Foundation. We thank you for your many years of good service, but your services are no longer required.'

'But you can't just...'

'Actually I believe that I can. And now that Lottie's getting married I thought I might start looking for smaller accommodation, too. So you see, there's really no place for you in London any more.'

'Alexandra?' Millie turned towards her cousin.

'Don't look at me.' Alexandra folded her arms pointedly. 'You're not staying here.'

'Or with me and Jasper,' Lottie chimed in.

'So you're *all* ganging up on me?'

'Yes.' Her mother smiled. 'Because we all want you to be happy. And you *have* been happy since you married Cassius, that much has been obvious. You've been like your old self, the free-spirited girl I remember. I don't want to see her fade away again. So blame it on me if you have to, do it to make *me* happy, but let yourself be happy, too. You deserve to follow your heart, Millie.'

'Oh, dear.' She rubbed the palms of her hands over her cheeks. 'I've been very foolish, haven't I?'

'It happens to the best of us.' Her mother smiled. 'But we won't tell anyone.'

They all jumped and then looked to one side as the

front door banged and George and Jasper's voices became audible in the hallway.

'That was quicker than I expected,' Alexandra called out to her husband.

'It's snowing again.' George peered tentatively around the door, looking as if he were about to bolt at the first sign of tears. 'Dashed cold, too. We thought we might take refuge in the library and open a bottle of sherry instead.'

'There's no need to take refuge.' Millie smiled. 'I've had a good telling-off and I'm thoroughly chastened.'

'Are you, by Jove?' He looked impressed. 'That *was* quick. My wife takes a lot longer when she scolds me.'

'*George.*' Alexandra gave him a look. 'We shall discuss that comment later.'

'I don't doubt it, my dear.'

'I have to get back to Falconmore Hall.' Millie stood up determinedly. 'As quickly as possible.'

'Not tonight, I'm afraid.' George tapped his nose with a sage expression. 'The roads will be impassable soon.'

'Surely it's not so bad?' Alexandra crossed to the window and looked out. 'Ah. Much as I hate to admit it, my husband is right.'

'But I have to go!'

'We'll see how it looks in the morning. In the meantime, I'm afraid I can't risk my coachman or my horses on a night like this. If only we had a sleigh.'

'Then I'll walk.'

'You'll do no such thing. Love is love, but survival is rather important, too.'

'But I need to put things right with Cassius!'

'And you will, but not tonight.' Alexandra gave her

a meaningful look. 'On the plus side, in this weather, at least we know he's not going anywhere.'

Cassius crumpled the piece of paper in his fist. She'd gone. Not just from the room, but from the house and for good. It was all too much, her letter said. She was sorry, but she could never belong there. She could never be a marchioness. The words had blurred as he'd read them, none of them concealing the real meaning beneath. She didn't love him.

He spun on his heel, making for the door that led to his adjoining chamber. His old army bag was stored in the bottom of a wardrobe and he tugged it out and stuffed a few items of clothing inside. She was gone. That was the one thought clamouring inside his head. But if she could leave, then so could he. He had to get away or he'd go mad.

'Kendrew!' he bellowed as he descended the staircase.

'Sir?' It took a few minutes for the butler to appear, looking somewhat more dishevelled than usual, but then he'd given him the day off, Cassius remembered vaguely.

'My apologies for disturbing you, Kendrew.' He shrugged on a greatcoat at the front door. 'Is there anyone left in the stables?'

'I believe the grooms are taking it in turns to look after the horses, sir. There should be someone.'

'Good.'

Kendrew looked alarmed. 'Do you wish to go somewhere, sir?'

'Derbyshire.' He made a snap decision. 'I haven't visited the hunting lodge yet. Not for ten years, in fact. Now seems as good a time as any.'

'But it's snowing again, sir. Surely it would be safer to wait until the roads clear again?'

'If it gets worse, then I'll stop at an inn. Don't worry, I've travelled through far worse.'

'And Lady Falconmore…?'

'Has left.' Somehow he forced the words past his lips.

'Left, sir?'

'Yes.' He rammed his hat on so forcefully he almost tore the seams. 'As it turns out, she and I aren't suited, after all.'

'I see, sir.' Kendrew looked awkward. 'In that case, how long do you think you'll be gone? I only ask because of the house and staff.'

'Tell the staff their holiday may be longer than they expected. Fully paid, of course. Or send a few of them to the town house in London. I'm sure the Dowager Lady Falconmore will keep them busy.'

'Yes, sir.'

Cassius made for the door and then paused on the threshold. 'Thank you for everything, Kendrew. I may not have been the easiest master to live with over the past year, but I couldn't have asked for a finer lieutenant.'

'It's been an honour, my lord.'

'Take care of yourself, Kendrew. And give my best wishes to Mrs Turner. I hope you have better fortune in marriage than I've had.'

Chapter Twenty-Five

Millie crept down the staircase, one slow step at a time. She could hear voices in the parlour, though fortunately the door was closed, allowing her to cross the hallway unseen. Stealthily she made her way into the dining room, opened the latch of the smallest window, threw a bag outside and then swung her legs over the sill. She didn't like what she was doing. She definitely didn't like leaving a window unlatched at night either, but if she closed it just so... She pushed it back into place and wedged a piece of folded up paper into the frame...*there*, hopefully it would hold until morning.

She pulled the hood of her cloak up over her head, picked up the bag and then crept around the side of the house, keeping to the shadows until she was out on the road. Once there, she threw a swift glance over her shoulder to make sure no one was following and then carried onwards, repressing a twinge of conscience. She'd feigned a headache and pretended to go to bed early, then stuffed some pillows beneath the coverlet in case anyone went to check on her later. She hoped that they didn't. On the off chance, however, she'd left *another* note on her dressing table to explain where she was going and why, not that it would be hard for anyone to guess. The last thing she wanted to do was to cause any worry, but at least this time she was better prepared for the weather, clad in four layers of clothing and carrying a bag filled with supplies. She was behaving recklessly again, but all she knew was that she couldn't wait until morning to go and find Cassius. In her panic, she'd done the worst thing possible and hurt a man who loved her, a man who'd lost so many people in his life already, whose heart had only just begun to heal. What if she'd broken it for good this time? What if he couldn't forgive her?

The fear hastened her footsteps away from the village and into the darkness.

'There.' Cassius placed a saucer of milk in front of the fireplace. 'Don't ask me for anything else.'

He lowered himself on to the hearth rug beside the kittens. This was all their fault. He'd been halfway down the main driveway before he'd remembered that they were still curled up in a box in his library and, with half of his domestic staff taking a holiday, there was no way of knowing when they'd be found. In the meantime, they might either have starved to death or torn his library to shreds, neither of which had sounded particularly appealing. With a weary sigh he'd turned his horse around, deposited it back in the stables, much to the lone groom's bemusement, and then stalked back into the house, collected the box of kittens and left again—on foot this time—scowling the whole while.

One fact had been infuriatingly obvious. No matter how much he wanted to leave, he could hardly travel to Derbyshire with a pair of kittens tucked under one arm. Which meant that there had been only one place left to go, one place where he could be alone to rage at the world.

He looked around at the gatehouse parlour. It was strange to be back. He hadn't visited since his night there with Millie and now he couldn't decide whether that was a good thing or just a means of torturing himself further. At least the kittens seemed happy, lapping up their milk enthusiastically before pouncing about and diving on each other's heads with gleeful abandon. At last they gave matching yawns and laid down side by side, nuzzling their noses into each other's fur. He watched them for a few moments and then reached for a cushion, deciding he might as well bed down for the night, too. It seemed the easiest thing to do, to stare up at the ceiling and reflect on the mess he'd made of his life, not to mention his marriage. *Especially* his marriage, in fact. All of the other things that had happened over the past year and a half had been outside his control, whereas falling in love... Well, as it turned out, *that* had been outside his control, too, but it had been *his* decision to say the words out loud. *That* had been his mistake. He should never have told Millie how he felt, especially when she'd been so brittle and withdrawn. For one scant day, he'd dared to hope she might actually share his feelings, but obviously he'd been wrong. His words had only scared her away and the result was that he didn't know which of them he resented more.

One of the kittens climbed on to his leg and then made its way slowly up his body to his stomach, kneading its paws into his shirt before twirling around a few times and then curling up into a ball. It must have looked like a good idea because a few seconds later the other one joined it, jumping straight on to his chest and nestling beside its companion.

So here he was. Cassius studied a mark on the ceiling and sighed. On his own again, lying on a fireside rug on Christmas Eve, weighed down by a pair of cats. It wasn't exactly where he'd been before Millie had walked into his life, but it was pretty close. It was even snowing again. If it hadn't been for his new companions he might have thought the events of the past two weeks was one long, surprisingly detailed and intermittently erotic dream. Except that the pain in his heart was undeniably real. It was too painful to be anything else. Somehow that wounded organ had recovered enough to love again, only to be crushed yet another time. He wished it hadn't started to heal in the first place. After Edward, Magnus and now Millie, too, he wouldn't make the same mistake again. He wouldn't allow anyone close enough to hurt him. If he could harden his heart through sheer force of will, then he'd turn it into a stone.

He closed his eyes, willing himself into oblivion for a few hours. Maybe then he could forget the way Millie had looked when she'd begged him to leave her alone, or how he'd felt when he'd discovered the letter she'd left behind. It was folded up now, in his jacket pocket. An intelligent man would probably throw it on to the fire and be done with the whole thing, but apparently he wasn't intelligent. For the time being at least, he couldn't let go.

He stiffened and then glowered at the sound of a knock. Now it seemed his mind was playing tricks on him, too, re-enacting the events of the night when she'd first arrived on his doorstep, but this time he was definitely ignoring it. This time he wasn't moving a muscle. This time... He opened his eyes at a different sound, a scrape like that of the front door opening, then a small thud as it closed again, followed by a light tread and a creak as if someone were walking over floorboards and then... He turned his head just in time to see Millie appear in the doorway.

'Cassius!' She gave a small shriek and flew across the room towards him, landing in a heap on the floor by his side. 'Are you hurt?'

'Millie?' He struggled upwards in surprise, eliciting a chorus of disgruntled meows from the displaced kittens.

'What happened? Are you injured?' She rubbed her hands frantically over his chest and shoulders. 'Where are you hurt?'

'I'm not...' He stopped. He'd been about to say that he wasn't hurt, but that wasn't true, was it? He'd been *very* hurt—and by *her*, the woman who was currently running her hands up and down his body, making him feel angry and aroused at the same time.

'I'm not injured.' He caught at her wrists as she started on his legs, holding them up between them.

'Oh!' She looked startled by the movement. 'Then why are you lying on the floor?'

'Keeping the cats company, what does it look like?' He scowled back at her. 'What are you doing here, Millie?'

'I was on my way back to the hall.'

'You were going back?' He let go of her wrists, his

gut clenching with a combination of hope and more anger.

'Yes, but then I saw smoke from the chimney and I thought it must be you. I knocked on the door, but you didn't answer so…well, it was unlocked so I came in.'

'Why?' He made his tone deliberately acerbic. 'Are you in need of shelter again?'

'No, I came prepared this time.' She jerked her head towards a bag she'd dropped by the doorway. 'I brought food and water and a blanket just in case I got stuck in the snow.'

'Impressive. No umbrella?'

Her eyes narrowed with a hint of defiance. 'There's a breeze.'

'Ah.' He gave a bitter laugh. 'You've been at the Malverlys' house presumably?'

'Yes.'

'Do they know you're here now?'

'No, I crept out.' She gave him an uncertain look. 'I needed to speak with you and it couldn't wait.'

'Really? I thought you'd said everything there was to say in your letter?'

'My letter was a mistake.'

'Another one? According to you, you've been making a lot of those recently.'

'I know.' She sat back on her heels. 'But I was confused then. I'm not any more.'

'All right…' He sighed and lay down again. 'Since you've gone to so much trouble, you might as well say what you came to say.'

'Very well.' She paused to draw in a deep breath. 'If you want me to leave again, then I will. I'd understand after everything you've been through—everything I've put you through, too. I might deserve to be sent away, but before you decide I want you to know that I'm sorry. Yesterday Lottie said some things about how I've changed and I panicked. She didn't mean to upset me, but I felt overwhelmed. So much has happened so quickly, not just between us, but with everything. I thought I was losing my way and living for my own selfish desires, but now I know I was wrong. It's not selfish to love, to be loved either and...'

'Millie, *what* are you saying?' he interrupted her urgently.

'I'm saying that I love you, too, Cassius. I knew it days ago, but I thought you might not want to hear it. You said you couldn't love me and I thought that maybe that was the sacrifice I had to make for being so happy, but then you said you loved me, too, and I was afraid it was all too much so—'

She didn't get any further as he grabbed her elbows and pulled her down on top of him, clamping his lips over hers and kissing her so deeply that he felt almost breathless by the time they finally pulled apart again.

'You left me.' His voice sounded raw.

'I know.' Her breathing was short, too. 'I'm sorry.'

'How do I know you won't do it again? How can I take you back knowing you might leave me again?'

'Because I won't, I promise.'

'I was leaving, too!' He spoke the words fiercely. 'I was going to Derbyshire. If it wasn't for those infernal creatures I'd be well on my way by now.'

'Oh.' She threw a look of gratitude towards the two kittens. 'In that case, I'm doubly grateful for them.'

He rolled her over, covering her body with his own and pinning her arms above her head. 'What if I can't bear the risk? You say you love me, but *who* are you, Millie or Amelia?'

'Amelia's gone.' She looked notably unperturbed by his ferocity. 'My mother dismissed her from the Foundation and nobody else wants her. Not even me. So you see, there's no place for Amelia Fairclough any more. Not there and definitely not here. Now there's only me.'

'Just you?' He swallowed, feeling his resolve start to break. *'Just Millie?'*

'Yes.' She smiled and craned her neck, pressing her forehead up against his. 'I know who I am and who I want to be now. I'm Millie Whitlock, Marchioness of Falconmore, your wife, and I'm not going anywhere unless you want me to. The only question is whether you want me to.'

'Of course I don't want you to!' He claimed her mouth again with a growl, pressing her down to the floor. 'The only place I want you is right here.'

'Here?'

'And now.' He let go of her arms, starting to unfasten the buttons at the neck of her gown, surprised to find another row underneath.

'What the…?'

She looked apologetic. 'I needed layers for the cold.'

'How many layers?'

'Four. Here.' She lifted her hands to help, squirming beneath him. 'Oh, dear, I can't seem to… Maybe if we…'

There were several loud popping sounds as Cassius tore four rows of buttons open simultaneously.

'And a corset?' He was tempted to laugh. 'There are chastity belts that are easier to get into than this.'

'I thought I was being sensible.'

'That sounds like Amelia talking again.'

'You're right.' Her eyes widened. 'Let me up.'

'What?' He felt another rush of panic. 'Why?'

'Don't worry, I'm not going anywhere. Just let me up.'

He shifted to one side dubiously, watching as she wriggled upright, then reached around to unfasten her corset.

'Can I help?'

'No, I...there!' She pulled the offending garment away, held it up for his inspection and then tossed it on to the fire.

'Um, Millie...'

'Would Amelia do *that*?' She tossed her head triumphantly.

'I think you might just have smothered the flames.' He grabbed her arm, pulling her away as a cloud of thick grey smoke wafted out of the fireplace and into the room.

'Oh, dear.'

He laughed and then started coughing. 'Loosening shackles isn't easy. We may both have a way to go yet.'

'But we'll do it together?' She looked at him hopefully.

'Together.' He agreed. 'Only in the meantime...' he picked up a poker and prodded at the disintegrating corset '...the fire's safe enough, but I don't think we ought to stay in here.'

'Do you think we should go back to the hall?'

'In this weather?' He grinned. 'Why bother when we have a perfectly serviceable bedchamber upstairs? Come on, you two.' He reached down, scooped up the kittens and then held a hand out to his wife. 'Let's go to bed.'

Chapter Twenty-Six

'A toast!' George lifted his wine glass and winked at Millie. 'To a very happy Christmas for all.'

'Happy Christmas!' A chorus of voices echoed around the dining table.

'And to reunions, be they familial or otherwise!'

'To reunions.' Cassius tilted his head towards Millie's, murmuring in her ear, 'This must be the strangest Christmas I've ever had.'

'Why?' She smiled teasingly. 'Just because we climbed in through a window at the crack of dawn and then hid in my bedroom until breakfast?'

'And then pretended that nothing wayward or untoward had happened. That's about it, yes. I'm afraid you may be a bad influence on me, after all.'

'Oh, I intend to be much worse from now on. I have ten years of being sensible to make up for. I may become quite wild.'

'I certainly hope so.' His lips brushed lightly against her neck. 'Is there any particular reason why we haven't explained ourselves, by the way?'

'Because that would spoil the fun, obviously.'

'Obviously.'

'And because it's our story.' She smiled secretively. 'I'm certain there are lots of things Lottie hasn't told me about her and Jasper. And Silas's letter was maddeningly vague. He mentioned a woman, but he didn't give any details. No, *they* can have their stories and we can have ours.'

'Then my lips are sealed. Until you want me to open them, that is.'

She blushed and then smiled as one of the kittens rubbed its way around Cassius's legs. 'Orestes has taken quite a shine to you.'

'Mmm.' He smoothed a hand over the small head. 'Do you know, I think I may be a cat person, after all.'

'Good, because I'm not sure two is enough.'

'I hope you're not planning to turn Falconmore Hall into a cat sanctuary?'

'No, but in the legend Orestes and Electra had a sister. On reflection, I don't want her to be left out.'

'Did they?' He thought for a moment and then clicked his fingers. 'Iphigenia, how could I have forgotten? She was sacrificed by her father Agamemnon, wasn't she?'

'There are different versions of the story. In some of them, she lived.'

'Then I prefer those versions, although it's still a curious name for a cat.'

'How about we shorten it to Ginny?'

'Ginny, Ellie and Orestes.' He nodded. 'Much better. I'll send word to the Petches that we need another sister.'

'Here comes the goose!' Alexandra announced loudly. 'Now, do we have enough food for everyone, do you think?'

Millie exchanged an amused glance with her mother and Lottie. The dining table was covered with steaming bowls of mashed potato, parsnips, chestnut stuffing, peas, carrots, gravy, apple sauce, a roast ham and even a game pie for good measure. There was so much food they could hardly see the linen beneath.

'I think so, Cousin.' Lottie smiled mischievously. 'Although I'm not sure we ought to share it with people who arrive without presents.'

'They're back at home.' Millie squeezed Cassius's hand at the word *home*. 'We'll send for them when the snow clears.'

'Well then, how about you give us a promise instead? Since *I* wasn't invited to your wedding, why don't you promise to throw a belated party to celebrate? For all our friends at the Foundation, too?'

'I think that sounds like an excellent idea.' Cassius grinned. 'Otherwise I fear my wife might start pining for a new project. She'll be overhauling the whole estate if I'm not careful.'

'I will not.' Millie gave him an arch look. 'Although I *did* have an idea for a local hospital. Maybe here in the village? I thought perhaps we might dedicate it to your friend.'

'The Edward Towse Memorial Hospital?' he murmured thoughtfully. 'I think he would have liked that. He always did have an ironic sense of humour.'

'Then it's agreed,' Alexandra announced decisively. 'Millie can start planning a hospital *and* a party. That should keep her busy for a couple of weeks.'

'Actually…' Millie looked around the table with a smile '…I've no intention of doing anything at all for the rest of the year. I want to have a proper honeymoon.'

'Next year is only six days away, dearest.' Her mother gave her an affectionate look.

'I'll take what I can get.' Cassius raised her hand to his lips and kissed her knuckles. 'Where would you like to spend it?'

'Oh, not far. I believe there's an empty gatehouse we might use?'

'I believe you might be right. Although we'll need a *chaise longue* and some novels.'

'And a box of macaroons, don't forget those.'

'Naturally. I think that sounds like a perfect plan. With any luck, we'll get snowed in properly this time.'

'I say…' George gave an emphatic cough. 'I don't know about the rest of you, but it seems to me like the food is getting cold.'

'You're right. We should eat…' Millie laughed '…after just one more toast.' She raised her glass, smiling around the table at the people she loved. 'To love, family and the future, whatever 1843 might bring.'

* * * * *